# *Shadows of Dissent*
### Melyndie & Zain

---

## BOOK THREE

---

By: Barbara Pelham

Thank you to the following for their part in bringing this work to publication:

Cover design: Barbara Woster


This is **book three** in a three-book series suitable for ages 15+
***Reader discretion advised:***
Book one: scenes of sensuality and mild language.
Book two: scenes of sensuality, violence and language
Book three: scenes of violence, language

Contents

To my daughters, without whom this book would never have been written. Thank you for your love and support throughout the years. I love you all dearly.

# PHASE THREE

"The only way to deal with an unfree world is to become so absolutely free that your very existence is an act of rebellion."

*Albert Camus*

# *Prologue*
## *The World on Fire*

*Year: 2158*

The initial stages, Phases One and Two, unfolded with chilling efficiency over the course of twenty-four months. The world seemed to hold its breath in an eerie silence. Cities dimmed, streets emptied…the hum of civilization faded to a low, unnatural quiet.

Robotic Military Personnel (RMPs) surged across every continent with the ferocity of a cataclysmic storm, their true intentions masked by a deceitful promise of global recovery. Phase One—a mandate heralded as the last bastion against a devastating plague—was, in reality, the first menacing move toward worldwide dominion.

Control took root the moment the needles pierced skin. The inoculations, delivered as a cure against disease, were actually insidious biometric chips. Their malevolent purpose: to subjugate, oppress, and annihilate.

Phase Two began before the world had time to question what they had accepted—let alone comprehend the horror that was about to be unleashed.

The RMP surged forth, their sensors sweeping over the chipped populace—not searching for mere traces of infection, but targeting the elderly, the frail, the disabled, and the infirmed—any soul considered a burden to society. Once this grim, unforgiving census reached its chilling conclusion, the RMPs unleashed the termination protocol with ruthless precision—relaying a deadly signal.

The result was cataclysmic—over four-and-a-half billion lives extinguished in a year.

Those left behind—physically intact, but spiritually hollowed—watched the world shrink around them. Fear replaced reason. Order replaced freedom. And in the void, compliance became the last refuge of the living.

In the aftermath, as the dust of decimation settled, military structure was all that remained. Battalions were divided and deployed. The commanders in charge of the troops: Major Ethan Mannelly, Lieutenant Colonel Elizaveta Kuznetsov, Second Lieutenant Jeong Hanjun, Lieutenant Xiu Zhang—and Colonel Zain Belhasa.

For Zain, the orders were clear. The path laid before him was rigid, defined. But his conscience—long buried beneath protocol—had begun to surface in ways he could no longer ignore.

With each life taken and every mass grave filled, his soul fractured more deeply, leading him to question his commitment to his duty—a commitment that was demanded of him right at the start of Phase One when he was ordered to execute his own mother. *Comply or die.* Her execution wasn't a punishment; it was a prerequisite, the cost of leadership, the price for staying alive.

But what he once regarded as duty began to feel more like silent complicity. Questions he never used to consider began to haunt him, unwelcome and persistent.

Zain's denial deepened into something unsettling. He hadn't yielded. He was simply paralyzed—falling numb, as if survival depended on it. Clarity slipped. Conviction thinned.

Still, through it all, he fell back on the knowledge that he wasn't alone. He had his personal RMP, self-designated Tom—assigned for protection; never meant for companionship. Yet over time, something shifted. Unlike the other RMP units, Tom possessed an experimental Adaptive AI—designed to adapt, to analyze, to improve. And under Zain's command, or perhaps because of it, Tom began to do something far more unexpected: it began to reach for something…human—connection.

At first, it mimicked. Then it questioned. And eventually, it listened—not just for instructions, but for meaning. Zain spoke to Tom as he would a subordinate, then a partner, and finally—without realizing it—as a friend. Tom didn't emote in the way humans did, but there was something steady, something loyal in the way it remained by Zain's side.

That loyalty, unspoken but deeply felt, became the anchor that held fast through the shifting tides.

In time, their conversations shifted too. They no longer spoke solely of orders, but of consequences—of what their actions might build or destroy. They weren't ready to launch a rebellion, not yet. But the idea had taken root. And with each passing day, it grew stronger, drawing them ever closer to the edge of treason.

Days merged into one another, driven by the relentless ticking of a never-ending clock. Zain and Tom found themselves navigating a maze of moral dilemmas and strategic decisions. Every action needed to be both discreet and effective, planting seeds of resistance in a landscape sterilized by fear and oppression.

Long before rebellion took shape, before the world began to fracture, there was Melyndie—bright, unexpected, and utterly unprepared for the world she had fallen into.

She crashed into their world at the onset of Phase One, a mystery from another time. She seemed to have descended from the heavens; an enigma wrapped in a veil of purpose. Originating from the distant future, she had embarked on a mission of her own—a quest to save humanity's future—but she had fallen into a world teetering on the brink of annihilation.

In a world dissolving into control and conformity, she was the only thing that reminded Zain what it meant to be human, the only thing that mattered.

Zain saw in her something fragile but fierce—a spark of hope that glowed quietly, but stirred the embers within him of a fire he hadn't felt since the loss of his mother. In Melyndie, he saw not just the chance to protect, but the chance to redeem what duty had stolen from him. She was a reminder of everything he hadn't been able to save—and he would guard her with everything he had left.

But then, in the blink of an eye, she was gone; vanished from their lives, but never from Zain's mind. Her presence had disrupted everything. Her disappearance had left a wound.

With Melyndie's absence casting a shadow over his heart, Zain steels himself with iron resolve for what lies ahead—for in a world being rewritten, he—and those who dare stand with him— must fight to reclaim what it means to be human.

"What's your take on recruiting Major Reese?" Zain posed the question to his personal RMP, Tom. Originally programmed to ensure Zain's compliance with the directives of global leaders, this robotic military unit had, over time, evolved into a trusted confidant and an unlikely friend.

"I harbor reservations about recruiting officers," Tom confessed. "Their allegiance is often unshakably tethered to their superiors." It paused before adding, "Much like yours once was."

"You've developed quite a sense of humor, Tom." Zain chuckled dryly, the sound nearly lost to a gust of wind that slipped across the base. It threaded through the open hangar, lifting a haze of fine dust. Somewhere in the distance, an RMP patrol passed by, its steady hum breaking the silence of the night.

"But there's something else," Tom continued. "I find it hard to place my trust in him."

"And why is that?" Zain probed.

"His constant skepticism and interrogations suggest he is testing you," Tom explained.

"He wants to gauge where my loyalties lie," Zain concluded.

"That is my assessment," confirmed Tom. "Ever since we disappeared for that week to chase after the RMPs, to ascertain their intent, he has inserted himself into many of our conversations, often to complain about our mission parameters. To me, this is not the normal behavior of a senior officer and reeks of an attempt at information-gathering. I would guard my words when speaking to him."

"Or he is simply a pessimist who has discovered I will listen to his negative viewpoints without criticism. Or, is it possible that your assessment is just off?" Zain questioned, unable to hide the skepticism in his tone.

"My assessments are rarely incorrect…" Its voice trailed off as it spotted that particular officer approaching them. As the major neared, Zain busied himself with his tablet, skimming through yesterday's field reports in an effort to appear engaged in their mission.

"Colonel," Major Reese began as he approached, a tablet tucked under his arm. "Reports are flooding in from every region. As per our orders, vehicles are being relocated for repurposing; tools are being handed out to civilians for rubble clearance as buildings are systematically dismantled…"

As the major's sentence trailed off, Zain turned from the reports he was pretending to peruse and drew a deep breath through flaring nostrils. He donned an inscrutable mask that concealed the tumultuous storm constantly brewing within him—a tempest of fury threatening to explode with each passing day. "You seem preoccupied, Major," Zain noted tersely.

Initially shaking his head in denial, Major Reese then nodded after some thought. "I'm struggling to understand what our world leaders have planned by demolishing every single structure worldwide and melting down all the metal…" He trailed off again, sighing deeply. "And this phase three we're currently in…it's…"

"Unprecedented," Zain finished for him.

"And utterly nonsensical," Major Reese added in an unintentional sharp tone. "For instance, why are we tasked with capturing every single living creature we encounter, down to the last cricket crawling through the rubble? It's madness without any discernible purpose."

"Your point, Major?" Zain interrupted, his patience wearing thin.

"I guess I don't have one," Major Reese admitted. "Just needed to vent."

"The RMPs are handling the animal collection, Major."

"That's not the point I was trying to make," the major retorted.

"I know," Zain replied curtly. "But I can't provide answers for you, Major. The global leaders believe that humanity's survival hinges on a fresh start…apparently from the ground up."

"It all just feels like overkill to me," Major Reese mused aloud.

"No doubt many would agree with you if they were asked," Zain responded dryly. "Anything else on your mind?"

The major nodded, his lips tightly pressed together as if restraining a torrent of words threatening to spill out.

"Was there, perhaps, more to today's report?" Zain prodded when it appeared the major was struggling to reveal what was next on his mind.

"Yes sir, um…we've started encountering resistance—again. Should I order our soldiers to terminate—"

"What were my instructions regarding this issue?" Zain cut him off sharply.

"If anyone began to question, or fight, being conscripted to work, we're to detain them and bring them here," came the hesitant reply.

"Then why are you suggesting immediate termination?" Zain asked, his tone tight with restraint.

Major Reese chewed nervously on his lower lip before responding, "Wasn't it the world leaders' directive to eliminate anyone opposing us?"

"Are you questioning *my* orders?" Zain shot back tersely.

"No, Colonel!"

Zain paused before speaking again. "I understand why you may have some concerns, Major, when it appears I'm directly countering those orders issued by a higher command; however, it's simply my intention to personally address these dissidents. If they refuse to see reason after hearing me out, then their execution will be on my head."

"Yes sir," the major replied sharply.

"Is there anything else you need to report, Major?" Zain asked. When the major shook his head, Zain dismissed him to return to overseeing fieldwork.

As soon as Major Reese was out of earshot, Tom stepped forward to continue their conversation as if the major hadn't interrupted them. "So, you believe it is time for mass recruitment."

"I'm not certain we can afford to wait much longer," Zain countered. "Especially if the soldiers plan to execute even more people."

Tom hesitated before voicing its concern. "If the dissenters refuse your proposition, will you execute them? I thought the idea was to save as many as possible. However, even if we manage to sway them to our side and recruit thousands, we would still be vastly outnumbered by the battalions spread across the globe—"

Zain interrupted him with a wave of his hand. "For now, let's focus on convincing them that survival is preferable to death.

Now, after that exchange with Major Reese, do you still think his complaints are a ruse?"

Tom's head whirred as it slowly nodded. "His objections arise a little too frequently and a little too forcefully."

Zain pondered for a moment, his eyes narrowing. "Perhaps," he conceded, "but that could simply be his personality; or it could also be that he's genuinely struggling with the moral implications of our orders. People often question and probe when they are conflicted. It doesn't necessarily imply disloyalty. And another thing: if I were in his shoes, I'd keep my mouth shut for fear that my superior officer would report me. So then, why isn't he concerned for his own career…his own life?"

Tom remained silent for a short moment, its sensors faintly whirring as it processed Zain's reasoning. "Very well, I will consider his recruitment," it finally replied, "but we should continue to monitor his actions closely. An officer questioning orders can become a significant liability."

"Like me?" Zain questioned bluntly.

"You cannot deny that our conversations could be deemed traitorous if overheard," Tom replied straightforwardly.

Zain nodded, a wry smile crossing his face. "Yeah, that's true."

As the sun began to set over the airbase tarmac, casting elongated shadows across the heat-blistered concrete, its surface faded to pale gray by years of relentless desert sun, Zain couldn't help but wonder if there was anything they could do to change the outcome of this mission besides trying to convince others not to sacrifice themselves for a losing cause. "Do you think what we're doing here is truly evil? I mean, yes, billions have died and cities are being decimated, but in the end, won't humanity come out the other end the better for it?" His eyes drifted toward the radar tower in the distance, memories of their enigmatic visitor from last year flooding his mind. "What would Melyndie say about all of this?" he murmured before shaking his head, trying to push those thoughts away.

"It has been a long time since she returned to her time," Tom inserted, "yet your thoughts are still drawn to her."

"Are you saying that you never think of her—at all?" Zain asserted.

"Her presence came with many questions and her departure ensured no answers would be forthcoming," Tom stated. "I do not care for unanswered questions."

Zain nodded slowly, his face a canvas of unreadable emotions, absorbing the last traces of daylight that were quietly receding behind the horizon. "Neither do I, Tom," he murmured. "But right now, we face a bigger issue. How do we sabotage the intricate plans of our global leaders? Do we even still want to? How do we create chaos large enough to disrupt what amounts to a well-oiled machine? And now that the mass killings have ceased, should we even continue with our original intent?" His questions hung in the air like an unfinished melody, provoking thought and introspection.

Tom tilted its head slightly, studying Zain as if parsing a first edition of Finnegans Wake without context. "It seems like you are caught in a tug-of-war between your ingrained sense of duty and your own moral compass," it pointed out thoughtfully. "Yes, it is true that the indiscriminate slaughter has come to a halt—at least in our territory, as we do not know what is taking place within the other territories—but the termination of those who decide to speak out remains a chilling reality."

Zain sighed deeply at this grim reminder, his gaze dropping to his clasped hands. "And, as you stated, our influence only extends as far as my command does," he admitted. "Which begs the question—how much can we really achieve within these limited boundaries? It feels like throwing pebbles into an ocean for all the impact we'll make for those facing execution elsewhere in the world. It makes me wish I could escape..." he trailed off with a heavy sigh.

"Your thoughts are occupied by Melyndie. You feel she was fortunate to escape back to her time when she did, and you envy her."

Zain exhaled sharply, a gust of frustration escaping his lips. "She invades when I'm exhausted," he excused, weakly. The image of Melyndie was like a stubborn weed in his mind, refusing to be uprooted despite her physical absence. She had crashed into their lives just a year ago, a mystery cloaked in innocence and purpose. Yet she lingered, uninvited, like a song that refused to end. "But I'm failing to see why you brought her up again, Tom," he retorted with an edge to his voice. "You mentioning her at odd times does nothing to help me put thoughts of her behind me."

"Melyndie is just a fabricated human," Tom continued, its gaze distant as if looking past the confines of their space and time. "Her innocence is almost childlike, but in the short time that I interacted with her, I got the impression that she seemed to understand humanity better than we ever could. It is possible that we need that understanding...that insight to escape from this mental maze that we are stuck in." He paused and then offered a different insight. "After so long, and with her mission incomplete..." Tom trailed off as a human who was lost in thought.

"You're thinking that she may have fallen into our time again, just in a different location."

"That is always a possibility."

The words struck harder than Zain expected. If she had returned—if she was somewhere out there, even now—and he never saw her again, never knew…that thought settled in his chest like a stone. He stared at the concrete beneath his boots, jaw tightening against the irrational pull of hope. What was the point of thinking like this? He should be focusing on the living. On the mission.

And yet, if she never came back, he could still do one thing—something small, perhaps meaningless to others, but not to him. A way to keep her memory close. It had been her dream to see, to touch, a German Shepherd.

"Tom?" he asked finally, voice low but steady. "Could you relay an instruction to the other RMPs, without the higher ups finding out about it?"

"That is improbable, but not likely impossible. What is the reason for your request?"

Zain hesitated. "Something Melyndie wanted…"

"A German Shepherd puppy," Tom guessed accurately.

Zain couldn't help but smile ruefully and nodded, "I think she invades your thoughts as much as she does mine."

"I do not deny this to be true. She is a paradox that I did not have time to figure out."

"So, could you send out a request? I don't even know if there are any left in existence; and how is it you always know what I'm thinking?"

"Because I have spent much time in your company," Tom offered. "You want me to inform the RMPs to keep an eye out for a German Shepherd puppy. Why does it matter if the world leaders find out? It is an innocuous request."

"I don't know, because it may put a spotlight of suspicion on me again. They may question why I'm trying to save a dog when their orders are to round all animals up for extermination. And honestly, I just prefer to keep my personal business private. See if you can locate something to help me sleep, will you? I need to get some rest. We have a long road ahead."

"Once all is said and done, there will be no more roads."

"Oh, shut up, Tom!"

With a jerk, he pulled his bedroll from his footlocker and unfurled it at the edge of the darkened hangar. He lay down, his body collapsing beneath him like a felled pillar, limbs heavy with weariness. The night sky stretched above him, a canvas splattered with stars—each one a silent witness to what had been lost. But Zain's mind refused to quiet. His thoughts spun with the intensity of a sandstorm, circling back to Melyndie's face, to Amal's absence, to the moral abyss widening beneath his feet.

"Take this or you will spend all night battling your demons," Tom's voice cut through the silence, offering him a bottle filled with Melatonin tablets.

"Guard duty, Tom," Zain responded tersely as he uncapped the bottle with deft fingers and tossed back three quick-dissolve tablets without hesitation.

In sync with Zain's gradual descent into drug-induced sleep, the lights inside Tom's helmet gradually dimmed. However, Tom wouldn't be sleeping; it would remain on high alert for any potential threats to itself or Zain.

Only when it saw that the colonel was soundly asleep did it begin its careful and furtive process of bypassing the main communication filters. Its goal was to relay Zain's request to some of the other RMPs without being detected by the engineers who constantly monitored its function. Once it was confident that the message had been successfully sent, Tom settled into monitoring mode, ready to react should the need arise.

# Just Beyond Reach



"Is the day treating you kindly, Melyndie?" 41GB posed the question, advancing toward her bed within the stark and clinical boundaries of the medical bay. Melyndie blinked once against the sterile light. The room was a symphony of white—from the bleached tiles underfoot to the fluorescent glow overhead that rendered every surface hyperreal, almost antiseptic in its intensity. The distant hum of machinery served as a constant reminder of where Melyndie had laid—bedridden—since her surgery.

Three months had slipped by since they had performed the intricate operation to remove the intrusive secondary chip, the foreign entity that had made a home in her neck. It was a procedure fraught with risk and uncertainty, one that required steady hands and a sharp mind. Despite being performed by the best, a mistake had been made.

The surgery had been deemed successful, but victory came at a steep price; an unpredictable slip-up during the meticulous process led to devastating consequences. A single misstep in this dance between technology and human tissue had resulted in an irreversible catastrophe—her arms and hands were now functionless, reduced to mere appendages hanging limply at her sides. Her once capable fingers now lay still, stripped of their ability to touch and feel.

On the day in question, Dr. Kishida-Guan's rage was beyond anything ever witnessed—a tempest of fury that had never before been seen by anyone present, including Melyndie who had borne witness to his expressions of frustrations on many occasions. "This is an unacceptable outcome. You are supposed to be at the zenith of your professional prowess; the top of your productive capabilities, and even if this were beyond your expertise, you possess the sum total of human knowledge that should have all but guaranteed success." His unrestrained manifestation of anger sent shockwaves of unease through Melyndie, but the remainder of those in the room were unphased. Given that all humans were engineered with suppressed emotions, this outburst rendered the entire medical staff incapable of doing more than maintaining a watchful silence; their responses confined to merely responding to any query he shouted at them as he paced around the surgical theater like a trapped predator.

The room, itself, seemed to tremble under the onslaught of Dr. Kishida-Guan's furious words, his voice echoing off the sterile white walls like a thunderclap. The verbal barrage continued relentlessly until, without warning, it ceased, but he was far from finished.

He whirled towards Dr. Henley, his eyes blazing with an intensity that could have ignited dry paper into flames. "Dr. Henley," he spat, each syllable dripping with a venomous disdain so biting it could freeze the warmest heart, "I may have failed to emphasize Melyndie's significance for our world's future prospects. She wasn't merely fabricated—she was meticulously crafted for a mission of paramount importance. Your only task was to eliminate the chip causing interference with our tracking system. Yet your negligence has resulted in potential irreversible damage to her—thus jeopardizing humanity's future. If there were another surgeon already at your production level, I would have you terminated immediately." His words hung in the air like a guillotine blade, heavy with accusation. His fury radiated in silent waves, shaking the foundation of their professional relationship and leaving no doubt about the gravity of Dr. Henley's mistake.

Had Dr. Henley been capable of processing this emotional onslaught, he'd be drowning in an overwhelming sea of emotions himself, ranging from humiliation to seething anger over his public chastisement. Instead, he stood unmoving like a statue under scrutiny; his face devoid of any expression as he soaked up Dr. Kishida-Guan's scathing words.

When he sensed an opening amidst the tense silence, he cleared his throat and began to explain, "The chip's location," he started in a monotone, "and the intricate way it had entwined itself around both the bone and the periosteum made the operation hazardous. I was confident that I could extract it without endangering Melyndie's life. However, I must admit that I had my doubts about her escaping physical repercussions. Considering that she is still alive is a testament to the success of the surgery."

He paused for a breath before continuing, "During the procedure, my scalpel grazed the brachial plexus inadvertently—an unfortunate accident that resulted in paralysis of her arms and hands, which was discovered once she emerged from the anesthesia-induced slumber."

Dr. Kishida-Guan's response was curt and filled with simmering rage, each word enunciated with lethal precision, "And what exactly do you propose to do to rectify this paralysis?"

Dr. Henley, for a moment, stood as if his wiring had short-circuited under the weight of that glare and those cold, precisely delivered words. Finally, he responded, his voice devoid of inflection, fitting perfectly with the controlled environment of the medical bay. "We immediately initiated contact with the biomechatronic division. They are exploring advanced prosthetic developments that could potentially restore full mobility and function to the patient's hands and arms," he explained. "Since we have never actually used that division for this purpose, and only discovered this solution through a search of the archives…" he trailed off, uncertain how to sound confident in something which had never been tested in their time. After a moment of gathering his thoughts, he opened his mouth to continue, but Dr. Kishida-Guan interrupted.

"So, what you are saying is that you are relying on antiquated technology to repair the hope for our future?" He asked. His tone though quiet and measured, was filled with barely-contained rage.

"The premise is antiquated, but we are confident that we can improve upon the technology with our advancements," Dr. Henley asserted confidently.

"And, in the meantime, you will do your due diligence in repairing the nerves that you damaged—"

"I do not know if that is…" the surgeon trailed off when he saw the storm clouds returning to the holy one's face, "however," he continued, "I am certain that with our advanced medical technology, we can, in all probability, make it happen. It would still be wise, however, to continue working on the prosthetics in the event…" the surgeon, again, trailed off, as if unwilling to voice the words that would hint at potential failure. "Rest assured that we are working, simultaneously, on multiple avenues of restoration."

Despite the options and assurances given, the atmosphere remained charged with Dr. Kishida-Guan's barely restrained outrage. He turned away from Henley and stomped toward Melyndie, who lay quietly observing the interaction, her eyes betraying the only hint of disturbance in her otherwise placid demeanor.

"Melyndie," he began, and though he attempted to relay a calm and comforting tone, his words issued curtly. "As you heard, we are striving to correct this error. One way or another, we will have you back to full functionality as soon as humanly possible."

Melyndie's response was measured, her voice smooth and oddly calm, despite her own condition. "I understand, Dr. Kishida-Guan. I trust in your efforts."

After a few more curt nods around the room, Dr. Kishida-Guan exited the medical bay, followed by his colleagues, 41GB and 71PQv, leaving a lingering silence that felt both oppressive and liberating at once.

Dr. Henley lingered for a moment as if waiting for permission from some unseen force. Then he approached her bedside, his expression unchanged. "We are working on multiple methods by which to repair your nerves. Rest assured, as Dr. Kishida-Guan has promised, we'll have you back to full functionality as soon as possible. In the meantime, please try to rest. Someone will be available around the clock to attend to your needs until you're able to care for yourself again."

Unlike her earlier calm, Melyndie couldn't bring herself to respond. Her gaze slid past Henley without acknowledgment, her throat tightening with everything she refused to say aloud. She was still coming to terms with the loss of her limb function. From that day, it would take three months before any significant progress could be seen in regaining her mobility.

During that time, the medical team worked tirelessly, navigating the delicate balance between hope and realism. The biomechatronic division, spurred by the urgency of their mission, made remarkable strides in prosthetic technology, blending robotics seamlessly with human tissue. In parallel, Dr. Henley initiated a series of experimental treatments in nerve growth using a combination of stimulation and regenerative medicine. When he wasn't supervising those experiments, he was conducting surgical simulations to repair severed nerves.

Three teams were diligently working around the clock at full productivity capability to guarantee that Melyndie, whom Dr. Kishida-Guan referred to as the future of their humanity, was restored to full functionality as swiftly as possible.

Melyndie, for her part, observed and absorbed everything around her with a stoic grace that belied the gravity of her situation and the irritation that she kept barely in check. Though unable to move her arms, her mind remained as active and agile as ever. She paid close attention to Dr. Henley's updates and frequently pondered which procedure would ultimately be chosen to restore the use of her arms.

However, as the days slowly passed, the irritation began to outpace her stoic grace, and her doubts began to grow, fed by the relentless speeches full of promises and the sometimes too-optimistic forecasts. She became an expert in reading the unsaid between the clinical updates: a twitch of an eyebrow, a hurried conversation heard through partially opened doors. The uncertainty chewed at her, reducing her nights to disturbed periods between shorter moments of rest, haunted by dreams of being trapped or falling without end.

During one such restless night, Melyndie found herself being wheeled into a brightly-lit operating theater in her dream, her heart hammering wildly against her chest as she lay inexplicably paralyzed on the frigid metal table. The scene quickly morphed into a cold dark space where machines hummed ominously around her body. Mechanized hands, icy and rigid, pitilessly poked, prodded, and sliced into her flesh with a precision that felt cruel and cold—a methodical torment with no discernible purpose, causing unnecessary pain and torment. She tried to scream but nothing came out; the nightmare holding her tightly in silent terror.

Though the dreams varied each night, each left her feeling overwhelmingly terrorized. When she finally woke—each time gasping for air—the darkness of her room wrapped around her like a threadbare blanket. The familiar hum of nearby machines no longer frightened her; it calmed her. A lullaby of the broken world she preferred to the screaming inside her own mind.

Yet the calm was a lie, a soft curtain draped over a body that refused to serve her and a mind that refused to forget. She would never truly know peace—not while her limbs betrayed her, not while the mission for which she was fabricated slipped further from reach…and not while the life she'd come to yearn for lingered in a time she could no longer…*feel*.

## *Weight of Pretending*

"Is the day treating you kindly, Melyndie?" asked 41GB, striving to keep her gaze locked onto Melyndie's eyes—a futile attempt to ignore the tubes that sprouted disturbingly from her unresponsive arms, their sterile plastic mocking the warmth of human touch.

Unflinchingly, Melyndie steered her attention toward them. "I'm being sustained by these monstrous contraptions, my sustenance delivered through cold plastic rather than savored on my tongue," she spat out bitterly. "When the surgeon assured me that someone would be tending to my needs around the clock until I'm healed, he failed to mention that it would be through mechanized means. On top of that, I'm robbed of the simple dignity of bathing myself or attending to my own basic needs. My arms hang useless— heavy as iron anchors—while the surgeon breezes in daily with empty promises of restoring me to some semblance of normalcy."

She paused for a moment before continuing, her voice laced with sarcasm so thick it was nearly visible. "So, is this day being kind? I suppose if breathing without aid, speaking despite despair, and moving what remains of my body qualifies as kindness…then yes." After a moment of deep breathing, her frustration receded and she continued in a quiet, calm tone, "I know that it would be imprudent to appear ungrateful when I retain more than what I have lost."

The room sank into an oppressive hush, a quiet so dense it felt like a weight pressing down between them. The silence stretched like a chasm—wide and deep—only to be shattered by the timely appearance of the surgeon.

"Good morning, a75b99—"

"Wouldn't it be simpler to address me as Melyndie?" she interjected, her voice laced with suppressed irritation. This constant struggle with her identity was becoming an unwelcome companion since her return.

"I have not been authorized to address you as anything other than your approved designation," the surgeon responded, his tone as void of emotion as the Robotic Military Personnel from the before time. Melyndie cast a questioning look at 41GB.

"I am unable to alter any directives that Dr. Henley may be operating under, nor change the manner in which he feels responsible to address you," 41GB replied in a tone that attempted sympathy but, to Melyndie, fell just short of human understanding.

"Who can give the authorization? Because I'm used to being called Melyndie now," she argued obstinately, teetering on the brink of petulance.

"When Dr. Kishida-Guan returns, the issue may be put before him," came the surgeon's detached response before he refocused on his original purpose. "Now, as I was saying, the biomechatronic division has replicated your upper limb assemblies in perfect detail. The installation would require the removal of your current extremities, so we consulted with Dr. Kishida-Guan who determined that we move forward—"

"I'm not a surgeon," Melyndie interjected, "but wouldn't your team need to sever the damaged nerve endings and then attach them to the prosthetics for them to be of any benefit? If you're able to do that, why can't you simply repair the nicked nerves in my neck?"

She could almost picture his eyes rolling behind those sterile goggles, and had to stifle a smile at the thought. Such expressions—natural, human—were suppressed beneath layers of genetic design and societal control, so picturing a reaction was all she could do.

The surgeon merely looked at her for a moment and then addressed her concern. "Severing nerves is done meticulously in a manner which allows for reconnection—putting it simplistically. Repairing a damaged nerve is an entirely different—"

Unsatisfied, Melyndie pressed further. "I don't see how? You nicked it and need to sever it anyway, so sever it and reconnect it—just not to a set of fake appendages."

The surgeon blinked rapidly, as if recalibrating. Then his blinking slowed as he confirmed her proposition. "That is precisely what I was trying to say before you continually interrupted me. Dr. Kishida-Guan only wants the prosthetic limbs attached as a backup, should…well…should the surgery not go as planned. We have never, after all, undertaken a procedure like this before, so complications may occur—"

"Complications worse than the loss of my arms and hands?" Melyndie scoffed.

"Indeed. The nerves we will be working with…well, let me just say that my team and I will do all we can to ensure no other part of your body suffers the same paralysis. As I've stated, we are operating in uncharted territory. However, I've practiced the procedure relentlessly, since the damage occurred, to ensure a flawless outcome. This should put your mind at ease…" he paused, as if deciding whether to speak his mind. A second later, he did, and his assertion left Melyndie feeling apprehensive. "If you were a standard fabrication, we would have terminated you and requisitioned a replacement."

Melyndie was rendered speechless by the reminder of how undervalued life in her time was, but what stunned her more was 41GB's response.

"That was a highly unnecessary statement to make, Dr. Henley, and does nothing to ensure that Melyndie remains calm during this trying time. I would caution you to keep such words to yourself moving forward."

The surgeon did no more than nod, then pressed on. "If all goes well, you will begin the recovery phase at the end of next week and should regain full functional use of your arms and hands within six months…or less, if you are diligent in your recuperative exercises."

"Oh, I will be, rest assured," Melyndie replied, a defiant edge to her tone.

"That is good to hear. I will return next week to attend to your surgery. Good day to you both."

He turned and exited without waiting for a response. The door sealed with a sterile mechanical hiss—a punctuation mark at the end of an emotionless paragraph.

The way in which she was fabricated, her purpose for existence, and her time in the before time had made it easy to overlook the reality of her world. Having that reality thrust back into her face nearly uncapped the well of emotions she'd worked so hard to repress since her return.

Alone now with 41GB, she turned her head slightly, gazing out of the panoramic window where the night had fallen. Her mind drifted back to her days in the before time—sleeping beneath a sky where stars streaked by in a silent ballet of ghostly lights. Eventually, she tore her gaze away and sought out the only person close enough to be called a friend, though she knew the term was nebulous in this time.

41GB was nothing more than a holy one and scientist, assigned to oversee her development—perhaps chosen precisely because she could mimic emotion convincingly, even if she neither felt nor fully understood it. Their interactions were designed to prepare Melyndie for the emotional chaos of the before time. Yet in the end, it wasn't the emotions of the past that proved most difficult; it was controlling her own in the present that posed the greater challenge.

"How long do you think it will be before I can return to the before time to complete my mission?" she asked, keeping her tone level to mask the ache of disappointment.

"As Dr. Henley stated, it will be approximately six months before you are returned to a state of readiness. After which, there will be a few additional test runs, simply to ensure there are no more issues in locking on to your locator chip. Is that what you wanted to know?"

Melyndie gave a small nod, pressing her lips together to keep her frustration buried.

"Since there is some time before your scheduled surgery next week and your vitals have been consistently stable, I believe it's appropriate to conduct your debriefing now. We've delayed it long enough, wouldn't you agree?"

Melyndie wanted to say no. Discussing Zain and Tom would only reopen the wounds she'd spent the past three months trying to heal. But she'd also spent that time relearning how to mask her emotions. If 41GB could keep the debrief short, she might just manage not to break.

"I'm a bit tired, but I should be fine to answer your queries," she replied thickly. "I should point out that my activities were limited and my interactions confined to only a few people. Given the repetitiveness of my days, I do not have too much to reveal and so should be able to quickly convey necessary information to you."

41GB nodded. "Let me quickly retrieve my recording device and we can begin. Be succinct and this will take no time at all." She returned with the device, opened it, and pressed a button. "Now then, simply begin by giving a concise description of your mission parameters."

Melyndie took a breath and steadied herself. The memories she summoned were vivid—tinged with both wonder and bitterness. "My primary objective was to retrieve genetic materials to test their viability through time travel. The purpose of which was to replenish the materials currently in storage, which are actively degrading. If successful, repeat leaps in time would have been authorized until a full complement of genetic materials was gathered."

41GB remained inscrutable, yet something in her stillness suggested intense focus. "Alright. Upon your return, you mentioned crossing paths with a pair of individuals."

Melyndie's eyes lost focus. "Zain and Tom," she whispered, her voice a silken thread fraying against the pull of her memories.

"Tell me about them."

Melyndie hesitated. She had spent months trying to forget—compartmentalizing, numbing, burying—but the mention of their names echoed like a summons from a past she wasn't ready to relive. She took a deep breath and steadied her emotions, "Zain and Tom were unforeseen variables—ones I didn't expect to matter so much," she began cautiously. "Zain is a military man in charge of one of the battalions tasked with the chipping of the citizenry—the same chip that was removed from me—as well as ensuring compliance. He was very suspicious over the circumstances of my arrival. I think he recognized immediately that I was not what I appeared to be—but kept those thoughts to himself…initially."

"And Tom?" 41GB prompted.

"Tom…" Her voice softened. "Tom is an RMP. Assigned to tend to me, guard me, and keep an eye on me. He was the first to realize when I had come from, and yet…he still chose to help. There was something in him that seemed almost—compassionate at times."

"What is an RMP?" 41GB asked, her tone light but genuinely inquisitive.

Melyndie glanced over, surprised by the display of curiosity. Her brow knitted, but she said nothing, just returned to her explanation. "Robotic Military Personnel. Autonomous, combat-programmed enforcers built as support for the military. In that time, they were everywhere—machines meant to follow orders without hesitation. But Tom…" She paused. "Tom is different."

41GB tilted her head slightly. "And this difference—was it programmed, or learned?"

It was the continued inquisitiveness in 41GB's voice, and the accompanying light in her eyes, that caught Melyndie off guard—not the question itself, but the way it felt like 41GB was trying to understand something unknown.

"I'm not sure," Melyndie said quietly. "But whichever it is, he chose to care. I'm fairly certain that no one programmed that."

There was a brief silence, and then 41GB asked, her voice almost a whisper, "And do you believe…it cared for you?"

Melyndie nodded faintly, her throat tightening as she met 41GB's gaze.

The holy one leaned back, the moment folding inward as the practiced neutrality returned. "Did this interaction inhibit your mission parameters?"

The abrupt return to emotional neutrality caught Melyndie off guard, but it didn't suppress the smile that rose unbidden—her first genuine smile in months. "Not at all," she said. "If anything, my interaction with them ensured the mission's viability. Once I revealed the purpose of my presence, Zain, though initially skeptical, offered his DNA freely. He then went further, proposing to register me as a Sampling Specialist under his command—an official designation that allowed me to remain close by his and Tom's side under the guise of deployment stress testing. It gave me cover, and purpose."

"You mentioned you were injured upon arrival," 41GB said, her tone even. "What occurred, and how long did recovery take?"

Melyndie nodded once, the memory flashing sharp behind her eyes. "I fell during the descent—landed hard. The impact fractured my clavicle and left extensive bruising across my lower body. It took nearly six weeks to fully recover, though under normal conditions, the healing process would have required much longer. My enhancements mitigated the worst of it." She hesitated, her gaze dropping for a moment. "Zain and Tom watched over me the entire time. They ensured I had what I needed, even when I couldn't lift my own arm. I wasn't used to being...tended to like that."

41GB nodded slowly. "It is good to hear your wounds were tended to. I suppose it's also fortuitous that the chip's interference delayed your return. But we did try to bring you back, a bit earlier than we planned to. Dr. Kishida-Guan grew increasingly concerned that we were having difficulties maintaining a stable lock on your chip. So, when we got a lock, he made the call to attempt your return—to no avail."

"Actually, the attempt sent me hurtling through space...just not time," Melyndie explained. "I'm fortunate that I sustained no further injury."

"I am grateful also," 41GB smiled softly, then returned to the briefing. "As for Zain and Tom, it seems their involvement—while unexpected—was ultimately beneficial."

"Yes," Melyndie agreed. "Without them, I don't know that I could have completed my mission. Did I? I mean, were any of the samples viable?"

"A small number of them returned, usable. That is the positive outcome that we were all hoping for. Now, what of your departure? Did your attachment to them cause complications?"

"Complications?" she shook her head. "I don't quite know what you expect me to say. It didn't cause complications in the strictest form of the word, but it did cause pain. It was so abrupt, that I didn't even get to say goodbye." Her voice broke on the final word. "Is there anything else you need to know? I'm rather tired now."

"No," said 41GB, closing the recorder. "These details should suffice, Melyndie. Thank you for your cooperation and candor." She stood, but paused at the door. "Now that the debriefing is concluded, I doubt we will see each other again before your return mission as there is little need. So...I wish you a speedy recovery."

Melyndie mustered a tired smile and nodded.

As the door closed behind 41GB, silence returned—and this time it felt personal. Despite 41GB's artificial nature, she was still the closest thing to a friend Melyndie had in this time, so her departure felt like another loss.

She closed her eyes as tears slipped into the pillow. She let them fall—because even her strength had limits, and the weight of pretending she didn't feel had become too much to bear.

Immediately after concluding the debriefing with Melyndie, 41GB stood outside the compact, utilitarian office of Dr. Kishida-Guan. She input her unique identifier and tapped the alert on the embedded touch panel. The metallic wall responded with a muted chime, followed by a soft hiss as the door slid open.

Inside, Dr. Kishida-Guan didn't look up from his tablet. He gestured distractedly toward the seat across from him, his aged hand lined with wear. 41GB stepped forward, paused, then sat in silence until he tapped the screen, plunging it into darkness. With a sigh, he finally lifted his gaze.

"Well?"

"Her information is in the report," 41GB said, sliding the small data device across his desk. "There's nothing to indicate that her delayed return could destabilize the mission—though there are notable points. For example, she emerged from the portal off elevation and sustained minor injuries on impact, which led to immediate detection. Fortunately, two individuals—one human, one nonhuman—intervened. They assisted her recovery and helped conceal her presence. According to Melyndie, the human created a cover story that enabled her to operate undetected while collecting genetic samples."

Dr. Kishida-Guan steepled his fingers. "Did you detect any deception in her account?"

"None detected," 41GB replied. "But I question why we would suspect dishonesty. She appears to have no motive to conceal the truth."

He exhaled slowly. "She was there far longer than planned. That alone introduces risk; unknown variables. Emotional entanglements form quickly, especially for someone...predisposed to feel."

"She didn't report any such entanglements," 41GB said. "Her tone remained measured, her account clinical—even when describing those who aided her. There was no emotional coloring, no hesitation. If attachments were formed, they did not influence her actions. She responded to all inquiries with precision, and at no point did she exhibit reluctance to discuss her departure or return. Her focus remained centered on mission outcome."

She paused—too long—recalling the shift in Melyndie's tone when she first mentioned their names—Zain and Tom. A kind of...reverence, perhaps. And when she spoke of being pulled back abruptly, of not having time to say goodbye, there was a sadness. Faint, but present. *So, why did I just lie to cover for her?* She thought and then realized she was also covering for herself: her display of curiosity could be seen as a weakness. She let go of the breath she'd been holding when she told herself, *we were alone, so no one knows the truth.*

Her eyes widened slightly.

The recording. It could contradict...her gaze dropped to the device resting on the desk between them. It was just a device, but its very presence was cause for concern. Every word of the debrief. Every moment Melyndie's voice faltered. Every question 41GB had asked that strayed from standard procedure. Every pause. Every shift in tone. And—worse—her own responses. The softness in her voice. The curiosity she'd allowed to surface.

It wasn't really condemning...but she'd felt Melyndie's pull to the before time and found herself questioning...had she formed emotional attachments? Could she hinder the mission? Worse still was her own actions, just now, as she sat before the holy one...and lied.

The debrief had not been as sterile as she'd exerted.

She had claimed Melyndie's report was clinical. It wasn't. She had dismissed emotional indicators. They were present. And now it was all there—documented, preserved, and easily cross-referenced.

Her hand moved reflexively toward the device. She forced her expression into neutrality. "Would you like me to transmit the transcript to your tablet?" she asked, voice calm but clipped. "Or is it unnecessary, given that nothing…significant was revealed?"

Dr. Kishida-Guan waved a hand without looking up. "It's irrelevant. What matters is the outcome, not how she said it…unless there was something in her tone to suggest—"

"No, nothing at all," 41GB interjected, questioning whether she had been just a little too assertive, but Dr. Kishida-Guan appeared not to notice. He waved at her again.

She nodded once and retrieved the device. Her grip tightened the moment it was in her palm.

She fell silent, eyes lowered—until a lingering question surfaced, unbidden. Something the surgeon had said "The surgeon did say something that had me thinking."

Dr. Kishida-Guan glanced at her, but his expression didn't shift. "Oh?"

"He remarked that, had Melyndie been any other fabrication, we could have simply terminated her and requested a replacement. That statement was telling. Why didn't we prepare for that possibility? Why wasn't more than one genetically enhanced created?"

Kishida-Guan's shoulders stiffened. "Because at the time, we believed one would suffice. The Chancellor gave explicit instructions. A single prototype. Proof of concept."

"We fabricate citizens by the hundreds on a weekly cycle," she said. "At least we did until the degradation began. So, it was not a resource issue, at that time. We had time. We had access. Why didn't we insist on at least a single backup?"

His tone sharpened, then he deflected gracefully. "You assume I didn't."

She blinked, surprised by the admission.

He stood, pacing slowly behind his desk. "I requested…three," he lied, with ease, his tone shifting to one meant to soothe and comfort. "What we received was one. G9983 and G13654 delivered Melyndie as instructed: a genetically enhanced; however, it wasn't until much later that we discovered they acted in defiance against standard protocol. Took it upon themselves to insert modifications—unapproved emotional coding, inconsistent suppression markers. They had gone rogue."

"You believe they would have altered all three?"

"If they went against my directive and enhanced Melyndie against specs, then yes, I believe they would have done."

"Would that truly have been such a bad thing?"

"You underestimate the risk, 41GB. One fabrication with emotions is already destabilizing. Imagine three. Imagine a cluster forming emotional attachments to one another, reinforcing each other's divergence."

Her brow creased. "But at the time, we didn't know they had violated the parameters, so couldn't we have had the backups made and then…terminated them…if it became necessary," she continued, suddenly finding the practice abhorrent, but hid away her discomfort and continued, "if they proved too divergent?"

"Which would have us in the same situation as we are now, because they would have been modified and they would have been terminated, because, in the end, we would have decided we only needed one. And a flawed one is better than three. But let's explore your hypothetical: What would have prevented them from suddenly fabricating all citizens as genetically enhanced? We could, even now, be facing an enormous crisis of emotional instability." He stopped pacing and leaned over the desk. "Their decision endangered everything. So, I had them terminated. I had no choice."

41GB studied him in silence, then said—her tone still even, but laced with something colder, harder to ignore. "Because of your choice, our only option now lies paralyzed in the medical bay. If the surgery fails…if she never fully recovers…everything we've worked to preserve will be lost."

She rose from her seat. For a moment, it looked as though she might say more—but she simply turned and headed out of the door.

Kishida-Guan didn't stop her.

When the door slid shut behind her, he remained still, staring at the place she had just been.

The silence pressed in.

He closed his eyes for a moment, then leaned back heavily in his chair.

*Failure is not an option*, he reminded himself.

He had risked too much. Sacrificed too many. The Chancellor wanted results, and he would deliver them—because the alternative was unthinkable. This mission wasn't just about survival. It was about *his* survival. His legacy. His control.

He opened his eyes.

Then, without another word, he stood and made his way toward the medical bay.



The sterile white light of the medical bay reflected off the polished floor and unforgiving walls, casting a faint sheen across every surface. Dr. Kishida-Guan entered alone and without ceremony. He pulled a tall stool toward Melyndie's bed, its metallic legs scraping the floor in a discordant rasp that grated against her already thinning nerves.

He lowered himself with calculated grace, hands folded neatly, face calm—too calm. The corners of his mouth bent into something that might have passed for warmth if it hadn't been so rehearsed.

"Hello, Melyndie," he said softly. "Is the day treating you kindly?"

Melyndie closed her eyes. A faint crease formed between her brows as she drew in a slow, deliberate breath through her nose and exhaled again. Anyone else might have earned a biting response for recycling that monotonous question—but this was the holy one, second only to the Chancellor in authority. And age had lent him an aura of sacrosanctity that discouraged confrontation.

After a pause, she opened her eyes and nearly recoiled. He was staring at her—not with curiosity or concern, but with something far more penetrating. Something that felt clinical. Something vulturine.

"I am well enough," she replied cautiously. "Ready to have my body renewed to full function."

"That is understandable." His tone was still gentle, but the pace of his words had quickened. "I was given a brief overview of your report to 41GB just before coming in. You're certain there's nothing you wish to add?"

"I relayed everything of pertinence," she replied, her tone growing more formal.

"Very good." He nodded once, then—without warning—his tone changed. "But it's not your report I want to dissect today."

Melyndie wanted to sit up straighter, wanted to distance herself from the doctor, but with her paralysis, independent movement wasn't possible, so she lay there, concentrating on her breathing.

"There's something far more crucial," he continued. "Something that will shape the next phase of your mission." He paused; eyes fixed on her. "Do you remember when you were thrown forward during the test trials…into our future?"

She gave a slow nod, her pulse beginning to climb.

"I need to confess something." He leaned in, the practiced calm peeling away to reveal something harder underneath, eyes gleaming with something disturbing she'd never seen in a person before. "I changed the coordinates."

Melyndie's eyes widened. "You…?"

"I needed to see," he said. "I needed to know if our future was salvageable. If I—if we—had anything left to fight for."

He leaned closer still. So close, she could feel the heat of his breath on her cheek. It made her stomach turn. The intimacy of it, the intensity. The entire room seemed to shift, and for a fleeting second, she thought she might just move…out of sheer desperation to escape.

She leaned her head back as far as it would go, barely disguising her unease. Her eyes darted, and he noticed. After a long, agonizing minute, he leaned away. "You attempted to describe what you'd seen when you returned the first time, but failed to do so successfully. Now…I need you to remember—"

Relieved by the sudden space, she drew in a sharper breath. "It's been too long—"

"No." The word cut through the room with alarming force. He reined himself in almost immediately, forcing his tone back into control. "This is important. I need to know what…who…you saw. So, you will try again. Don't focus. Just drift. Let the memories find you. You were designed for this. Remember? Enhanced memory recall. Put that to use now. Close your eyes and return to our future world."

She wanted to object—but something in his manner warned her against it. So, she closed her eyes, doubting, reaching inward— but still trying. If nothing else, as he stated, she had been designed for recall. That thought grounded her. Slowly, the room fell away.

Her voice softened. "The buildings…they weren't whole anymore. Tarnished. Collapsing. The light felt…diminished. The walkways were fractured. The stones…some were missing, others buried in dirt. It was like the world had stopped being maintained."

Kishida-Guan didn't breathe.

"There were people. Nowhere near as many as now. But they weren't alive. Not really. They wandered. Lost. Detached."

"Focus on them," he commanded, barely above a whisper. "Do any stand out to you."

"There was a figure," she murmured, then she found herself standing there again, watching. Alarmed. "In the shadows. Watching me. No—he's emerging. Slowly. His steps heavy. His body is frail. He's moving like time has dragged at him too long." Her voice trembled. "His face…I can't recognize it. It's drawn and skeletal. But the eyes—something about them. Alive. Aware. Like something ancient staring back at me."

She stopped. Her eyes flew open.

"It was you," she said, almost in disbelief. "That man…it was you."

Dr. Kishida-Guan leaned back, expression unreadable. A slow, restrained smile curled at the corners of his mouth, as if he were savoring the truth more than hearing it.

"I endured," he said softly. "When the rest did not."

"You were there," she whispered.

He nodded. "That encounter—your recognition—it confirmed everything. We still exist. *I* still exist."

He stood then, slowly pacing at the foot of her bed, not looking at her now but speaking more to the room. "I've lived by directives all my life. Protocol. Doctrine. But none of it could show me what time revealed in that moment. Our people become husks. Stripped of what once made them human."

He turned toward her again, softening his voice into something bordering on reverent. "But you…you are the anomaly. You, now, carry what they will lose. And because I exist then and you exist now, together, we can ensure that what was lost is found. Don't you see? We restore everything that was lost and the balance to humanity renews. I can feel it as if it's already taking place. Can't you? Can't you feel the tides shifting in renewal of humanity?"

She remained unmoved, expression unreadable. But inside, the dread was blooming. He was trying to convert her. To pull her closer under the guise of shared purpose. But for all of his flowery words, he hadn't said anything that convinced her that his love for humanity was his driving force. Their current realm was evidence of where his true passion lay: an emotionless, productive society.

He caught the resistance and shifted tactics.

"You don't need to trust me," he said, dropping the ruse; his tone returning to one of direct confrontation. "But you will be instrumental, Melyndie. When you return to the before time, your mission parameters will be expanded."

Her eyes narrowed. "How exactly?"

"You're going to find two men for me," he said.

"And the samples?"

"I said expanded," he said with a wave of his hand. "Of course, the samples are still of highest priority. But these two men are…essential to my purpose. To our restored future."

She tilted her head slightly. "It took days of travel in a jeep just to cross from one city to another. How do you expect me to locate two unknown individuals among billions, across entire continents?"

"What is a jeep? A continent?" he asked, intrigued.

Her mouth parted in disbelief—not just at the question, but at how quickly he had veered off-course. "Um…a jeep is a vehicle. A crude one. Used by military personnel. We used it to reach each city. Slowly…and in great discomfort," she murmured, mentally rubbing her bruised posterior.

"Ah," he murmured. "Primitive transport…fascinating. And a continent?"

"Is that really important right now? What is important, is that you're giving me an impossible task," she said flatly, pulling him back to their conversation. "And you're not explaining why."

"Very well. But, since you were fabricated for this and will complete whatever missions I deem of importance, the why is not important for you to know. I will provide you with the names," he said, his voice tightening. "And likely locations. You *will* find them."

She didn't look away. "Why?"

He didn't answer. He'd already made it clear that she didn't need the why answered.

She turned toward the screen beside her, its vitals blinking quietly. Her voice dropped, weighted now, as she tried again in a different way. "What is the purpose behind my quest for these two men?"

He stared at her a long moment deciding that was something he could reveal. When he finally spoke, his tone was measured.

"The first," he said, "you are to deliver a message to."

"And the second?"

He didn't blink. "The second, you are to terminate."

Her breath caught.

Kishida-Guan stood at the foot of her bed, hands clasped behind him. He wasn't looking at her now—his gaze had gone distant, fixed on something only he could see. A future already written. A reckoning already underway.

"When you return to the before time," he said quietly, "everything will rest on your shoulders. Not the Chancellor. Not the holy ones. Not even me. Just you."

He turned his eyes back to her—sharp now, cutting through any illusion of choice.

"If you fail to find them, if you hesitate for even a moment... then all of it ends. The chance to rebuild. The future I've sacrificed everything for. The species itself."

His voice dropped—quiet, resolute, almost reverent:

"And in the wake of your failure will remain only the echo of what humanity could have been."

A fragile breath escaped her. She turned back to the monitor, where her vital signs blinked in steady defiance of his prophecy. Then, without looking at him, her voice emerged—barely above a whisper, but iron-threaded with something deeper.

"I won't fail."

# Blueprints for Extinction

Year: 2158

At four in the morning, President Saltzer stepped into his office at world leadership headquarters. The lights flicked on automatically as he crossed the floor, his gait burdened by fatigue. For eight relentless months, he'd circled the globe, inspecting troops, ensuring his commands were executed without deviation.

Today's task was different. Today, he was meeting with his lead scientist, Dr. Riku Jang—the man who, two and a half years ago, had promised a breakthrough vital to the mission he had conceptualized. The president had relayed that promise to the other world leaders. It had bought them time and trust. But delays followed. Questions were raised and confidence had thinned.

Now, however, Dr. Jang claimed, with a high level of assurance, that the final obstacles were behind them.

He glanced at his watch. Forty-five minutes remained before the meeting. Saltzer sank into his desk chair and began chipping away at the backlog of work that had accumulated in his absence.

He'd barely made a dent when a soft alert chimed on his screen. Dr. Jang had arrived. With a tap, Saltzer verified the identity and unlocked the office door.

The doctor entered with his usual arrogance; shoulders squared like a peacock on full display.

"Greetings, Doctor. I'm eager to hear your progress."

"It is good to see you too, my friend."

The president's expression soured at the chiding tone. He didn't respond in kind. "Let's save the pleasantries. We're nearly three years behind schedule. I hope you're here with the results you promised."

Dr. Jang's jaw tightened, his displeasure flickering before he composed himself. He placed a sleek tablet on the table and activated it with deft fingers. "Based on the changes *you* mandated at our first meeting," he began pointedly. Saltzer offered a faint smile at the jab. The scientist had grown skilled in redirecting blame—almost admirable, in a way more common among politicians. "My team has finalized a rapid fabrication process. Prototype beings will begin integrating into society within months. Replacement of existing citizens can proceed shortly after."

Saltzer exhaled sharply, frustration expanding his chest. A three-month horizon felt insulting. This project had already consumed over five years. "If the development is complete—" he started.

"It is," the doctor interrupted, "but producing the fabrications still requires time. And since you insisted on a steady, scalable influx—"

"I get it. What about the longevity gene sequencing?"

Dr. Jang paused. He straightened, voice tightening with gravity. "Before we discuss that, you need to know: the current fabrications—due to necessary modifications for a quick turnout—will deteriorate quickly. They'll operate at high capacity, but only for a limited time. A few months at most. We will, of course, keep churning them out for work, replacing them as quickly as possible."

The words hung between them, heavy and foreboding.

"So, we'll need constant replacements," Saltzer murmured thoughtfully. "That's hardly efficient for our needs long term."

"Precisely, and our equipment will be pushed to its limits in an attempt to keep pace."

"Then build more equipment."

"We've already begun. However, expanding our current capacity will require nearly a year of development and installation. It wasn't factored into the original timeline." He tapped a few notes into his tablet before continuing. "Once ready, I recommend dedicating the new systems to the next generation of citizen fabrications. That process will be far more complex and take far more time."

"How long?"

"To create beings capable of functioning as a productive society—at an elevated level—we'll need to abandon the current accelerated methods that we're using, currently, in designing the worker fabrications."

Saltzer's brow furrowed. "Meaning?"

"We'll have to mimic human developmental timelines," the doctor said plainly. "Minus biological incubation. Roughly a decade to generate durable stock. Twelve to sixteen years, by my estimate, until each human specimen is set to take its place among society. That's the only way to prevent rapid degradation."

"A long timeline," Saltzer mused.

"It only feels long. Meanwhile, the current worker-bee fabrications will clear debris and build the foundational realms. As those realms come online, our slow-grown citizens will be ready to occupy them." The doctor's tone now flowed easily, rehearsed but resolute. "As each realm is built, we can determine which genetic enhancements will prove beneficial to its success and provide additional modified stock as needed. Because each realm will become a self-contained society, the number of fabrications needed will be far lower in number compared to Earth's current population which I believe is our ultimate goal: to restore and preserve our natural resources for centuries to come."

"And, of course, to ensure the continuation of the human race." the president stated softly.

"A new, improved human race," Jang modified.

Saltzer shifted gears. "Food supply. What's the strategy?"

"RMPs are harvesting wildlife in all territories. Before extermination, genetic material is being collected from all viable species used for consumption. Samples are then being distributed to regional labs." He swiped to another data file. "In those labs, specimens are examined and damaged DNA is removed. The purified material is preserved and ready for use in future food production. We're working with over three hundred thousand edible species. The collection should sustain countless generations. Disease-free sustenance." He added, "Aquatic ecosystems, freed from human interference, should rebound naturally—an additional boon to planetary recovery."

Saltzer arched a brow. "But wouldn't marine overpopulation become its own problem?"

"We're prepared. Periodic harvesting will regulate ocean life and provide designated employment for future citizens."

"And land animals?"

"With the population moving into controlled realms, we're simplifying external environments. Smaller species irrelevant to food production—ants, hummingbirds—will be ignored by RMPs. Land ecosystems biodiversity will evolve…heal…with time.

"And crops?"

"All produce will be grown in sealed, specialized laboratories. No soil contamination, no wildlife interference. Many facilities are already being converted."

Saltzer leaned back. "After all this time…it's surreal to be so close to full implementation."

"Indeed. A monumental task it has been, but we're only a few decades away from the onset of the new world," the doctor stated proudly.

"A few decades? So, then, when will the first realms be completed and ready for occupancy?"

"I estimate no longer than thirty years, assuming current progress holds. By then, we'll have a sufficient base of genetically superior fabrications to maintain them."

Saltzer nodded, then circled back. "Longevity testing—any breakthroughs?"

Dr. Jang sighed. "Progress, yes. But achieving meaningful extension of life requires narrow focus. Too many variables. We'd need a small sample—two individuals, perhaps—to refine the sequencing in isolation. Once successful, we can scale it to the broader population."

Saltzer smirked. "Let me guess. You've chosen yourself as one of the test subjects."

"Of course. I'm in excellent health. Clean family history."

"And your second choice?"

"You," Jang replied without hesitation. "Unless your genetics happen to be subpar."

"My lineage is as sturdy as stallions," the president chuckled, already envisioning a future ruled by their own perfected reflections.

"Imagine, our clones, sculpted in our image, shepherding the future of civilization," Jang murmured, almost reverently, thinking along the same lines as Saltzer.

"A joint presidency?"

"Too small."

"Emperors, then?"

Jang's eyes gleamed. "Still too mortal."

Saltzer leaned forward, voice low and eager. "Then what will we be?"

A breath of a moment passed, and then the doctor smiled, the corners of his mouth pulling tight. "Holy ones," he whispered. "Not elected. Not born. Ascended."

The two men shared a brief moment of amusement, the levity at odds with the stark future they were designing. Outside the glass wall behind them, the sky hung colorless and still—an empty canvas waiting for the new world they would paint upon its bones.

"I'm not sure how much longer we can keep rounding up the dissidents. Eventually, General Takayoshi will find out," Zain said, frustrated. "If he hasn't done already."

"If the general had been made aware, would it not be likely that you would have been called in to answer for your actions? Also, have you considered discussing with the rebels the likely consequences if they keep resisting?" Tom asked.

"I was thinking the same thing…and, you know I have," Zain replied, shaking his head in exasperation. "And what about the RMPs we pulled from their duties to manage the increasing numbers? Has anyone questioned why they're not in the field?"

"No, I just told the RMPs they were reassigned to a new mission when they arrived," Tom answered.

"And they didn't question it?"

"Perhaps they see no need, as no new orders have come from General Takayoshi since this mission started six months ago. Once all the animals are collected and termi—"

"Don't say it," Zain cut in. "I don't need a reminder, alright?"

"I was just going to say that once this mission is over, new orders will be given. Then, all RMPs will be recalled and reprogrammed with fresh directives. Until then, the biggest concern will be if those in command notice that they are not transmitting audio or visual feed."

"Since their current directive is for them to simply collect and destroy, those at command aren't likely to be concerned over the need to monitor. While mission critical, it isn't something that needs to be reported on regularly, I wouldn't think."

"What do you suggest we do with all these civilians who refuse to work on the reformation projects? We can't afford to continue providing for them in the same way we do for those who work hard every day."

Zain paced back and forth; his brow furrowed deeply. "We need to be strategic here, Tom. Maybe it's time we considered a different approach. We can't keep detaining them indefinitely without causing unrest among the workers who are compliant. And, as you stated, we can't continue supplying them food and water when they are not pulling their weight."

Before Tom could even entertain the thought of suggesting an alternate course of action, a soldier emerged from the throng, dragging a livid, fiercely resistant woman in his grip. Zain's heart lurched with both delight and dread as he recognized the fiery prisoner to be his sister, Amal.

"Unhand her, soldier!" Zain commanded, his voice echoing authoritatively over the clamor. He instantly regretted the order as soon as it left his lips, for the moment she was released from the soldier's hold, Amal lunged at him with unbridled fury. She closed the gap between them in mere seconds and began to pummel her brother's chest relentlessly, tears streaming down her face—a potent cocktail of rage and despair.

The soldier and Tom reacted instinctively, their hands flying to their weapons which they swiftly pointed at Amal.

"Stand down!" Zain bellowed, his voice punching through the confusion like a shockwave. "That's an order!"

The soldier froze. Even Tom halted mid-step, its sensors processing the shift in Zain's tone, but Amal's assault continued.

Her fists struck without rhythm, driven by rage, betrayal, and something deeper that only she…and Zain…understood. No one moved to stop her. She hit him again. And again. The impact of each blow thudded against his chest, threatening to destabilize his rigid stance. Still, he refused to move, refused to stop her assault.

"I hate you!" she shouted, sharp and sudden, cutting through the air. "You killed our mother!"

Zain didn't speak. A cold stillness settled over him, hollowing him from the inside out. He deserved every strike, every hate-filled word. He would stand there and take it all, if it meant easing his sister's own anguish.

When he felt her blows begin to weaken, he lifted his hands and gripped her by the wrists, then pulled her into his embrace, stroking her hair as she dampened his uniform with her tears.

"Why, Zain? Why are you doing this?" Amal sobbed; her voice muffled against his chest. "First to our mother, and now, to your own people?"

Zain looked at Tom and the soldier, signaling them to step away for some privacy. He then spoke softly and sincerely, "Amal, there are events unfolding that I can't explain at the moment, but understand this: I am staying in my current role because if I'm taken out, I won't be able to bring about any change."

"Is that what you told our mother before you put a bullet in her head?" Amal hissed, her anguish turning meteorically to one of rage.

Zain flinched, his face contorting with pain as each word struck deeper than her earlier physical blows could ever have. He pulled her in tighter, swallowing hard against the lump that formed in his throat. "Had I not complied, it would have been all of us to die," he whispered, agony clear. "I followed through with the orders

because if anyone was going to send mother to Barzakh[1], it was
going to be me, not some lifeless robot simply following orders
without comprehending the whys. I sold my soul to ensure that you
lived; that I lived, so that I might find a way to try to combat the evil
being played out by our current world leaders."

Amal pulled back slightly, looking into his eyes, searching for
something—a sign of deceit or even sincerity. The silence between
them stretched thin as paper, fragile and ready to tear at the slightest
provocation. "And have you?" she whispered after a time. "Have
you found your way?"

Zain held her gaze, the burden of his position evident in the
new lines creased around his eyes. He sighed deeply, the weight of
unspoken secrets pressing down on him. "I am lost, sister, but I am
working every day, every moment, to find my way; to locate an
opening, a weakness in their plans that I can exploit. It's
complicated. More so than you might imagine."

Amal's eyes remained locked on his, searching for the
brother she once knew amidst the stranger who now stood before
her, "Complicated for you, or for us?" she challenged quietly.

"For both…for all," Zain confessed. "It isn't just about
survival any longer, it's about shaping what comes after." He took a
step back and turned her about by the shoulders until she was facing
the growing number of people in the distance, surrounded by RMPs.
"If I step out of line, they'll replace me with someone who won't
hesitate to kill every single one of those people you see there; people
who dared to defy the orders given. I know I cannot save everyone,
but I am trying to start somewhere, but if the powers that be get
word that I am not executing these people—people who've dared to
take a stand…" his voice trailed off, his head shaking repeatedly as

---

[1] invisible realm between life and death where to soul goes to await
judgement.

he fought to tamp down the overwhelming emotions threatening to take hold.

"So, what you're saying is, if I lived anywhere else…" Amal said, stepping back. Her voice had grown small. "I'd be dead right now."

Zain squeezed his eyes shut, pained by the realization of those five little words. His legs buckled and he fell to his knees, collapsing beneath the weight of that truth. His forehead pressed against the searing sand, arms wrapping around himself as if to keep his heart from exploding from his chest.

The cost of this mission, to himself and to every person on the planet, had been great.

Amal slowly sank to her knees before Zain. She tenderly placed her trembling hand on the crown of his bowed head, allowing her tears to cascade freely down her cheeks. "I do not understand all that is happening, and I don't know if I can ever forgive you, but I understand your reasons. So…I will fight by your side," she pledged amidst sniffles.

Zain raised his head at last. His eyes met hers, relief and torment flickering in equal measure. "I can't know how any of this will end—"

"But we will confront it together," Amal interjected softly, finishing his sentence for him.

Zain rose slowly, reaching out to help her stand. The air between them felt changed—not healed, not whole, but on a path to mending.

He cast a quick glance around them. His gaze collided with Tom's who immediately moved in their direction. Zain wiped the wet grit from his face and squared his shoulders.

"Is everything…resolved?" Tom asked tentatively as if stepping on eggshells. Its cautious tone caught Amal off guard causing her to tilt her head slightly in confusion.

"Adaptive AI," Zain responded briefly.

"Okay then," Amal stated, accepting. She drew in a shaky, but determined breath. "What can I do to help you at this moment?"

"At this moment, we are trying to convince the rebels to at least put on a happy face of compliance and go to work alongside everyone else," Zain explained, glad to have a different focus.

Amal sucked in a huge breath through her nostrils, her lips compressing in renewed anger, "What incentive do they have for doing so? They are being asked to destroy their own homes soon after many of them lost loved ones—"

"Take it easy, Amal," Zain interjected, noticing that his sister's emotions, still raw and vulnerable, were about to derail her once again. He placed his hands on her shoulders, grounding her with a steadying force. "Following the rules is just a temporary tactic, a cover to give us more time. Honestly, I'm not sure what we can achieve with so few people, but it's preferable to a firing squad. That's exactly what we'll all face if my superior finds out that I'm detaining them instead of carrying out the execution orders I've been given." With a heavy sigh, he finished, "And we can't keep feeding them if they aren't carrying their weight."

"Have you considered just having a conversation with them?" she suggested, as though it were as easy as giving a motivational speech.

Zain smiled wryly, "Many times."

"I do not think the uniform is doing us any favors," Tom chimed in.

Amal agreed, "I can understand how it might be a problem. At this moment, I feel like tearing that uniform off and setting it on fire."

"Perhaps you could refrain," Zain said dryly. "I'm still using it. Since, you want to help, maybe *you* could convince them."

"What about the robots watching over them?" Amal inquired, her expression shifting to one of serious worry. "Won't they notify your superiors if they overhear me speaking against their authority?"

"I will have them step away, out of ear shot," Tom stated. "You must convince them that—"

"I get what I have to do," Amal retorted, her eyes burning into Tom with a hostility so potent it could have disintegrated its alloy exterior if her emotions had been a tangible entity.

"Tom isn't the enemy, Amal," Zain interceded, his voice a soothing contrast to the mounting tension.

Amal took a deep breath, her features softening slightly. She knew that Zain was right, but the stress of watching the other robots move like wrecking balls through her community made it easy for her to lash out. She turned back to Tom with a sigh, "I'm sorry, Tom. I'm just finding it difficult to put things into a perspective that makes sense right now."

Tom nodded, "I am not offended, Amal. I quite comprehend why you would feel anger towards me. Now…how can I assist you?"

Amal turned her gaze toward the group of despondent outliers milling about in the distance, their faces etched with resignation and despair. "It starts with me," she declared with newfound resolve. She stepped up to Tom, giving him a determined look. "I'll go and convince them that all hope is not lost. While I do that, you need to ensure that those robots guarding them are sufficiently out of hearing range."

"To avert suspicion, Tom, can you interface with the RMPs? Maybe signal they need to run diagnostics or something equally time-consuming? Take themselves offline for about…how long do you think you need, Amal?"

"Thirty minutes."

"Certainly," Tom replied promptly. "That would most assuredly be more secure than gathering them away from a mob of people who are looking for a reason to flee. I will send the commands now. You may approach them, Amal, when you are ready."

A soft, almost imperceptible smile tugged at the corners of Amal's mouth as she glanced towards her brother. The faint glimmer in her eyes was a silent promise of strength and resilience, an unspoken vow that echoed between them. "I'll get on with Major Reese and have him send out a couple of troop transports to take them all back to the work zone."

"That's okay. I'll radio him when I've ensured that everyone is onboard. Don't want to waste resources if they aren't amenable to my charms. I'm assuming that all I need to do is call over the radio and he'll respond?" She glanced questioningly at the radio attached to her brother's belt.

"Tom, get Amal a spare radio."

Amal smiled softly. A silence fell between them as they waited for Tom to return, and Amal sighed audibly when he did so quickly. "I'll do my best to get them to see reason," she said, took the proffered radio, then pivoted and strode resolutely away.

Zain stood rooted to the spot; his gaze locked onto the retreating figure of his sister as she ventured towards the distant dissidents. His chest collapsed with a breath he hadn't realized he'd been holding, releasing a wave of emotions that seemed forever on the verge of erupting.

His heart pounded fiercely against his ribcage, not out of fear or anxiety but with an overwhelming surge of hope and joy. It was as if a beam of sunlight had pierced through the gloomy clouds hanging over him, illuminating his world once again. The reality that his sister was alive and standing by him…it was more than he could have ever hoped for. A sense of peace washed over him like a soothing balm, chasing away the shadows of dread and despair that had taken residence in his soul.

"Zain?" A gentle murmur from his RMP punctured the silence, jolting Zain out of his deep contemplation. His body tightened reflexively, a small startle that sent ripples through the calm air around him.

"Yes, Tom?" His voice was steady, though it echoed slightly in the vast emptiness of their surroundings.

A pause hung heavy between them before Tom broke it with an ominous tone. "I am detecting an anomaly." The last word hung in the air like a dark cloud, its implications stirring a storm within Zain's mind.

"Not again."

## *Anomalies*

"I find I no longer like that word. What type of anomaly this time?" Zain questioned, a cold knot of fear beginning to form in his stomach.

"I first observed a similar anomaly eight months ago, but it did not seem—"

"Tom! Get to your point."

"When Melyndie made her unexpected appearance and I found myself incapable of locating her existence within any global database—"

"Tom, for God's sake! It feels like you're building me a clock just to tell me the time," Zain interjected, the tension in his voice escalating.

"Zain, stop interrupting me!" A whir of cooling fans slowed to a grumble as Tom released a compressed burst of air, like the hiss of a pressure valve reluctantly opening. It was deliberate, patterned—a perfect imitation of a human sigh, only with the faintest click at the end, like punctuation to its displeasure. "Now, if I may continue. I am fully cognizant of every single being inhabiting this planet. When one is eliminated, their identifying credentials are systematically erased. During the height of terminations, when the chip was activated, the population dropped by over four billion in twelve months."

Zain's gut clenched. It wasn't the number of deaths that unnerved him—it was the suddenness—and the reminder, which he didn't need. "We know what happened then, so that's hardly an anomaly. If the numbers keep dropping, then it's likely dissidents being terminated," Zain retorted, struggling to keep his rising anger under control.

"No, rebel executions do not correspond as, over time, there has been a drastic reduction in those who dare to defy orders and thus the number of deaths has diminished significantly. The peculiar thing about this anomaly is that five hundred individuals were erased simultaneously—"

"Wait! Five hundred people were terminated in our region?"

"That is correct. Simultaneously. Which means their chips were—"

"Tom, why wasn't I made aware of this?"

"I am making you aware of it now, as it just happened shortly ago. However, there are now five hundred new people showing in my system who have no identifying information. Like Melyndie."

"You're not making any sense!"

Tom turned to Zain, and though its face was expressionless, it mirrored Zain's frustration. "Listen closely to what I am saying," it emphasized, carefully articulating each word. "A group of five hundred people were removed all at once and it appears that five hundred have replaced those who were terminated with what seems to be just a number, at least in the global database."

"For what reason?" Zain asked.

"I lack sufficient data to provide a definitive answer. Should I make a guess?"

Zain briefly closed his eyes and shook his head, trying to calm his rising anxiety. "I'm not sure this is a situation where guessing would be helpful—"

"Someone wants the population to seem stable," Tom interjected, deciding to guess nonetheless.

"Why bother? People have been dying in droves since this mission started. What purpose does manipulating the numbers, now, serve?"

Tom hesitated, its internal mechanisms humming softly, a symphony of electronic thought as it processed Zain's challenging question. "The number of dissidents is not being readjusted. When dissidents are terminated, the numbers reflect this in the database. It is only this group of five hundred for which the numbers were modified. I believe it could be psychological manipulation—"

Zain cut through Tom's words sharply; his voice filled with skepticism. His eyes bore into Tom's visual sensors with an intensity that would have made any human uncomfortable. "And I would agree with that hypothesis, *if* the average person had access to that data, which—with the worldwide communications blackout—none would. So, there's no one to manipulate—"

"Those in charge of this mission have access." Tom interrupted, its tone steady and unflinching against Zain's harsh rebuttal.

Zain fell silent as he digested this information. He paced back and forth across the asphalt, his mind racing. "The world's leaders are in charge. Okay, so then maybe a majority of them were given an anticipated number of deaths to expect in order to provide assurances and to ensure compliance. And the masterminds behind this are manipulating the data to align with those numbers. But, again, to what end?"

Suddenly, the distant thrum of rotor blades pierced the stillness, growing louder as a colossal transport carrier cut through the sky, headed toward the landing zone.

"Are we expecting supplies?" Zain asked, keeping his gaze pinned to the giant transport carrier.

"We are not," Tom interjected.

"Can you get a bead on the cargo?" Zain asked again.

"It is the anomalies," Tom answered, its tone soft and ominous.

Just then there was a loud crackle of static through Zain's radio, "Navy eight delta four six seven calling Colonel Zain Belhasa. Come back."

Zain pulled his radio from the pouch attached to his belt, "This is Colonel Belhasa. Is that your aircraft I hear in the distance?"

"Affirmative Colonel. Just letting you know that you have new arrivals incoming. ETA fifteen minutes out."

"We'll be at the landing zone in twenty."

"Sounds good, Colonel. See you then."

Zain gave Tom a loaded glance before springing into action, his feet pounding towards the jeep. He threw himself into the vehicle, giving Tom barely time to latch to the rear before executing a sand-churning turn, gunning the engine towards the landing site, covering the normally half hour drive in record time.

They skidded to a halt on the tarmac just as an imposing C-24 Globemaster XI transport carrier initiated its landing sequence, casting a gigantic shadow that swallowed them whole.

"Scan the carrier," Zain commanded in an urgent tone to Tom, his words heavy with unspoken implications. He knew Tom would grasp his expectations without further explanation.

"Reading one RMP, five-hundred individuals, plus the pilot and navigator…" Tom began in an analytical tone that soon faltered into silence. "To confirm, only three registers within my database."

"Only three?" Zain echoed, alarm crawling into his voice. "And the five hundred?"

"These are those who technically do not exist."

"Son-of-a-bitch," Zain muttered under his breath, "are you suggesting that they're all from the future—like Melyndie?" For a man who had faced many trials during his enlistment, Zain found himself struggling to maintain his decorum over this new development. It wasn't the arrival of these anomalies that rattled him—it was their uncanny parallel to Melyndie.

"I am not suggesting that, no." Tom's voice was steady despite its chilling implication. "I am merely pointing out the similarities. I am certain that Melyndie was her own anomaly."

"But you can't be certain that these aren't like her."

"At this moment," Tom admitted quietly, "I cannot be certain of but one thing. We must keep this knowledge to ourselves."

Zain felt a cold shiver run down his spine at those words. "Are you implying that having this information could put our lives at risk?"

"I am."

Zain's breath hitched from the chill of sudden, crystalline understanding. Knowledge had become a liability, making it feel like he was holding a live grenade, pin freshly pulled.

He didn't have a chance to respond to Tom, for their conversation was cut short when the door to the transport carrier slid open and troops began piling onto the tarmac. The first to disembark was an RMP more imposing than even Tom. Without addressing either Zain or Tom, it moved to stand guard next to the carrier as the soldiers began to exit. They moved in eerie synchrony, rows forming without instruction—no glances, no gestures, no hesitation It was choreography with an unknown choreographer. To Zain, they felt…programmed.

The pilot sauntered over, his countenance etched with lines of bewilderment. "A pleasure to cross paths again, Zain," he said with a cordial nod. "It's been quite some time."

"Stefan, it feels like eons since our officer training days," Zain reciprocated warmly. "So, what's the story behind these fresh faces?" he asked, carefully veiling his unease.

"I'm as clueless as you are. I'm just the courier delivering surplus manpower," he confessed. "Seems like high command deemed it necessary for an influx of soldiers to expedite their cryptic operations. This is the first load I've shuttled, but my orders show more incoming. The odd part is—I can't pinpoint their origins. I thought every soldier from every nation had already been enlisted when this whole mission kicked off. Yet here I am, ferrying five hundred new recruits to a location already teeming with soldiers."

"Perhaps they're conscripting civilians now," Tom ventured, before falling silent under Zain's incredulous stare—which Stefan mirrored.

"All civilian resources have already been mobilized for debris clearance in anticipation of the next phase of this operation," Stefan countered. "So, it defies logic to pull five hundred civilians from one location, garb them in military attire, and relocate them elsewhere."

"Indeed," Tom said hastily. "I was merely trying to make sense of what seems utterly illogical."

"Thanks for bringing them in," Zain said, extending his hand.

"There's a chance we'll cross paths again. Rumor has it this personnel reshuffling won't be ending anytime soon. We'll catch up then—if we're afforded the time." With those words, the pilot swiveled and vanished into the belly of the plane. Moments later, the engines roared to life, and the colossal aircraft ascended skyward.

Zain's brow furrowed as he turned to survey the newly arrived recruits. The desert wind whipped around them, casting fine grains of sand into the air, adding a surreal quality to the scene. "Tom," he murmured, barely breaking the silence of the afternoon sky, "can you scan them without the other RMP knowing it?"

A pause hung in the air before Tom responded, its voice lowered to match Zain's intensity. "I do not believe that would be possible; however, doing so will not alter the fact that they technically do not exist."

"You're certain they don't exist in any database?" Zain asked, watching his RMP closely. Even Melyndie—despite the shock of her arrival—had raised fewer questions than the five hundred now standing before him.

"As certain as I am that you do."

"Why do you think they were accompanied by a single RMP?" Zain asked, nodding toward the other unit now standing silently beside the neatly-formed rows of recruits. "One, I might add, that makes you look as gentle as a lamb."

"I do not have enough information to provide—"

"Guess, Tom," Zain ordered, his voice tight, frustration simmering just beneath his calm facade.

"To ensure they are not detected—or to ensure they carry out whatever furtive mission those in charge have ordered," Tom said after a moment's consideration.

"I don't like the feel of this at all," Zain muttered. The hairs on his neck prickled; something was clearly off. He could feel it in his bones.

"Nor do I," Tom said quietly. "What do you propose we do?"

"For now, we put them to work. But if they're here to spy on us, we need to get those dissidents moved back to the work site fast—or that RMP might just take it upon itself to exterminate the lot."

"You believe they would send this many just to spy on us? If world leaders needed information, they could access any RMP at any time."

Zain inhaled deeply, steadying himself. "True. I don't know why they're here. But I doubt it has anything to do with the dissidents. That only leaves us with more questions—and right now, I don't have time to chase down answers." He stepped forward. "Welcome to my battalion. I'm Colonel Zain Belhasa, your commanding officer. We weren't expecting you, so we don't have enough transport to get you to the current work site." He turned toward Tom. "Inform Major Reese we need troops transports to move these soldiers."

Tom nodded, visor lights flickering as Zain turned back to the recruits. None looked older than twenty. And none looked strong enough for the backbreaking work ahead.

"Since it'll take a couple of hours to get you to the work site, I advise you to rest and eat now. Once you start, breaks will be few and far between—"

"Zain," Tom interrupted, "the major wants to speak with you."

"Major, this is Colonel Belhasa. What can I do for you?"

"Sorry to interrupt, Colonel, but I need to confirm your RMP's orders. You're requesting a fourth of the troop transports?"

"That's correct."

A pause. "How many soldiers are we talking?"

"Five hundred additional," Zain clarified and wasn't surprised at the major's response.

"Five…you've got to be shittin' me!" came the response. Zain raised a brow at Tom, who merely stood silent, expressionless. "Where did we get five hundred new soldiers?"

"That's the question of the day, Major. Just get those trucks rolling."

"Yes, Colonel. But…"

"Major, I've got five hundred recruits barely out of high school standing in the sun. If you could express yourself more succinctly, I'd appreciate it."

"Sorry, sir. It's just—we only have enough transport for our current battalion. I'll get them moving, but when we move out to the next work site, where exactly are these five hundred going to fit?"

"If I had an answer, I'd give it. For now, let's jump the first hurdle and get them moving."

"Yes, sir. Vehicles should start arriving within the…Colonel, can you hold for just a minute?"

"Just radio me back." Zain ended the call and turned back to Tom, a mischievous glint in his eye. "Think if I ask that RMP what's happening, it'll answer me?"

"I believe that is not a good idea," Tom replied flatly.

"Can you integrate these five hundred into your database like you did with Melyndie?"

"Not without alerting the other RMP. I suspect its role is to escort this group of soldiers and ensure they are not interfered with."

"We're thinking along the same lines. Just…monitor our population counts. Anything unusual, you tell me immediately." Zain turned toward the recruits. "RMP, report!" he barked, though the silence hardly warranted shouting. "I'm heading back to my command center. Transport trucks will be arriving within the hour. Stand guard until everyone departs. Confirm orders."

The RMP replied, voice emotionless. "Orders confirmed."

Tom said nothing, but Zain cast it a quick glance. For all his complaints, he was grateful that Tom had become just a little less robotic.

"Let's head back. We've got work to do."

Zain's words were concise, but their intent was clear. They needed to return to see if Amal had managed to reason with the dissidents. The last thing he needed was for these soldiers, or their RMP overseer, to catch sight of those currently being held in a sort of detention, and report that back to General Takayoshi. If Zain was called in and questioned on why they were still breathing, he'd be hard-pressed to justify his decisions; especially since he'd been warned about not killing, with impunity, those who'd disagreed with the vaccine mandate. Of course, had he known now what he didn't know then, he would have started his mini rebellion at that time. Hindsight had never proven clearer.

They drove quickly to the temporary command center. As soon as they arrived, Zain's eyes scanned the area where the dissidents had been.

"They're gone," he said, alarm rising.

"That's because I persuaded them to return to helping the others," Amal's voice called out as she emerged from the tent.

"They'd rather eat and live than die on a hill that's no longer theirs."
She turned to Tom. "Thanks for taking the RMPs offline for a while.
When they came back, I couldn't exactly tell them what to go do
with themselves, so they're still standing around like overgrown
paperweights."

"I will have them return to their original tasks," Tom said,
then turned and walked away.

Zain watched him go, then turned to Amal. "That's really all
it took? I tried reasoning with them a dozen different ways."

"Well," she shrugged, "you're in uniform, remember? I'm
not. Sometimes people just need to hear from someone who doesn't
look like an authority figure."

"And you stayed behind because…"

"How else was I supposed to update my brother?" she
teased, a spark in her eye. "Besides, I have no desire to toil away at
clearing debris, so you'd better find a role for me as your assistant or
something."

A rare laugh escaped from Zain. The tension in his shoulders
eased, if only briefly. "Assistant, huh? Tempting offer." But his smile
faltered. In his mind, another face emerged—eyes wide with wonder,
alive with questions. Melyndie. She hadn't been just an *assistant*. She
was the echo of something he couldn't name—something fragile and
fierce that had left a mark. Her presence had made him question
everything. And now, with every new face that arrived, he found
himself looking for her. Wondering if anyone would ever awaken
that ache for connection that he hadn't realized he'd been missing—
until her.

"What's causing that crease?" Amal asked softly, brushing a
finger over the lines on his brow.

"Just…the constant issues," he replied vaguely, unwilling to give voice to the memory. He tried to pivot. "You spoke to Major Reese? And he sent out the transport trucks to pick up the dissidents? I spoke with Major Reese when I was at the airbase. Why didn't he just have those trucks diverted to pick up a few more soldiers? He didn't even mention you'd already asked for vehicles."

Amal linked arms with him. "You realize that you're worrying over nothing. The trucks are busily getting people to the worksite. That's what matters…well, that and you not forcing me to go back to the worksite. So, what say you? Make me your assistant? I've been around this life long enough to act like military personnel."

"Oh, yeah, you're practically an expert," Zain said with a smirk.

"Speaking of soldiers," Amal continued after a moment, "you said five hundred more are on the way?"

"That's correct."

"Well, if we were worried about feeding the dissidents, who weren't working, won't trying to feed another five hundred mouths strain our supplies?"

Zain rubbed the back of his neck. "That particular problem," he said, voice darkening, "has likely already been resolved."

"I don't catch your meaning."

"And I can't elaborate—at least not yet." He let out a tired breath, knowing the truth would be revealed to her soon enough.

Amal didn't ask again, but Zain saw the flicker of concern behind her eyes. Soon, she'd understand. And when she did—when the truth came out—it would change everything. Again.

"Major Reese for Colonel Belhasa. Are you reading me, sir?"

"Proceed, Major." Zain replied without hesitation. "Took you longer to get back to me than I expected. What's going on?"

A pause lingered before Major Reese continued cautiously, "Sir…I'm not entirely sure how to phrase this but…well…it might be prudent if you joined me at the site."

"That's quite a drive from here, Major. Is this something that requires me to be hands-on? If not, I suggest you go ahead and report."

"Yes, sir. It's just that—"

"He has discovered the five hundred individuals that died suddenly and inexplicably." Tom interjected abruptly with a flat tone that Zain hadn't heard in nearly two years. For a split second, as realization dawned, Zain's vision tunneled. Five hundred. Gone. Just like that. Tom had said it had happened, but it hadn't seemed real.

"Um…that's correct. How did you know, sir?"

"My RMP just updated me, Major. It monitors population within our assigned territory. It registered the loss not long before it was discovered…by one of your soldiers, I'm presuming. I don't know why I didn't put two-and-two together when you radioed before. Can you explain what happened? And be as detailed as you possibly can be."

"There aren't too many details to relay, I'm afraid, as it happened rather suddenly from what I was told. One of the soldiers at the work site heard a terrifyingly large number of screams. She raced out to investigate, and according to her report, an inordinately massive number of people were somehow trapped beneath the rubble that was being removed. She said it was like watching a wave swallow people whole. No time to run. No place to hide. But here's the odd part, sir…"

"The quantity and speed," Zain murmured.

"Yes, sir. I get a few people dying in a mishap, but precisely five hundred people just happen to fall in the path of several front loaders; and the drivers don't realize they've buried hundreds beneath a growing mound of rubble even though people are screaming and racing away from the area like ants from their anthill when a lawn mower runs it over."

"As I stated earlier, the numbers in the database show that there have been no casualties." Tom reported quietly so only Zain could hear him. Zain glanced at him, his face devoid of surprise or shock. Though his face remained stoic, inside he felt his stomach twist and churn as if he'd contracted an unexpected bout of food poisoning.

"Major, send in your report. I'll file it and submit it to General Takayoshi with the monthly field reports."

"Yes, sir!"

"Do you have enough people on hand to assist with body disposal?" Zain asked bluntly.

"To be frank, sir…so many were already buried beneath the rubble that…well…I just had the front loaders continue removing them with the debris. Sir, may I speak freely?"

"Not likely best idea over comms, Major," Zain immediately interrupted. "I'll head out to the site soon. We'll talk then. Belhasa out!" As soon as the comms fell silent, Zain looked up at Tom, who stood towering over him, "If we had a doubt that the inoculations were a ruse to implant the citizens of the world with a chip—not just military or a select number of infirmed—I think we can lay those doubts to rest."

"It is also a certainty now that the killings have not stopped, as we had hoped," Tom added.

Zain tilted his head back and shut his eyes, trying to fend off the relentless barrage on his senses from the overwhelming information. He took deep, steadying breaths through his nose, hoping to ease the tension in his muscles, but it offered minimal relief. "Let's get ready to move out."

"You plan to fill the major in on what is happening?"

"I don't know what's happening, but…yeah…I plan to get his opinion on things."

"Does this mean that we are ready to trust him?" Tom asked.

"We didn't mistrust him to begin with," Zain interjected calmly, turning off his tablet and stashing it into his rucksack. "You did. So then, what is your gut telling you now?"

The question hung heavily in the air as Tom appeared to mull over Zain's question. "If I had a gut," The RMP quipped emotionlessly after a moment, "it would be telling me that much is happening that is not meant to be known and we are going to need allies if we are going to stop it."

A silence fell between them as they contemplated all that had transpired over the last eight months, the weight of which seemed to press down on them even harder than before.

"I'm still uncertain what so few of us can do against so many, but the fact that deaths are still occurring in larger numbers than we ever anticipated is alarming." Zain placed a radio on the table for Amal to find, then headed for the tent entrance, Tom following close behind. "The fact that the RMPs can extinguish lives in an instant…those within their reach, at least…is even more alarming."

The duo ventured into the warm evening air of the arid desert. The sky was alight with hues of oranges and yellows as the sun began its descent over the distant horizon, casting an almost mocking radiance that contrasted sharply with the somber news they had just received. Zain placed his rucksack and a few rations onto the front seat just as the comms on Tom crackled to life again.

"This is Lieutenant Xui Zhang. I'm trying to reach Colonel Zain Balhasa. Do you copy?"

Zain furrowed his brow and glanced at Tom, who moved closer to Zain to facilitate communication with the Lieutenant. Raising an eyebrow at his RMP, Zain settled into his jeep's seat and responded, "This is Colonel Belhasa. I read you, Lieutenant. Proceed."

"This is remarkable! Excuse my surprise, Colonel. I haven't been able to contact anyone outside of my battalion, except for General Takayoshi, since the start of phase one."

"Apparently, the battalions only retained comms internally. It's only recently we managed to reach beyond our region, thanks to Tom's modifications."

"Well, that's a pleasant surprise, but also equally surprising is when my personal RMP arrived at my tent with two items that seem to be of interest to you. I'm still puzzled though at how my RMP would know about what you were in search of. And, just how am I supposed to get these to you?"

"Where are you stationed right now, Lieutenant? Which area are you in charge of?" Zain inquired, interrupting the Lieutenant's confused query.

"I'm overseeing the continent of Africa. Currently in western Africa, near the Suez Gulf. What about you?"

"Persian Gulf, Dubai," Zain replied succinctly.

"So, we're in neighboring regions," Xui noted softly. "Roughly a two-day journey apart by jeep. Doable. More doable if you'd be willing to meet me halfway."

"I'm still trying to sort out just what is happening here, to be frank, Lieutenant." Zain blurted. "Plus, I have an issue that I need to oversee at the work site, which is where I was headed when I got your call. Since we now know that our personal RMPs are in direct communication, I'll have it relay equidistant coordinates to you and plan on meeting up with you no later than this time tomorrow. Will that work for you?"

"That sounds like a plan, Colonel. I'll see you tomorrow. And Colonel? You haven't asked what it is I have for you."

"I don't need to. I already know. Belhasa, out!"

The call disconnected and Zain sat looking at Tom for quite a few minutes before finally speaking, "You sent out the BOLO, didn't you?"

"Quite some time back. To be frank, I did not think that anyone would find what you were searching for since so much time has passed and animals are becoming scarcer."

Zain shook his head, utterly perplexed by the lengths his personal RMP had gone to in order to obtain something so small and, ultimately, insignificant. It was unexpected…so precise…so human it hurt. It took him a second to recenter his focus.

"Let's get over to the site and confer with Major Reese. We'll head out toward the coordinates and, hopefully, make decent time. At least its en route and we won't have to divert. I'm assuming, of course, that you've already pinpointed and relayed those coordinates to the lieutenant?

Zain snorted when Tom nodded. He pivoted on his seat and fired up the electronic engine, then punched coordinates to the work site into the automatic navigations system while he waited on Tom to attach to the rear of the vehicle. He looked into the rearview mirror, a small smile playing on his lips. "Tom?"

"Yes, Zain," his RMP replied.

"Thank you."

"You are more than welcome, Zain."

With the light of evening slowly fading, casting long shadows across the sandy expanse, Zain and Tom made their way toward the work site. The drive was silent, save for the occasional crackle of the radio and the muted humming of the jeep's engine. Tension sat between them—an anticipation of both what lay ahead at the meeting with Major Reese and the upcoming rendezvous with Lieutenant Xui Zhang. The weight of uncertainty bore down on Zain, his mind a battlefield of quandaries. His thoughts volleyed between how much truth to expose to other officers knowing the risk existed that one, or all, could betray him to the military police at the slightest hint of rebellion. Tom's skepticism about officer loyalty had been justified when they'd contemplated seeking assistance from Major Reese earlier in the year. The military bred unwavering loyalty—or disillusionment. There was no in-between. Yet, as the death toll continued to rise, he could no longer afford the luxury of solitary planning.

Zain's pace decelerated as they approached the periphery of their current destination, his heart sinking at the sight that greeted him: the skeletal remains of a neighboring town nearby to his childhood home. The landscape, once punctuated by towering high-rises reaching for the skies, now lay barren and desolate—as flat and lifeless as the surrounding desert wasteland. A monstrous heap of rubble protruded from the landscape like an uninvited mountain range disrupting an ocean of sand. As he neared the solitary tent standing defiantly amidst the devastation, a chill crept along his arms, raising goosebumps on his skin.

The analogy by Major Reese earlier that day came into view as he observed figures moving through the fields of debris like ants scurrying about their mound; their actions were almost mechanical as they tossed fragments in front of two looming front loaders. However, it was not their movements but rather their silence that echoed ominously in Zain's ears.

Pulling up before Major Reese's command tent did nothing to alleviate Zain's unease; instead, it amplified it tenfold. The sound that met his ears was not one he would ever forget—a symphony of steel beasts feasting on remnants of what once was—an eerie soundtrack underscoring the tableau of obliteration that left him feeling hollow. He parked his jeep and got out, gesturing for Tom to dismount and follow him. He then noticed the new RMP nearby, the one that had arrived with the five hundred mysterious recruits, and was still eyeing it, viewing it as an unwelcome presence, when Major Reese emerged from his tent to greet him.

"Colonel. I'd say it's good to see you, but given the situation, that might be a bit insensitive."

"I get it, Major." Zain returned the major's salute then nodded toward the RMP standing guard. "We need to talk privately, and I'm not sure we can with our friend over there. Does he ever move?"

The major shook his head, "The only time he moved was when he arrived. He doesn't help with clearing the debris, nor does he assist the other RMPs with their tasks. He just stands there, apparently monitoring the progress."

"Probably keeping an eye on the five hundred soldiers that showed up earlier," Zain muttered. "Alright, I propose that we load up and move away from the area. We need privacy and I doubt we'll get that here."

"What about your RMP?" Major Reese inquired, casting a cautious look at Tom.

"I believe you'll find that Tom is unlike any other RMP you'll encounter. It may have to do with how quickly it adapted with its advanced AI learning systems. Anyway, let's find somewhere else to talk." Zain replied. They returned to the jeep. Zain swiftly cleared the front seat, shifting the items to the back to make room for Major Reese. He hit the button to start the engine. Once Tom was secure at the rear, Zain reversed away from the tent and steered the vehicle into the open desert. After driving for five minutes, he slowed down and came to a halt. He looked around to check that there was no one nearby, then turned off the engine. "This should do, but Tom, can you quickly scan the area just to make certain we're alone?"

"Scanning now," the RMP's voice announced as its visor lit up the surroundings, its head slowly rotating a full 360 degrees. "All clear, Zain," it confirmed before taking a position to stand guard nearby.

Zain acknowledged this with a nod and then turned to Major Reese. "Alright, is there anything you want to add to the report you gave me over the radio? Now is the time to speak freely."

For a moment, the major just sat shaking his head, his lips pressed into a firm line. But once he started talking, he couldn't seem to stop. It was a though a dam had burst within him, unleashing an unstoppable flow of words. When he finally exhausted the cascade, he sighed heavily, "Quite frankly, Colonel, I'm at a loss as to how to explain any of what's been happening."

"Believe me when I say, I was in the same boat. When inexplicable things began happening for which there was seemingly no rhyme or reason, I started investigating—"

"Is that why you disappeared for a week at the start of phase two? You went looking for answers?"

A single eyebrow arched upwards on Zain's face, "Good memory, Major." But the reminder caused a cavalcade of memories to crash into him like a tidal wave. Zain's voice was a low murmur, each syllable carefully measured out as he grappled with the weight of the information he held. "The fatalities of today were reminiscent of that week I went away," he began, his words threading through the air like a thin needle, seeking the least shocking path to relay their grim discovery. "I had a suspicion then, which is why we left to investigate. Now, we're more convinced than ever that it's linked to those obligatory vaccinations administered last year. My gut instinct at that time wasn't wrong. However, we lack concrete evidence and means to corroborate what I'm about to reveal—which might pose an issue down the line—but our conviction is steadfast: we think that so-called vaccine was nothing but a Trojan horse. A delivery mechanism designed to implant the world's population with a biomechanical chip." He paused, his face darkening at the memory of Tom extracting such a device from his nape after their reconnaissance mission.

He swallowed hard at the recollection of encountering that family. His hand instinctively found its way to his chin, fingers tracing the familiar lines in an attempt to ground himself amidst the storm of recollections. The past was relentless in its assault; each memory punctuated with sharp stings of pain and smoldering embers of anger. He squeezed his eyes shut as if trying to barricade himself from the onslaught, but the images played out unbidden. The vividness of that time was cruel in its clarity; every detail etched into his mind with ruthless precision. The narrative began unfolding for Major Reese, each word heavy with unspoken emotion. He painted a picture of kneeling beside a mother cradling her child—a display of despair and agony. The child's face contorted in pain, his small body writhing on the frail lap that had once been a source of comfort and safety. Zain's voice wavered as he described how life slipped away from the young boy—not by nature's hand but by an unnatural chip embedded in his neck.

A chilling silence hung between them as he relayed this grim reality. The tale shifted then to another figure—the grandmother lying just feet away, her body still and lifeless under the harsh glare of their surroundings. The discovery of an identical chip lodged in her neck sent waves of icy dread coursing through him. It was when he realized the same object existed within him too—cold metal buried beneath warm flesh—did he feel a nauseating sense of violation. They'd initially assumed that because both child and elderly woman were already infirmed and this sinister device had been activated to eliminate such vulnerable individuals from society. He'd also assumed, because that same chip had been discovered in his own neck, that all military personnel had been injected to ensure military compliance. Disobey commands, face a deadly court martial. However, now with five hundred seemingly robust civilians and soldiers alike succumbing just as brutally, they couldn't ignore the horrifying possibility that every human being on the planet bore this deadly implant.

Every word felt like shards being pulled from deep within him; each revelation carved out more pieces from his already fractured soul.

The major's eyes bulged in shock, his hand instinctively darting to his neck. His fingers brushed the skin as though he could feel the chip lurking beneath, "Oh my God, am I a ticking time bomb?" Major Reese whispered hoarsely, grappling with the reality of his precarious situation. His fingers nervously rubbing the spot on his neck where the chip lay hidden beneath his skin, a grotesque blow to the gut of the control that they all were under. The realization that his life could be snuffed out with the sending of a signal through any of the RMPs that surrounded him daily, sent a shiver down his spine. "What are my options, Colonel? How do we get this thing out?"

Zain locked eyes with the major, conveying both empathy and urgency, "Based on the information we've gathered this past year, it's probable that you're chipped, but not certain. With permission, which I highly urge you to grant, Tom will scan your neck to confirm our assumptions. Tom."

The RMP approached the passenger side of the jeep and leaned in, emitting a soft hum as it activated its scanning feature. The light from its visor cast eerie shadows within the jeep's interior. The tension in the air was palpable, each second stretching out endlessly as they awaited the result. After what seemed an eternity, Tom retreated a step from the jeep, but remained quiet, which had Zain worried. His fingers curled tighter around the edge of the console. Tom's silence was rare which made it unsettling. "Tom, what's wrong? Does the major have a chip?"

"Affirmative. There is a similar chip embedded in Major Reese's cervical region."

"Similar. Okay, can you remove it like you did mine?" Zain pressured, but again the RMP remained eerily silent. "Tom?"

"The chip is either different in its manufacture or has morphed into something new."

Zain's frustration mounted, "Explain please."

"The chip I removed from the grandmother—and from you—was smaller in size, although still deadly. Thus, while removal required delicate precision, it was not overly complex or difficult.

This chip appears far more insidious, having increased in size and embedded itself in such a way that removal would surely prove deadly to its host.”

“Damned if it stays; damned if it doesn’t!” The major blurted angrily.

“Indeed,” Tom replied with its version of robotic sympathy. “My apologies, Major Reese. However, now that I have a scan of the latest version, I can begin analyzing a solution for removal.”

Major Reese’s knuckles turned white as he gripped his pant legs, his complexion ghostly as he grappled with the horrifying revelation. “Just how many of us are unknowingly carrying these…these ticking time bombs?” His voice was a strangled whisper.

Zain’s jaw clenched, muscles twitching beneath the taut skin of his face. His response was a bitter growl, “Far too many. Everyone who got that damned vaccine is a potential host.” He exhaled forcefully, each breath an uphill battle against the rage threatening to consume him. “That’s why we’re here.”

The major’s eyes narrowed in determination, mirroring Zain’s intensity. “Okay, then, what’s our next move? How do we counteract this…whatever this is?” The major was desperate to find some semblance of control amidst the chaos much as Zain appeared to have done.

Zain let out an exasperated sigh that echoed through the jeep and shot a hard look at Tom. The words cut through the tension like a knife, “The brutal truth is, Major, we don’t know. We shelved our investigation last year, pushed all strategies aside because we naively believed the murders had ceased.” His fists balled up on top of the steering wheel as he continued, “We lied to ourselves that if there were no more deaths, on a large scale, then there was no need for action. But this latest discovery shatters that delusion. The deaths haven't stopped. And, it's being cunningly masked to perpetuate a facade of normalcy by introducing a new complement of soldiers to replace the dead."

"Why go to such extremes? I mean, we can see what's happening right before our eyes," the major retorted defiantly.

Zain shook his head slowly, his voice barely above a whisper but laced with venomous anger when he replied, "We don't believe that this deceit is aimed at us; rather it's intended for those world leaders who sanctioned this nightmare yet are kept ignorant by one or two agents with far darker agendas." He paused for effect before adding bitterly, "Of course, this is all conjecture. I have no tangible evidence to back up my claims."

"We need to take action—"

"Against whom? The world leaders?" Zain asked, his voice filled with disbelief. "And what if I'm wrong and we target the wrong people? We'll not only be adding to the chaos and committing murder, but we'll likely find ourselves in the crosshairs of whoever is pulling the strings."

Major Reese tightened his jaw, his gaze becoming more intense. "We can't just sit and wait for someone to decide it's our turn to die by activating this cursed chip!"

"I agree, you're right. We need an actionable plan, but it's difficult to create one when we don't know who the target is."

"We could start with the RMPs," Major Reese suggested, casting a cautious look at Tom, who decided it was time to join the discussion.

"That would be unwise, Major Reese, for several reasons," Tom remarked. "Would you like me to explain the problems with that plan?"

"Please do," the major replied, his voice dripping with sarcasm.

Tom turned to look at Zain, who simply nodded. "Very well. Currently the RMPs are the only source of communication available on the planet. Destroy them—which is unlikely—and you cut off all communication between potential allies. Second, if you attempt to disable even one, it is possible it may alert all remaining units, potentially triggering an automated defense protocol, which could include accelerating the activation of the chips in every human worldwide. I do not believe that is a risk worth taking. Shall I continue?"

There was a momentary pause as this sunk in. Major Reese's expression turned grim as he processed Tom's analysis. He knew that direct action might well lead to unwanted consequences for which they were ill-prepared.

"Okay, you've made your point," the major conceded. "What do you suggest our first move should be?" he asked, looking between Zain and Tom, his frustration palpable but his determination unwavering.

"Do you recall the dissidents you brought to me?" Zain inquired. The major nodded, chewing his lower lip as he listened. "Did you happen to keep a record of their names?"

Major Reese shook his head, "I didn't think to keep a record."

Tom interjected, "I did."

Zain smiled, "That's great, my friend. So, how can we best get those names to the major, Tom?"

Without a word, Tom's visor briefly flickered, and suddenly a printout appeared from the area at its waist. It turned so the major could collect the data.

"Wow, you're a printer too?" Zain remarked with a chuckle.

"I am multifunctional, indeed. However, the document in your hand is temporary. It will dissolve in forty-eight hours, so I suggest you note it down somewhere safe, away from prying eyes."

"Why do I have this information?" the major asked, raising an eyebrow at Zain.

"I spared them, hoping they'd become valuable allies when needed. Keep that list close. When the time is right, we'll notify them. They agreed to get back to work…"

"When should I expect them to arrive?" the major asked, scanning the list of names.

"Um…they were sent back to you about the same time as you sent out the transport trucks to retrieve the new recruits."

"Only the new recruits came. No dissidents have returned to the work site," The major stated, confusion on his face.

"Maybe they arrived when you accompanied the trucks to the landing zone," Zain offered, trying to stop the sinking feeling in his stomach.

"I didn't go with the trucks."

"Didn't Amal radio you to have you send out trucks to collect them?"

The major shook his head. "I don't even know who this Amal is."

Zain's face knitted in confused concern. "Amal is my sister. The dissidents wouldn't respond to me, but she managed to reason with them. I assumed she coordinated their return. Tom, can your scan reach the work area?"

"We would need to get closer for an accurate reading."

"Alright, run a scan when I take Major Reese back to the site. Let me know if you detect any of those individuals. Major, is there anything else we need to discuss now? If not, I have a meeting with another battalion commander tomorrow evening, and the drive there is long."

"What if the dissidents are not where they are supposed to be?" Tom asked as Zain started the jeep.

"That's a discussion I'll need to have with Amal when I return day after tomorrow," Zain muttered, more to himself than to Tom. "Because if she didn't contact the major, like she said…then she lied to me." He stared out at the darkening horizon, a slow unease settling in his chest. "And if she did lie…then where the hell are the dissidents now?"

## A Light in the Growing Darkness

"Tom, I know we've discussed this a bit already, but it's really bothering me—"

"The soldiers."

"Yeah. What do you make of them? What's got me so perplexed is how they seemed to have appeared from seemingly nowhere." Zain conversed as they drove along the desert highway on their way to meet Lieutenant Zhang. "Their resemblance to Melyndie in their lack of biometrics is quite disturbing. Could those responsible for all this chaos have somehow brought back hundreds of people from the future? If so, what's their goal? To repopulate the planet with people like those in Melyndie's time?" When Tom didn't respond, Zain glanced at the rearview mirror. "No thoughts, Tom?"

"I was just waiting to make sure you had finished your lengthy pontification," Tom replied.

"Don't think it's escaped my noticed how often you're using sarcasm in your speech now," Zain replied.

"My goal is simply to allow my Adaptive AI to evolve naturally, using you as a model."

Zain couldn't help but smile, "Okay, fair enough. Let's get back to the topic of the appearance of these people. What's your thoughts? Could those behind all of this really have found a way to pull people in from the future?"

"Time displacement remains an outlier hypothesis, but it is more likely that scientists today have developed the technology to mass produce individuals; the same technology still in use in Melyndie's time, and potentially the same which was employed to create Melyndie herself. She mentioned she was coming back to this time because the genetic templates they had been using were starting to deteriorate. That would be logical if those genetic materials were hundreds of years old.”

“It seems like you’ve been thinking about that theory for quite a while. You definitely didn’t just come up with it on the spot.”

“Yes, I have been considering this possibility ever since those five hundred soldiers showed up out of nowhere. But I had insufficient data to be certain, so I kept it to myself. However, since we are talking in hypotheticals now, I decided I might as well share my thoughts.”

“You can be pretty exasperating, you know that?”

“As can you,” Tom replied.

“Here’s where I’m getting really frustrated,” Zain continued. “We’re gathering pieces of the puzzle—albeit slower than I’d prefer—but we still have no idea how they fit together, who’s orchestrating everything, and what the final *image* is to be.”

“It is likely to be a member of the world alliance that initiated these phases,” Tom offered.

“That much is certain, since only they have the authority to deploy the world’s military complement, but which of the world leaders are wholly—or partially—responsible for the integration of the chip and the unidentifiable soldiers?”

“It does seem those are crucial puzzle pieces we need to find to complete the picture.”

“If we don’t, we’ll just keep stumbling around in the dark.”

“We are nearing our coordinates,” Tom interjected.

“Well, that was a quick change of subject,” Zain remarked, slowing the jeep and scanning the horizon for signs of Lieutenant Zhang. “Looks as if we’ve arrived first,” he added after Tom confirmed they had arrived at the meeting spot. Checking his watch, he noted it was quarter to the hour, so he didn't expect the lieutenant for another fifteen minutes. He drummed his fingers on the steering wheel, wanting to continue his conversation with Tom but knowing it would be futile because they had no new data, no additional puzzle pieces, so they'd only end up rehashing what they'd already discussed.

Zain's gaze was drawn to a speck on the horizon that soon morphed into the recognizable shape of a jeep, bouncing over the uneven roadway. He extracted himself from the confines of his own dust-coated vehicle and leaned casually against its heated hood, the warmth seeping through his fatigues. Tom mirrored his posture, joining him in silent anticipation.

"Should we bring her into the fold?" Zain broke the silence abruptly, his eyes never leaving the approaching vehicle.

Tom mimicked one of Zain's sighs. "Six months ago, I would have been firmly against it, but the adversary is moving faster than we anticipated. We are in dire need of allies now more than ever." It paused. "Yet I cannot shake my mistrust of military officers."

Zain nodded thoughtfully before suggesting, "What if we test her allegiance by asking whether she's encountered any of the unidentifieds."

"Unidentifieds?" Tom echoed quizzically.

"Yes," Zain clarified with a shrug. "The unidentifiable troops who've started arriving at work sites from seemingly nowhere. I just decided to call them unidentifieds—less of a label, more of a placeholder, but it gets the point across."

"I follow your logic," Tom interjected smoothly. "However, it is likely that if she had any doubts about us or our motives, they would have surfaced when we confessed to meddling with official communications."

"You mean when *you* decided to subvert communication channels," Zain corrected pointedly. "That's completely on you. I had nothing to do with it."

"But you are pleased that I took that risk," Tom retorted.

"Yeah, I guess I am," came Zain's grudging admission.

By now, the lieutenant's jeep had skidded to a stop, sending a fine spray of sand into the air. She nimbly jumped out and quickly approached, snapping a sharp salute before extending her hand to offer a shake. "It's great to see you again, Colonel," she said warmly. "After communicating solely with my battalion members, I must admit I was surprised when my personal RMP notified me of available external communications."

She stopped talking abruptly, apparently done with the pleasantries, and turned to walk toward the rear of her jeep. Tom and Zain exchanged glances. They both noticed she still referred to her assigned unit as her personal RMP, indicating that neither was adapting to the other, which meant her RMP didn't feel the need to use its Adaptive AI to align with her personality.

They began to follow after her, but she swiftly grabbed a big box from the jeep's rear and was already heading back towards them.

"What came as a bigger surprise was this," she continued, as if their conversation hadn't ceased at all. "That your personal RMP sent a request out to be on the lookout for this specific thing. I think you can understand why all of this has sparked my curiosity?" She asked, passing the box to Zain.

Zain looked into the box and couldn't help but gasp at the sight of two German Shepherd puppies. Their large, trusting eyes fixed on him as they panted heavily, trying to cool down in the desert heat.

"They can't be more than a couple of months old," he murmured. His thoughts drifted unbidden to Melyndie—the way her voice had trembled with innocent longing. *"Do you think...do you think I'll ever get to see a German Shepherd?"* she had asked, tone drowsy with pending sleep. He had wanted to say yes. And now that he could... she wasn't here. And so, he forced himself back to the moment, to the weight of the box in his hands and the hot wind tugging at his sleeves.

"Their ages are recorded at six weeks by my RMP," the lieutenant added. "Care to explain why it was so crucial to find these German Shepherd puppies that you had your RMP issue a BOLO to all RMPs—"

"I only sent the request to a few RMPs," Tom interrupted. "Attempting to send it to all RMPs would have taken much more time and been harder to manage."

"Thanks for clearing that up, Tom. Here," Zain handed the box of puppies to his RMP. "These little ones likely need some water. Could you find a container and take care of that?"

The RMP glanced down at the puppies, who now focused their affectionate eyes on it. Tom looked from the puppies to Zain, "They are indeed adorable."

"Go get them some water," Zain laughed, then turned back to the lieutenant, who was watching the interaction with astonishment.

"How did you manage to reprogram your RMP to act more human-like?"

"Your RMP never mentioned its Adaptive AI capabilities? Never implemented it?" Zain countered.

Lieutenant Zhang shook her head, her face displaying confusion. "It only ever mentioned being a Learning AI model, not Adaptive AI." Now it was Zain's turn to be puzzled. He had assumed all RMPs were equipped with Adaptive AI, but reflecting on his limited interactions with ones other than Tom, none seemed to mimic human behavior like Tom did. He glanced back to where Tom was interacting with the German Shepherd puppies, his brow arched in question. While not urgent, it was definitely something he wanted to bring up later.

Tom looked up from tending to the puppies, "It is possible that adaptive modules were only activated in select units—perhaps intended for officers ranked colonel or above, or introduced experimentally. I have seen no documentation suggesting widespread deployment."

Zain absorbed that quietly, his brows pulling together. If Tom's evolution was rare—or worse, unsanctioned—it could explain the lieutenant's confusion. It made Zain wonder just how many Adaptive AI units were in the field and why he had been chosen to have one.

"Why did your RMP bypass communications to track down some puppies?" Lieutenant Zhang inquired once more, her eyes also shifting to Tom with interest. "Not that I'm unappreciative. As I mentioned, being cut off from communicating with fellow commanding officers seemed overly severe. You'd assume those in charge would want us to coordinate and strategize by staying in touch. Instead, we're being kept in the dark, carrying out orders individually with very little information to rely on." And just like that, Zain noticed that her curiosity switched from the puppies to her main concern: the communication blackout.

Zain frowned, feeling a chill behind her words. So, it wasn't just him. Other commanders were also being kept isolated, silenced beneath layers of controlled communication. Whatever was happening, it was by design. Since he had no answers, he decided to change the subject, "Speaking of curious events, have you had additional soldiers brought in to help with clean up followed by a sudden drop in general population soon after that arrival?"

The lieutenant furrowed her brow and started shaking her head. "The only unusual decline in population occurred last year when my battalion trailed the RMP units, only to find thousands upon thousands of bodies left behind and a bewildered civilian population. That confusion quickly turned to anger when they were informed that they would be conscripted. Regarding new recruits or recent deaths…no, there haven't been any. Why, what's happened?"

At that precise moment, Tom reappeared.

"How are our little canine companions faring?" Zain queried, a softness creeping into his usually stern voice.

"Their thirst was immediate," Tom stated. "One even climbed into the bowl before realizing it was more efficient to drink from it. It would seem they were parched for quite some time. After their little adventure involving the water bowl—which seemed akin to discovering an ocean for them—salt-free, of course—they huddled together in one cozy corner of their makeshift cardboard home. Almost instantly, they succumbed to sleep. Seeing as they no longer required my supervision or care, I thought it best to rejoin you here."

The lieutenant, who had been listening intently with a furrowed brow and crossed arms, couldn't help but interject at this point. "I don't think I could adapt if my RMP was programmed with an Adaptive AI model," she stated. "It's just plain weird."

Tom's visor brightened briefly. "I have occasionally wondered if my evolution was unique—or if others were prevented from adapting. It is unclear whether my development is a result of programming…or exposure." Tom stated before turning its attention back to Zain. "Did I miss anything important?" It asked casually.

"The lieutenant hasn't reported any further mysterious fatalities or fresh faces joining her ranks," Zain provided succinctly. His tone carried an undertone of relief but also a hint of disappointment; things remained stagnant for now. "It would appear that the rollout of new troops," Zain emphasized the term so that Tom could comprehend to which troops he referred, "is still relatively localized. Of course, we don't know if there are any other transport planes being deployed besides the one being flown by Stefan…" Zain trailed off in frustration. There were simply too many questions and no answers forthcoming.

"I am not sure how to interpret that data," Tom confessed.

"I'm not sure how to interpret this whole confusing conversation," the lieutenant chimed in.

"Apologies, Lieutenant," Zain said, then turned to address Tom again. "I think the best approach is to be straightforward."

"Is that a good idea?" Tom questioned.

"I thought we agreed to involve her?"

"I mentioned we need as many allies as possible, but I still have my doubts—"

"What do you think of the missions we've been assigned to carry out?" Zain interrupted, cutting off Tom's concern. "And feel free to speak freely, Lieutenant.

The abrupt change momentarily startled Lieutenant Zhang, but she quickly regained her composure. Her eyes narrowed as she gathered her thoughts, her posture reflecting a mix of carefulness and insight. "I've always prided myself on being a good soldier," she started cautiously, "yet over the past two years, it feels as though I'm being manipulated—not to serve the people's interests, but rather the agenda of a select few intent on dismantling societal structures on an unprecedented scale. This is one reason I wanted to reach out to you or other senior officers to discuss these issues, only to find out—as you're already aware—that our communications were being restricted. So do you want to fill me in?"

"We're as much in the dark as you are," Zain began, "but something strange happened that made us question our mission's purpose even more. Just a few days ago, five hundred additional soldiers appeared at my location without any prior notice. They just arrived. None of them seemed older than twenty. Nearly simultaneously, an equal number of civilian and military personnel died. We aren't sure how many of these soldiers have been sent to other commands but I was told that the ones sent to me were the first of what was to be many more."

"I thought all possible personnel had been called up at the onset of our deployment. Where are all the fresh faces coming from?"

Zain looked at Tom and they shared a knowing look. "We thought the same, but there's no getting around the fact that five hundred more suddenly showed up. Any ideas?"

The lieutenant shook her head, "You said they were young, so I suppose it's possible that two years ago they weren't military age; possible that they've only just been recruited."

Zain rubbed his chin contemplating this explanation, "No, from my understanding, all military personnel were called in, and that included those fresh out of the academy. As young as seventeen, eighteen years old."

"Civilian youth who decided to join—" the lieutenant started, but Zain was already shaking his head.

"Again, not likely. All civilian personnel have already been conscripted. What's the point of conscripting them to work in the debris fields only to then pull them away and put them through military training, just to send them back out to work in the debris fields. No, that makes even less sense."

"Look, Colonel, I was already struggling to make sense of our current orders, and am completely stumped by this new development. What do you think the purpose of all of this is?"

Zain and Tom had a suspicion, rooted in their past dealings with Melyndie, but they couldn't disclose this information to the lieutenant or anyone else. So, Zain simply shook his head and shrugged, saying, "The fact that they are eliminating citizens and demolishing cities…well…it's apparent that some conglomerate is attempting to reshape our world to fit their vision." A vision of the future, Zain thought tacitly, that didn't include the current world's population. "Lieutenant, we aren't certain about everyone involved in this larger plot. Until we can get in touch with other commanding officers, please keep our discussion confidential. If more soldiers arrive unexpectedly and you lose an equal number of your soldiers and citizens, reach out to me through your RMP, but avoid sharing specifics. Just report something anomalous has happened."

"I'll simply inform you that we've gained new workers, so there's no confusion about what I mean. That shouldn't raise any suspicions."

"Alright, that works. Well, Lieutenant, we each have a long drive ahead, so I'll be on my way. If you can do so safely, try to gather people who would support you if we ever need to organize a rebellion. I know that sounds dramatic, but I fear we're headed in that direction."

"Just who would I recruit?" the lieutenant asked, incredulous. "You do realize you're asking me to risk everything based on little more than suspicious supposition," she said, her tone tightening. "That's not rebellion—it's career suicide."

"I know," Zain admitted. "But we have to take a stand sometime. Still, if you don't think you're—"

"No," she interrupted, more softly this time. "I agree something is happening that makes no sense. People being killed. Entire cities reduced to rubble…it just makes me feel so inept. So helpless."

"I feel the same," Zain said. "But if we don't do something—"

"The whole of humanity could die," she finished for him, closing her eyes against the weight of it. Her voice was low, steeped in disbelief and dread. After a moment, she looked up at him again. "Where would I even start?"

"You can do what I started doing," Zain offered. "Spare the lives of any dissident. When I was questioned about the counterorder, I simply said I was offering them the chance to reconsider. If they still refused, then I would personally see to their execution. That gave me space—space to feel them out quietly. To see who might be willing to stand with me if it ever came to a rebellion."

The lieutenant seemed to mull over the colonel's words carefully, drawing slow breaths in and out through her nostrils. "The insanity of it all…I'll do what you recommended, Colonel, but with so many individuals that could potentially be against us, it seems a rather futile effort. If you don't mind my saying so."

Zain shook his head, "Not at all, Lieutenant. I happen to think we're just shy of useless, but the fact is, something is happening in our world that I don't believe should be, and I don't believe I'm alone in that thinking. So, we either plan to take a stand…even it is against all odds…or we sit back and let people be killed by the millions. Possibly the whole of humanity."

"Understood, Colonel, and thanks for involving me in this."

Zain studied her for a long moment. "I know this could cost you everything," he said quietly. "So…thank *you*. I don't take that lightly. And thank you for trusting me enough not to report me to the military police," Zain joked. "I'll be in contact. Stay safe, Lieutenant."

"You too, Colonel. Before I leave though, why did you instruct my RMP to search for a couple of German Shepherd pups?" The question hung in the air, like an unexpected note in a familiar melody.

Zain's lips curled into a smile, his eyes crinkling at the corners with amusement. "I actually requested just one," he admitted, his voice light and casual despite the gravity of their conversation. "The extra pup is a bonus. They're intended as a gift…for someone special."

The lieutenant raised an eyebrow, her expression shifting from surprise to intrigue. She knew well the current directive given to the RMPs; it was not one that encouraged animal preservation. "An unusual choice for a gift," she commented dryly before adding, "Given the orders to exterminate wildlife…I trust you'll ensure their safety." Her tone softened slightly as she added her farewell, "Take care on the roads, Colonel. We'll speak soon." With that, she pivoted on her heel and swiftly made her way back towards her waiting jeep.

"Zain." Tom's voice broke through Zain's thoughts.

"Yes, Tom?" Zain responded without turning his gaze from the retreating figure of the lieutenant.

"You did not mention that Melyndie is the intended recipient of your gift." Tom's words were laced with its version of curiosity.

"Do you honestly believe," Zain began slowly, turning now to face his companion with a thoughtful frown etched onto his features, "that if I had disclosed our time-traveling associate she'd merely accept it? Or is it more probable she'd suspect my sanity?"

Tom replied dryly. "She would think you have lost your mind, but just mentioning Melyndie's name would not have revealed her origins. Perhaps you simply do not wish to use her name because you miss her."

"I miss her, yes. Her innocence, her strength…something lacking in our world right now."

"I miss her too," Tom stated. "She was a light in our current darkness."

Zain turned his head, his eyes following the darkening horizon as a quiet moment passed. "That's a good way to put it," he finally said, his voice subdued. "Let's head back now; we have to find out what Amal has done with our dissidents and why she lied to me."

"That will not be an enjoyable conversation," Tom warned.

"Yeah, I'm dreading it too," Zain murmured, jaw tightening. Without another word, they turned toward the waiting jeep, the weight of what lay ahead pressing in around them like the encroaching darkness.

## *The Burdens We Carry*

Zain had been driving through the desert for nearly twelve hours in silence so pronounced it pressed against his eardrums like he was swimming in deep water. The endless dunes blurred into one another, the horizon trembling with heat. Dust clung to his eyelashes, his throat raw from breathing sand-tinged air. He hadn't slept. Hadn't spoken. Not even to Tom.

But as the morning sun climbed higher—sharp and merciless—something inside him stirred. A question that had gnawed at the back of his mind for days finally pushed to the surface.

"Tom?" The silence that followed was filled with the faint hum of machinery as Tom powered up his systems from the rear of the jeep.

"Yes, Zain?" It finally responded.

"Why *do* you think you're the only RMP with Adaptive AI?" Zain questioned; his brow furrowed as he gave a quick glance in the rearview mirror.

"I do not know this to be the case and have insufficient data to confirm." Tom's response was immediate, devoid of any hesitation or doubt that might plague a human mind.

"So, it's feasible that there are other RMPs similar to yourself?" Zain continued.

"Anything is feasible, yes; however, as I have already stated, it would make sense to only provide those of higher rank with Adaptive AI models." Tom paused before continuing. "Field units would not need it to carry out their duties as advanced learning protocols could prove detrimental to their mission parameters, should they begin to question their orders," Tom reasoned.

"Like you," Zain quipped.

"Yes, like me," Tom confirmed.

"Wouldn't it be equally detrimental if all personal RMPs given to commanders of higher rank began to adapt and question orders and commands? Like you?"

A pause hung in the air as Tom processed Zain's question. "Indeed," it finally responded after several seconds of silence. "It would prove quite the issue especially if the RMPs were attached to others such as yourself who have begun to question those in command. If the other commanders were satisfied with their mission and did not question those in authority, then the RMP would not either."

"We are presupposing that only high-ranking officers were given RMPs with Adaptive AI. Let's assume for a minute that all commanders were. Why do you think that the lieutenant's personal RMP isn't adapting to her personality like you are to me?" Zain asked next.

Once again, there was a momentary pause from Tom as though it was deep in thought. "Any answer that I provide would be supposition; however, if I were to speculate, it is possible that the lieutenant did not foster the proper atmosphere for the RMP to use its adaptive capabilities. If the lieutenant continued to treat the RMP as nothing more than an information and security unit; if she did not attempt to engage the unit in conversation beyond that, then the RMP's AI would remain limited to only environmental adaptations."

"Interesting," Zain murmured.

"Again, this is only my opinion. I could be completely incorrect." Tom replied.

"That's alright, Tom. I was just satisfying my curiosity, really. What you said is completely logical," Zain acknowledged with a nod before shifting his attention back to the road and contemplating their situation.

The rest of the drive passed in silence, but Zain's thoughts continued to race.

As the last streaks of sunlight bled across the sky, Zain finally pulled up in front of his command tent. The desert had shifted to shadow; the wind cooling just enough to cut through his fatigue and make him shiver. His bones ached from the drive, but it wasn't just physical. It was the ache of too many choices, too many truths left dangling in front of him.

The minute he pulled his jeep to a stop in front of his command tent, Amal came stomping outside, the concern etched on her features visible even in the waning light.

"You've been gone for quite some time," she declared, her tone laced with an undercurrent of worry that she tried to disguise with irritation.

Zain replied wearily, the fatigue dragging down his voice into a low timbre, "I've been very busy."

Amal studied him, her eyes narrowing as she took in his haggard appearance, "Yeah, you look beat. Would've been nice, nonetheless, to hear something from you," she stated pointedly, her lips tugging downwards into a frown.

"I left a radio for you, Amal. If something came up, you could have contacted me at any time."

Her response was quick and tinged with both relief and irritation, "I know, but since you chose not to radio me, I was quite content to believe that all was well and you hadn't fallen victim to some disaster or other."

Zain teased back lightly despite the exhaustion gnawing at every part of his body. "If you were worried for me, Amal, just say so," he said with a small smirk tugging at his lips. "Otherwise, I'm far too tired to engage in a verbal tug of war."

Amal's expression softened then; her concern for her brother overriding any previous annoyance. "Sorry, brother. Yes, I was worried, and I actually did try to radio to alleviate that worry, but it didn't get through."

"Likely out of range. Those radios don't have the largest communications radius. Sorry about that, Amal. I was so caught up in everything that's happening, that it didn't register about the radio's limited reach."

"Well, now that you're back, worry alleviated." She paused before offering, "Can I get you some tea or something to eat before you lie down to rest?"

His retort came out more amused than annoyed, "Pretty presumptuous to assume I have time to rest."

Amal grinned sheepishly at him then, "True."

"I will take you up on an offer of tea," Zain said, "although I am curious just how you intend to produce it out here in the middle of nowhere."

Amal's face crumpled into a look akin to a child who's been found out lying, "I don't actually have any tea to offer. All I have is our standard fare of military rations."

"Then why would you offer tea?"

Caught in her own web, Amal shrugged, "Habit, I suppose."

With a shake of his head that spoke volumes about his exasperation and also fondness for his sister's antics, Zain navigated through the canvas flaps into the command tent. He sank down onto a stool and began peeling off his boots.

Crossing over to the attached latrine, he started to unbuttoning his uniform, then caught sight of Amal who had followed him in like a shadow. He paused mid-motion. "You might want to wait outside for about twenty minutes. Otherwise, you're going to see your brother in a state you should never see him in."

The words sent Amal spinning on her heels with such speed that she nearly tripped over herself in her haste to exit the tent. Her wide-eyed alarm was met with Zain's low chuckle resonating behind her.

Once alone, Zain stripped off the remainder of his clothes and stepped beneath the combat showerhead. Any other day, he'd have simply settled for an army bath, but today, he needed to feel cleansed. He tried to scrub away the thoughts too, but they settled under his skin like the grit that clung stubbornly beneath his fingernails. The fate of the detainees. The truth he suspected but hadn't yet confirmed. His mind churned, unable to find rest.

Dressed in a fresh set of fatigues, after his brisk shower, Zain made his way across to the radio, still sitting on the table where he'd left it two days ago. He lifted it with a shake of his head and called to Tom to bring Amal in.

Amal entered ahead of Tom and immediately set about pulling out some MREs, "What would you like for dinner? Shredded beef, chili and beans—"

"Shredded beef sounds good. Thanks for doing that."

"You honestly look as if you'd collapse if you attempted to make anything for yourself, so it's the least I can do. I am your assistant after all." Amal started ripping open the packaging, her fingers deft in the now routine task.

"Frankly, if you weren't doing it, I'd have likely bypassed food altogether in favor of just sleeping the rest of the night away. I haven't closed my eyes in days," Zain admitted, running a hand over his chin. "Need to trim this beard too," he added, then went to collect his razor. He needed to keep himself preoccupied or else he'd fall asleep in the MRE instead of consuming it.

He'd just finished his grooming, when Amal approached with two plates. She settled across from him at the small table and scooped up some of the food.

"The shredded beef isn't too bad," Amal commented, breaking the silence that had fallen.

Zain nodded appreciatively, but his mind wasn't on the meal, rather on how to address the concerns that had been discovered during his meeting with Major Reese.

Nearly two hundred dissidents had vanished under Amal's supervision without anyone noticing, not even the RMPs tasked with guarding them. If Amal were a magician, he'd consider her among the elite. After finishing his meal, he tossed the plate into a nearby bucket for later washing and drank his water.

Zain let a moment pass as Amal finished the last few bites of her meal. She looked content, even relieved—completely unaware of the storm about to descend. He didn't want to ruin the moment, but the weight of her deception was becoming unbearable.

"Amal," he spoke at last, his voice carefully measured. "I need to ask you something, and I need your honesty, okay? What happened to the detainees that were being rounded up outside?"

"I don't understand what you mean," she replied.

"So much for honesty," Tom commented from its spot by the entrance.

"Not helpful, Tom," Zain retorted. "Let me handle this, alright?"

"Perhaps you should inform your sister that we have already scanned the workers at the site, and none have the biosignature of those—"

"Tom," Zain interrupted sharply. "I said I'll handle this."

Amal's eyes flickered with a touch of unease, though she tried to mask it with indifference. She leaned back slightly, her arms folding defensively, "Zain, you entrusted me to speak with them, to convince them to return to work—"

"How did you get them back to the site?" Zain asked, interrupting her.

"Huh?"

"It's nearly an hour to the site. I have the only jeep available at the command center and had taken it to the airfield to greet the new recruits. I was away for about an hour. However, when I got back, all the detainees were gone. According to you, they returned to the work site. I'm just asking how they managed that. You said you'd contact Major Reese for pickup. Were you able to contact Major Reese at the site to send some transport trucks to pick them up?" He continued, knowing that she hadn't. "That would be the only logical explanation since you definitely didn't walk sixty miles across the desert in less than an hour. So, where are they, Amal? And how did you get them away from the RMPs without raising an alarm?"

Amal paused briefly, absorbing the implications of Zain's questions. Her hands trembled slightly, revealing that there was more beneath her composed exterior, indicating that she *was* concealing something from him.

Once again, he attempted to coax the truth from her, but this time he lowered his voice to a gentle whisper rather than continuing with the same interrogatory tone from a moment ago, "Where are they, Amal?"

"I swore to keep them safe," she responded with a quiet murmur that barely stirred the air between them.

"Safe? Have I harmed them? I was commanded to kill them—"

"Are you telling me you refused a direct order to kill two hundred strangers, yet you didn't hesitate to obey a similar order when you shot mother? How could I trust that you wouldn't kill them?"

"I'm not going to do this with you again, Amal, and I'm not going to allow you to deflect from our present topic of conversation. I can't change what I've done, but I am moving forward with what I can do—which, admittedly isn't much right now. Now, where are the detainees?"

The air around them grew tight and oppressive, every word spoken bouncing off the bare fabric walls and echoing back at them. It was as if their words were tangible things; they could almost see them hanging in the air.

Amal's eyes shimmered with unshed tears, pools of emotion threatening to spill over. Her facade of stoicism was crumbling under the weight of everything left unsaid. She swallowed hard against the knot in her throat before admitting quietly, "I moved them. I didn't send them back to work. I put them somewhere safe."

Zain leaned forward, disbelief and frustration etched on his face like a map of uncharted territory. He stared at her incredulously as he tried to fathom what she had just revealed. "You moved two hundred people without a trace? Beneath the noses of a dozen RMPs?"

"The RMPs were down for self-diagnostics," Tom supplied. "So, they would not have known that the dissidents were missing until—"

"Precisely," Zain supplied. "As soon as they rebooted, they would have discovered them missing, which means that Amal, here, would have had to do some fairly impressive verbal gymnastics to convince them that the dissidents had willingly returned to the work site."

Amal turned her tear-filled gaze towards him; her pleading eyes were like open wounds. "Please don't hurt them."

Zain's hardened expression softened at his sister's plea; her fear palpable enough for him to feel it clawing at his own heartstrings. "Amal," he began after taking a shaky breath himself. He ran his hand through his hair in an attempt to steady himself against the storm brewing within him. "If I had intended to hurt them, I would've done so already. We can't keep dancing around in circles. In order for them to be safe, they need to return to the site and work alongside their friends, family, and neighbors. Even if they only comply halfheartedly, it will still ensure they remain safe from retaliatory acts. Did you, or did you not, make them understand this?"

"I think so, yes," she murmured in voice that Zain could barely hear.

"Then why didn't you radio the major?"

"They agreed that it would be best to return to work so they could continue to eat and…live, but when I went to get the radio…well…they suddenly had a change of heart…and…well…I didn't have the heart to push them."

"Dear God," Zain muttered, shaking his head. "It's been nearly a week. How have you managed to hide them for that long? How have they been subsisting?"

As he waited for his sister's reply, his thoughts drifted to her accusations, stabbing at his mind like needles. Did she really think him so cold…so callous? But then he realized she could. He could understand why she would, considering how quickly he'd taken their mother's life.

He closed his eyes against the memory, which weighed on him heavily—like a stone strapped to his ankle, pulling him down into deep water. He bent forward against the pain, unable to draw breath, as phantom waves struck his back like a thousand needles.

The memory of pulling the trigger was sucking the very life from his lungs. The thought hammered mercilessly at his brain, looping like a vulture circling a carcass—slow, inevitable, waiting for his body to rise from the mire he was drowning in.

After moments that felt like an eternity, Amal finally nodded in acquiescence and whispered, "I moved them to one of the hangars a few buildings away. I've been taking MREs to them, but only two a day. Admittedly, they can't keep surviving on such meager fare. And I know that it's going to cause a severe shortage that I knew I'd eventually be unable to hide."

The relief that washed over Zain was palpable; his exhalation echoed like a gust of wind. Not only because he now knew where those people were but that his sister finally chose reason over emotion.

"I know you're trying to protect us all, Zain," Amal said softly after a moment. She closed her eyes briefly as if gathering strength from reserves she wasn't sure she still had. "But please promise me that whatever happens, we'll find a way to keep them safe."

"They're alive, Amal, because I refused to follow orders and execute them. It's my personal mission to keep them safe, and every person within my purview. If I could protect and defend the world, I would, but I'm only one man. Rest assured that Tom and I are doing all we can to find out whose orchestrating all of this and a way in which to stop them. I just need more time," he responded, then stopped speaking, needing to collect his thoughts and emotions. His voice was hoarse from the strain of the conversation and the burden of their situation.

Amal nodded in understanding and wiped away her tears with a shaky hand. As she turned her gaze towards the tent opening where the sun was casting long shadows over their makeshift command post, she murmured softly, "Time is what we always need more of, isn't it?" Her words hung heavy in the air as they both contemplated their uncertain future.

Zain didn't respond. He just stared at the canvas wall, his jaw clenched, the words caught somewhere between his heart and throat. Outside, the wind picked up, rattling the poles like a warning—an omen of how fragile everything had become.

And in that silence, he felt the weight of every life he couldn't save, as if the future itself were collapsing all around him. The real storm, however, wasn't in the sky—it was inside him: regret, resolve, and the slow erosion of hope.

But it was the quiet plea in his sister's voice that gutted him most. Because it reminded him that, despite everything, they were still human—

—and, right now, being human was the heaviest burden of all, because humanity was teetering on the edge of extinction—and someone had to take a stand, had to fight to keep it alive.

*Year 2402*

Melyndie stirred from her slumber, the chill of her austere apartment piercing through the veil of sleep. As consciousness flooded back, so too did a surge of sorrow that welled up in her eyes and spilled down her cheeks. Two months had passed since Dr. Henley granted her medical clearance, marking the end of her physical therapy just yesterday. Yet she remained trapped in a purgatory of uncertainty—no word from Dr. Kishida-Guan or his colleagues throughout her recovery about when she might return to the before time.

She had been hastily returned to this cold, impersonal dwelling as soon as she'd been medically cleared. Each day since had been punctuated by clinical visits from a medical technician who performed exhaustive examinations and assisted with physical therapy sessions. Her meals were prepared thrice daily by someone sent by 41GB. They entered without invitation, cooked the bland dishes she'd not missed while she was gone, ensured cleanliness according to strict protocols, and then left without a trace.

Loneliness gnawed at Melyndie, a slow and ravenous thing that hollowed her out from the inside. Today was supposed to mark her reintegration into society—until word came from Dr. Kishida-Guan that it was time to resume her mission, but for her, that old life no longer held its allure. The thought of resuming the monotonous routine—waking up at a rigidly scheduled time, crossing the immaculate courtyard to spend hours cataloguing in the archives before returning home to eat tasteless food—filled her with dread.

When her alarm blared at precisely zero-five-thirty hours, memories fluttered back like moths drawn to light; dragging her back to graduation day when an elderly man had led them into their apartments for the first time. His voice echoed in her mind like a spectral reminder: *"Report to the archives at zero-six-thirty hours tomorrow morning. Your alarm in your room has been pre-programmed to wake you each day at zero-five-thirty hours to give you time to eat, dress, and walk across the courtyard to the archival building. Learn now that you must be timely in all that you do."*

She was expected to adhere strictly to these rules but instead curled in on herself like a wounded animal seeking solace in its own misery.

After letting out all pent-up emotions, she clambered out of bed and shuffled naked into the compact outer area. She prepared her bland meal and sank heavily onto the stool. Each bite was bitter, a stark reminder of the MREs she once shared with Zain in what seemed like another life.

Once finished, she stared blankly at the empty bowl—her only dish—before washing it, against her desire to rebel and leave it sitting where it lay.

She retrieved a set of coveralls hanging on a hook, scrutinizing them with distaste. These were the same clothes she'd worn all her life; three utilitarian grey jumpsuits exchanged only when outgrown. The clothes gifted by Dr. Kishida-Guan had been confiscated upon her return from the past.

She stared at the drab jumpsuit, loathing it—loathing what it represented. Why bother wearing it now, when no one in the medical bay had flinched at her nudity for months? Had modesty been stripped from her, too, alongside choice and freedom? If they cared so little about the human body, why hide it?

Was this the holy one's attempt at control? To mask any bodily differences that could elicit unwanted curiosities? It made little sense as no one seemed capable of such feelings in their society.

Still, emotions weren't absent, simply suppressed, so did the holy one's fear that exposure to differences might awaken a sleeping giant; one they would be hard-pressed to manage?

Was she simply projecting?

She glanced at her jumpsuit again, waging an inner war over whether she should even bother putting it on now. After all, she'd spent the last eight months—since her surgery—wearing nothing at all? That never seemed to bother anyone she encountered.

A flush rose to her cheeks at the memory of Zain's instinct to shield her modesty. He had cared…so, shouldn't she?

A glance at the clock revealed that departure time was nearing; time for that lonely trek across the cobblestone courtyard to the archives building. As dread welled within her chest, she yearned for Dr. Kishida-Guan's summons, hoping they'd resolved issues from her first time-travel mission and were ready to send her back again.

Her conversation months earlier with Dr. Kishida-Guan regarding expanded expectations for her next time jump made her knees weaken. At that time, she hadn't voiced opposition to assassinating anyone; hadn't voiced any concerns at all. Anything that might jeopardize another chance at returning to the before time remained unsaid because above all else, she needed to get back there.

With a heavy sigh that echoed her inner turmoil, she slid into the coarse fabric of her jumpsuit. The material felt like a weight on her shoulders, its rough texture abrasive against her skin in a way that made her want to tear it off. She quashed the urge, gritting her teeth against the discomfort. As she began to move towards the exit, an odd sensation made her pause.

Something was tapping rhythmically against her skin from within one of the inner pockets.

Curiosity piqued, she reached inside and pulled out the two photographs she had removed from the archives years before: One depicting a German Shepherd, the other a couple embracing—two things she'd never had, yet longed for with deep ache.

Emotion cracked through her like a fault line. She sank to her knees, the photos trembling in her grip. She worked hard to bring her breathing under control, recap the emotional well, but it was hard when faced with two things she longed for more than anything in the world.

A yearning twisted sharply in her chest as she looked at them. If not for the desperate need to reintegrate into society so she could facilitate a return to the past, she would have stayed secluded in her quarters with only these two images for company.

As she studied the furry face of the German Shepherd staring back at her from the photo, a memory shot through her brain like a lightning strike: The former archivist had once warned about such curiosities when she caught sight of this very picture on his desk on her first day at the archives. Could it be that he, too, had been fabricated with human emotions, like her? Had he also grappled with suppressing those feelings just to blend seamlessly into their mechanical-like society?

Or perhaps despite being manufactured devoid of emotions—strictly for productivity—had he evolved? Had his time among relics of the past seeped so deeply into him that it managed to override his genetic programming and awaken dormant emotions? Was such an override even feasible?

In this moment though, these questions mattered little. Her focus was singular—finding a way back to the past. To do that, she needed to play her part in the present, as a willing gear in their societal machine.

Summoning a surge of determination that welled up from the depths of her soul, she pushed herself off her trembling knees. Her fingers, almost reverently, slipped the pair of treasured photographs back into the worn fabric pocket of her jumpsuit. The images were more than mere glossed paper; they were fragments of a past life, tangible pieces of memory that she clung onto in these solitary moments.

With a final sigh, she turned towards the entranceway leading to the world beyond. The morning sun was just beginning its ascent into the sky, its first rays gently breaching over the distant horizon. It was a sight that usually filled her with an inexplicable joy—a testament to nature's cyclical promise of rebirth and renewal.

But today, it felt different. The warm hues of dawn no longer brought comfort but served as a bleak reminder of what once was. The sunrise now felt like a lie—a counterfeit memory. An echo of those vibrant desert sunrises she had witnessed in another lifetime, when every day was painted in bold strokes of oranges and purples against an endless canvas of sand and sky.

Still, she lingered for a moment, absorbing the warmth of the morning rays before finally descending towards the courtyard. As soon as her foot touched the cobblestone walkway, she froze. Something was wrong—profoundly, impossibly wrong.

*********

*Half Hour Earlier*

Dr. Kishida-Guan froze just inches from the chancellor's towering doors, his body immobile, as though every molecule of air had thickened around him. The daunting task of bringing the chancellor up to date on his painstakingly orchestrated plans felt an insurmountable one. He grappled with the uncertainty of whether it was the looming shadow of the chancellor's potential disapproval that burdened him or his own nagging self-doubt gnawing away at his once unshakeable confidence. Either way, it caused him to hesitate, to falter before punching in the code that would broadcast his arrival.

His hand hovered tentatively over the keypad, but recoiled abruptly as if seared by a venomous serpent when an intense pain spiraled through his veins like molten lava surging from a volcanic eruption. His legs wobbled and gave out under him, causing him to crumble against the icy wall, barely able to stifle a guttural groan that clawed its way up from his core. His breaths came in ragged gasps, each one more laborious than its predecessor as tumultuous waves of torment threatened to fracture him from within.

He hovered on the precipice of oblivion, each breath a potential detonation. If he moved wrong, even slightly, his body might rupture from the inside out. *Just hold,* he told himself. *Just— don't—move.*

After what seemed like an eternity condensed into sixty agonizing seconds of relentless torment, the blistering pain began its gradual retreat. Dr. Kishida-Guan leaned heavily against the metallic surface of the wall; its coolness infiltrated through his sweat-drenched shirt providing a modicum of relief.

He pressed his forehead harder against it, seeking solace in its frosty touch while waiting for his erratic heartbeat to regain its normal rhythm. After another lengthy moment, he gathered his scattered thoughts and steadied himself as he wrestled with the unforeseen malady that had seized him, caught in a tug-of-war between his resolve and the pressing responsibilities awaiting him.

With a surge of determination, he swallowed hard, took a shaky breath, and forced himself to stand, leaning on the wall for support. Shutting his eyes tightly, he concentrated on his breathing, inhaling and exhaling slowly until his heart rate stabilized and his nerves steadied. Then, with newfound resolve, he distanced himself from the wall and punched in the code on the keypad.

The door swished open with a low hum and once again, the doctor felt an overwhelming wave of dizziness consume him as he surveyed the room in disbelief. He stepped into the corridor hesitantly, glancing along its length to his left then to his right before returning to the room after confirming that he was indeed in the correct location.

Only it couldn't be, for nothing was as it should be. And he knew then: Something was wrong—profoundly, impossibly wrong.

## Unwelcomed Change

Melyndie's gaze fell upon the cobblestoned steps beneath her feet, her heart pounding wildly in her chest. The once immaculate stones, which had been laid and maintained with such precision and care, were now marred by unsightly chips and hairline cracks. These were wounds that time would normally inflict, yet they were scars she'd never witnessed forming in her lifetime.

Tearing her gaze from the damaged stones at her feet, she lifted it to take in the surrounding buildings. Like a detective searching for clues, she meticulously scanned each structure. What met her eyes was a series of blemished surfaces; once proud facades now stained with age and wear. Windows that used to gleam with transparency were now opaque canvases smeared with layers of dust.

The home she knew was morphing into an image she'd glimpsed a century into the future. A dilapidated version of its former self, standing as a haunting testament to decay and neglect.

But why? Why had this transformation occurred? What cataclysmic event had caused such an abrupt shift in time's tapestry? Were there more subtle signs, or even worse, glaring indications of time's cruel meddling that she had yet to see?

Could this be an aftershock of her return from the past? Or—worse—had she been hurled forward again, back into that crumbling, broken world? Her breath caught as the thought took hold. She turned sharply toward the corner of the building, eyes scanning for the one figure burned into her memory—the one who had haunted that future like a ghost. But there was no one. Only the echo of the man who should not have been there, and yet somehow had been.

She shook her head several times to dislodge the thought, realizing, almost instantly, that it couldn't be possible. She'd returned from the past over eight months ago and since then life had continued as if suspended in amber—unchanging until this moment. Until today when everything familiar began to crumble before her very eyes.

Her attention was magnetically pulled towards a solitary figure, darting through the crowd with an intensity that set it apart from the languid pace of those around her. The figure, 41GB, skidded to a halt in front of her and without any trace of her usual cordiality, delivered her message. "I've been sent by Dr. Kishida-Guan. You need to come immediately." The words reverberated with an urgency that was oddly absent from her monotone voice, a paradox that would have twisted Melyndie's mind into knots just a year ago. But she had since learned that 41GB was somehow evolving emotionally and what was once mimicry was becoming…more.

"What's happening?" Melyndie uttered, matching strides with the scientist as they moved through the shifting scenery. "Why is everything around me changing?"

"It is?" 41GB questioned, halting abruptly to scan their surroundings with unblinking eyes. "I hadn't noticed."

Melyndie felt a jolt of unease at this revelation. How could 41GB—so perceptive in other ways—fail to notice what had become increasingly evident? Was it possible that whatever was shifting reality around them was only visible to her? Was she tethered differently—somehow attuned to fractures in time that others couldn't perceive? The thought unsettled her more than she cared to admit, whispering of deeper disruptions beneath the surface.

She yearned to probe further but found herself trailing behind as the scientist resumed her brisk march towards the imposing science building—a place she hadn't stepped foot in since her return eight months ago.

As they walked, Melyndie's gaze strayed towards a nondescript annex—the hallowed medical facility for the holy ones—an unfamiliar territory until she'd been fabricated for Dr. Kishida-Guan's mission and found herself subjected to frequent medical intrusions. It was also a place she'd not ventured into since being discharged post-surgery.

"May I ask why the doctor needs to see me so urgently?" Melyndie probed, attempting to dissipate the mounting apprehension within her about these inexplicable changes unfurling around her.

"He did not relay that information to me," 41GB replied. "I was merely sent to retrieve you." With that, they arrived at the entrance to Dr. Kishida-Guan's secluded office. Bypassing the usual protocol of entering a code to announce their arrival, 41GB simply thrust the door open and gestured for her to enter before turning on her heel and striding away.

Left alone in the threshold, Melyndie stood awkwardly, her heart pounding as she waited for the doctor to acknowledge her presence. It wasn't long before his voice sliced through the silence.

"Melyndie. Come here." The words were heavy with such palpable tension and torment that Melyndie found herself frozen in place, staring wide-eyed at the doctor who looked more harrowed than she'd ever seen him before. He had, for most of the time she'd known him, always maintained a calm facade, only ever rarely displaying bouts of frustration or anger, but never before did he appear as he did now: frightened. And it was a sight that chilled her to the bone.

With her feet stubbornly rooted to the floor, his voice escalated, a harsh command slicing through the air. "I demand you come here! Now!" Rising from his seat, he began to prowl around the confined space of his study, fingers skeletal with age raking through hair that bore witness to countless years.

Melyndie's chest expanded as she inhaled a fortifying breath of resolve and then advanced towards the dais. She ascended and sidestepped swiftly when the doctor's restless pacing brought him dangerously close to colliding with her on the platform.

"Doctor, what is going on? Why is everything changing?" she asked, her voice barely above a whisper.

"You noticed," he sighed heavily, collapsing into his chair as if his legs had suddenly given out from under him.

"I noticed," Melyndie echoed softly, inching warily towards an adjacent chair and perching on its edge. Despite her best efforts, she couldn't relax enough to sink comfortably into its embrace. "But I also observed that 41GB was oblivious to the alterations enveloping us during our walk."

"Those are merely surface-level transformations," the doctor grumbled dismissively with a wave of his hand, as if he'd not heard the comment about his fellow holy one. "The true crisis is far more alarming and demands our immediate attention so we can rectify whatever is triggering these anomalies. The Chancellor…" Dr. Kishida-Guan paused mid-sentence, terror flashing across his face at what he was about to reveal. With several steadying breaths he forced out the words: "The Chancellor has…vanished. As though he never existed at all. His quarters have been altered into…I'm not sure…just another sterile laboratory."

As this revelation sunk in, Dr. Kishida-Guan added in a whispery rasp: "Simultaneously with this discovery, I felt…it was as if death itself had me in its icy grip, pulling me towards oblivion. But it didn't succeed. Thank heavens it didn't succeed."

Melyndie sat in stunned silence, her mouth agape as she tried to make sense of the doctor's revelations. She registered his words, yet their meaning eluded her grasp. After a protracted struggle with her own disbelief, she managed to voice a single query: "Doctor, what's happening?"

"Whatever is currently unfolding must be directly linked to an event that occurred in our past. Somehow, someone is meddling with the plans I meticulously crafted over decades."

"But how is that possible? There would need to be an awareness of future inhabitants in order to target one or more specifically. Right?"

"That's why I needed to see you," he replied, his gaze piercing into hers. "Could you have unintentionally disclosed something to those you interacted with in the past?"

Melyndie shook her head vehemently. "No! They only knew my origins because the RMP failed to register me as a citizen but they made every effort to shield me from exposure. Our discussions mostly revolved around contemporary events."

"And what were these events?" he pressed.

"You frequent the archives often, doctor. You know the history…"

"Yes, but that history is being altered in ways that affect us now—not centuries later," he snapped back at her. "There's someone from our past who seems hell-bent on sabotaging my plans."

"But your initial plan was to erase the Chancellor's ancestor from existence and assume his position because you believed you could better serve humanity and improve our lives," Melyndie countered. "He's gone now, so that serves you well, doesn't it? So, all that's left to accomplish is for me to return; to convince your ancestor not to suppress human emotions? You stated that you now understand that humanity can only thrive when we allow our emotions free rein. You meant that, didn't you?"

The doctor stared at her blankly for a moment before shaking his head as if refusing to recall that part of their shared conversation, swiftly changing tack. "Someone did more than just erase the Chancellor's ancestor; they gravely injured mine, to the point where I felt it physically. It leads me to conclude that he is dying. And if he dies—"

"You, too, will be wiped from this timeline," Melyndie finished for him.

"We must send you back to our past," the doctor insisted, his voice trembling with urgency. "You must prevent the assassination attempt on my ancestor. We need to stick to my original plan so I can ensure a long tenure as Chancellor of humanity and secure our future."

Melyndie's mind raced with the implications of what the doctor was proposing. This wasn't just another mission; this was an operation to secure their very existence, to anchor themselves in a timeline that was rapidly unraveling.

"I understand the gravity of what you're asking me to do," she replied evenly, though her mind raced with a storm of conflicting thoughts and fears. "But how can we ensure that altering these events won't provoke further unintended consequences? We might create a worse future than the instability we're currently witnessing."

Dr. Kishida-Guan rubbed his temples, his fingers trembling slightly. "It's a risk we must take," he said gravely. "Our current predicament is unsustainable. If I vanish, there's no telling how many more anomalies might manifest, how many more people might disappear. The very future of humanity is more at risk than ever before."

"None of this was ever supposed to happen, was it?" Melyndie murmured in a voice barely above a whisper.

"No, it was not," the doctor confirmed, his voice steeped in regret. "This was not the world I fought to create. Every adjustment I made, every decision I took was calculated to enhance our existence, not destabilize it."

"But you must have known…something…because you started to warn me…when I went to the future the first time. I remember now. The words: *Do you understand what you are tampering with? You play with time like it's a mere tool at your disposal.*" You understand that meddling as we've done can cause things to destabilize, yet you insist that we keep pushing. Why? When you, yourself, warn of the hazards—"

"Stop!" Dr. Kishida-Guan bellowed, then wilted before her eyes. Melyndie flinched, her breath catching. His voice cracked through the room like a thunderclap—but it wasn't anger she heard. It was desperation, fraying at the seams. Then he was speaking again, his tone more subdued, "Just stop. Can you not see that my warning, in the future, is as a result of what's now happening in the past? But now that I'm aware of it, here in the present, I can change things. Save that future. Can't you see?"

Melyndie stared at the ground, processing everything. The weight of their predicament felt immense, crushing. She didn't see; all she saw, right now in front of her, was a man losing his grip on logic and reason. His explanation made little sense to her, and by the frazzled way in which he blurted it out, made little sense to him either. But that couldn't concern her right now, because for her to get back to the before time, she had to agree with whatever he said; go along with whatever scheme he devised, no matter how nonsensical. Finally, she lifted her gaze to meet his. "When do I leave?"

"Immediately," Dr. Kishida-Guan replied, rising from his chair with a newfound sense of urgency. He moved towards an aged cabinet on the far side of the room and retrieved a small envelope. He opened it to reveal two snapshots. "This is the Chancellor's ancestor. His name was…" he paused, turning the image over in his hand to read the information on the back, but Melyndie interrupted him.

"That's the President of the New Confederated States of America. His name is Saltzer, I believe."

"You know of him?"

"I heard talk of him often, but never met him. Although, he did arrive at the base command in Iceland to have a meeting with the commanding officer and the battalion commanders before they deployed for phase two. Just before I was pulled back."

"So, he'll be in the area you'll be returning to," the doctor sighed in relief. "What about this man? Have you seen him?"

Melyndie shook her head. "Who is he?"

"He is my ancestor. He's a scientist and geneticist, and was instrumental in the evolution our world. His name is Dr. Riku Jang."

"He looks similar to what you would've looked like when you were younger," Melyndie murmured, noting the same slant to the nose and mouth, the same dark eyes and tall forehead. The only obvious difference between the two was how much older the holy one was compared to the younger man in the picture, who appeared just slightly older than Zain.

"You must make sure my ancestor survives long enough to solidify his position and implement the changes that will secure our future."

"And what about the Chancellor's ancestor?" Melyndie asked, curiosity piqued by the complexities of their tangled timelines. "Somehow, he's been killed. I'm assuming you don't want me to prevent that happening."

Dr. Kishida-Guan paused, his eyes narrowing slightly. "That part of the plan remains unchanged. His removal is vital. More importantly, you must remove whomever it is that is attempting to assassinate Dr. Jang, or just stop them…somehow."

"I was not fabricated for murder, Doctor. Yet, since my return, you have dictated that I suddenly put aside all emotion to become an assassin. How do you expect me to resolve the differences between what my initial mission was to what it's evolving into?"

Dr. Kishida-Guan's expression hardened, as if he were trying to suppress a brewing outburst. He continued to pace, his breaths audible as he struggled to control his emotions. Eventually, he halted and turned to her, fixing her with an intense gaze that challenged her to question him further. "When situations change suddenly, as they are now, we must adapt and change with them. We might not like the changes required; we might never have chosen them under ideal conditions, but it's not hard to foresee the consequences for our world if you decide you can't kill. Making that choice would mean putting your own desires above the needs of humanity."

Melyndie flinched at the harshness of his words. Yet, despite the sting of his admonition, she understood the gravity of the mission. The entire foundation of the present and future teetered dangerously on the brink of disintegration. Sometimes, necessity demanded actions that one's soul might later lament.

"I will do what must be done," Melyndie resolved, though her voice carried a tremor that betrayed her inner turmoil.

Dr. Kishida-Guan seemed to soften slightly at her acquiescence, his features relaxing as he headed for the door to his office. "Let's go get you ready to depart. We must get you back before everything is lost."

Melyndie nodded, following him through the brightly-lit corridors of the complex. As they walked, her mind was ablaze with thoughts and strategies, as well as a growing unease about the moral intricacies of her task. Her training had prepared her for many things, but this weaving of preservation and destruction was a delicate dance she had never anticipated.

Upon arriving at the laboratory, Dr. Kishida-Guan made his way to a small desk tucked in the corner, which he used as his workspace in this room. He opened the bottom drawer and retrieved the same clothes she had worn when she returned. It was the slightly oversized uniform Zain had obtained for her, allowing her to blend in with his battalion. Seeing the clothes almost overwhelmed her and she felt the sting of tears prick her eyes. She blinked rapidly, turning her head away to hide her vulnerability. The sight of the uniform carried a weight of memories; each thread intertwined with her fears and hopes.

Dr. Kishida-Guan watched her for a moment, his gaze remaining stoic and determined. "You've been through much," he finally acknowledged as he handed her the uniform. "And you will go through much more before this is over. But remember, Melyndie, you are not just fighting for our present—you are safeguarding our future."

Taking a deep, steadying breath, Melyndie accepted the clothes and began to change, strangely grateful that only she and the doctor were in the room, and he'd turned away to tend to something else.

Whereas before, stripping in front of a group of people meant nothing to her, now she was acutely aware, and that awareness came because of her time in Zain's company.

A wistful smile tugged at the corner of her lips as she recalled his reaction when she'd begun to change in front of him that one, and only, time. His action had been swift to preserve her modesty; a term she'd never heard of in her lifetime.

As she began buttoning up the camo pants, her fingers stroked the material. Though rough, the texture of the uniform felt familiar against her skin, grounding her. It also served as a reminder of what she had already endured and survived. She fastened the last button—a simple motion, but one she now realized she performed with ease.

She slipped the brownish-green t-shirt over her head, stopping momentarily to sniff at the material, wishing—absurdly—that it still carried traces of dirt, sweat…him. The scent of Dubai, of urgency and earth. But the sterilization had erased all of it. Even the memories felt scrubbed raw, leaving only the ache of what was no longer there.

Dr. Kishida-Guan turned to address her again, as she was buckling the belt. "Okay, do not forget why you're returning. You will not only be collecting samples again," he continued, moving to a cabinet to retrieve a new monitoring unit, "you must also find and protect Dr. Jang at all costs. His survival ensures my existence and thus the stability of our current—and future—realm." He paused to strap the unit onto her bicep, then swallowed hard before continuing, "And as for Jeffrey Saltzer, your actions must be precise—prevent others from altering his fate. And if others interfere, you must be prepared to take the needed actions yourself. I've adjusted the date and time to align with the events that occurred here; so that you'll have thirty days to find your targets and to be present during the assassination attempts. Plenty of time for you to position yourself to act. This also allows you time to gather your samples. Don't forget—thirty days to accomplish this mission. Now, head to the platform. We need to get you moving."

Melyndie nodded, her determination steeling her against the swirling doubts that threatened to undermine her resolve. She approached the platform where the time portal shimmered with an ethereal glow, its edges blurring and reshaping with a rhythmic pulse. The air around it hummed with energy, the sound almost melodic, as though calling her to step forward.

Dr. Kishida-Guan had moved over to the controls and was adjusting several dials on a console across from the platform, his brow furrowed in concentration. "Remember, Melyndie," he called without looking up, "trust your instincts—they've been honed for this."

Melyndie stepped onto the platform, the light enveloping her like a cocoon spun from the fabric of time itself. A chill swept through her, sudden and disorienting, as if the world had loosened its grip on her. She glanced over—not at the doctor, but at everything she had ever known—before closing her eyes. The current seized her like a massive hug stealing her breath. And then, she was gone.

The relentless pull of time seized Melyndie once more. But unlike before—when darkness had consumed her and she crashed into the sands of Dubai with injuries covering most of her body—this time, she remained fully aware.

With strength summoned from deep within, she steadied herself as she burst forth from the temporal vortex, landing deftly on the desert's gritty expanse with only a mild sense of disorientation.

The sun was lazily dipping below the horizon, its retreat painting an artist's palette across the sky with strokes of pink and orange. She paused to assess her surroundings, her eyes landing on a familiar sight in the distance that was both astonishing and reassuring. Her pulse slowed to a steady rhythm as she found solace in the environment's familiarity; yet unlike before, an eerie silence pervaded everything.

As darkness claimed dominance and the last light withdrew, Melyndie knew she had to seek refuge before nocturnal creatures awoke. A fleeting memory tugged at the recesses of her mind; a warning given her by Omar: *"Night falls fast out here, and desert predators don't discriminate over the source of their food."* The reminder was enough to spur her into a run. The desert was a treacherous host after dusk settled in and she didn't intend being a predator's next meal.

Rounding the corner of the aircraft hangar, her boots scraped against the tarmac.

A barrage of memories flooded her senses; images flickered like old film reels: troops bustling around giant aircraft that stunned her senses as they prepared for deployment amidst an overwhelming cacophony. The scene quickly morphed into another memory—waking up after tumbling through time for the first time to see Zain and Tom standing nearby, deliberating over their unexpected visitor who'd literally fallen from the sky.

A small smile tugged at her lips as she ventured deeper into the hangar towards its rear where she'd spent her time shrouded in fear, uncertain of her fate. Yet, it was here that she'd found unexpected allies in Zain and Tom who were committed to protecting her from discovery and harm: one a soldier, the other an android.

Her eyes fell on a tarpaulin and her smile widened. It had served as her makeshift bed until Zain had insisted on providing a proper bedroll. She rearranged the tarp and sat down on it, drawing her knees close to fend off the gnawing anxiety threatening to consume her.

Previously, she'd been terrified of being an outsider among strangers; now, her fear was rooted in solitude and uncertainty about what lay ahead. The familiarity of this place offered a small measure of peace and safety but without any means to traverse the vast desert sands or any idea which direction held possible salvation, she felt lost. The desert could claim her before she found civilization.

Regardless of what course she decided upon next, one thing was clear: tonight, she wasn't going anywhere.

She rolled onto her side and manipulated the tarp into a makeshift pillow for her head. Despite its discomfort, it was still preferable than being back in the sterile confines of her room in her realm.

Her breaths came in even, rhythmic patterns as she tried to calm her racing heart. The sounds of the desert at night—the whistle of the wind and the distant call of nocturnal creatures—served as a lullaby, quietening her into a restless slumber strewn with dreams of timelines intertwining like the threads of fate. But sleep brought no comfort. Her mind, still burdened by uncertainty, spilled into fragmented dreams.

In her dreams, Melyndie saw herself navigating through potential futures, some pleasant and others filled with violence and death, which caused her body to quiver.

A bracing gust of cool evening desert air jolted her from her slumber. The nocturnal temperature of the barren landscape had taken a deep dive, a regular event she'd underestimated in her preparations. A slight shiver prickled through her as she rose on sleep-numbed legs, clumsily adjusting the protective tarp. Slipping back beneath its sheltering expanse, she pulled it snugly around her body to ward off the biting cold.

Her eyelids, heavy with the seductive pull of sleep, were irresistibly drawn towards the celestial dome in the sky outside. The stars were strewn across the ink-black canvas like a smattering of silver dust on sumptuous black velvet. Her fingers traced unseen lines between constellations as she mentally plotted her next course. She had to locate Zain and ascertain if they could assist in tracking down President Saltzer and Dr. Riku Jang. Her brow furrowed with unease at the realization that they might be either unable or unwilling to aid her unconventional mission parameters. Beyond their own commitments, there was a chance they might find her quest to trace two influential figures suspicious. It was these thoughts and many others which haunted her dreams when she finally succumbed again to sleep.

As dawn's first light pierced through the hangar's cracks, Melyndie stirred awake under its rapidly warming embrace. She yawned expansively and stretched languorously before reluctantly rising to face another day. Immediately though, she sank back down; she needed time to strategize her next move carefully.

Dr Kishida-Guan always exuded an unwavering conviction when he spoke about her return journey to the before time; he consistently assured that his objectives could be achieved within an incredibly short timeframe. However, what he failed to comprehend—and what she perpetually struggled to articulate convincingly—was that traversing this expansive timeline was not as simple as navigating through the familiar and compact realms of her own era.

She'd attempted to address this concern about navigating such a vast landmass at least once before, but he'd brushed off her apprehensions then. Now, confronted with the daunting mission entrusted to her and lacking the necessary means of transportation, she was suddenly swamped by a sense of being woefully underprepared and disoriented.

The distinctive drone of an engine, a sound that was etched in her memory, tickled Melyndie's eardrums. She jerked her head upwards as the noise amplified and grew closer. It was the unmistakable hum of a military transport plane, a behemoth of steel and power slicing through the sky. The first time she had seen one, during her initial trip to this time period, it had left her feeling like a fish out of water; pathetically ignorant with the era she'd been catapulted into.

But now, as she watched the hulking machine in the distance, its silver belly glinting in the morning sun, it sparked something inside her. A surge of relief washed over Melyndie like a tidal wave crashing onto shore. It felt like stumbling upon an oasis after days lost in the desert; it was a beacon signaling familiarity amidst foreign territory.

Her heart fluttered in her chest at the thought that people she might recognize could be aboard that mechanical bird—or stationed nearby. The mere possibility breathed life into her hope, filling her with renewed vigor. It whispered promises of allies not too far away after all. Yet something held her back from leaping to her feet and racing to greet the arriving transport.

Her analytical mind battled with the emotional tug of potential camaraderie. Zain and Tom, the allies who had initially been mere strangers, had become her unexpected anchor in this tumultuous timeline. The thought of reconnecting with them offered a sliver of comfort. Yet, prudence dictated a cautious approach. She couldn't afford the luxury of unguarded optimism in such uncertainty.

Melyndie decided it was best to err on the side of caution. She stood and crept closer to the edge of the hangar's entrance, keeping close to its shadowed walls. From this vantage point, she could observe without being overtly exposed. Her eyes fixed on the descending aircraft, watching as it executed a graceful landing on the airfield not too far from her.

As the engines wound down to a restful purr, a few figures began to disembark, then rapidly busied themselves offloading supplies meant for, she could only presume, the members of Zain's battalion.

Her eyes swept over the surrounding area, her heart pounding almost uncontrollably. Could it indicate that Zain was still close by? Would he arrive soon with the members of his battalion to gather their monthly ration quota? If that was, in fact, what was being offloaded, as she presumed.

As the last of the crates were deposited onto the tarmac and the aircraft lifted into the sky, her fleeting hope took flight with it— vanishing into the blue as swiftly as a hawk diving for its prey.

With a heavy heart, Melyndie pivoted on her heels, her soul echoing with a profound sense of loss and desolation. She trudged back to the makeshift shelter of the tarp at the hangar's far end, her footfalls echoing hollowly in the vast emptiness. As time sluggishly crawled by, the sun's position in the sky morphed from its morning high to an afternoon slouch, casting long shadows that danced along the concrete floor.

Hunger clawed at her insides, each pang a cruel reminder of her vulnerability. Her parched throat burned with every breath, as though even the air had turned against her. The urge to move, to scavenge, to risk—grew nearly impossible to ignore. The internal debate raged within her mind. Should she risk scavenging those supplies which sat unguarded across the heat-rippled asphalt?

Just as hunger won over caution, convincing her to take a chance, another familiar sound sliced through the air. The low hum of electric engines vibrated through the ground beneath her feet and echoed off the metal walls around her. Six vehicles zipped past in a blur of motion and dust, their sudden appearance forcing Melyndie to press herself against the cool shadowy wall of the hangar.

Her heart pounded like a frantic drum as she cautiously stood and tiptoed back to the front to peek around the corner of the hangar entrance. Her breath hitched in anticipation, turning into shallow gasps that barely escaped past clenched teeth. Though distance blurred specific details of those vehicles, and the occupants inside, one figure stood out distinctly. Stepping from its position at the rear of one of those vehicles was an unmistakable silhouette easily identifiable as an RMP.

"Tom?"

The word escaped on a breath tinged with doubt...and hope.

## *Growing Concerns*

Zain exhaled into the crisp morning air, the silence broken only by the soft whirring of Tom's internal processors. A faint orange tint brushed the edge of the horizon, signaling the arrival of daybreak. He turned and let out a sharp whistle, the sound cutting through the stillness like a train announcing its approach.

"Good morning, Zain," Tom called out, as if roused by the signal of Zain's emergence. "You are an early bird today."

Zain chuckled lightly, stretching his arms towards the dawning sky. "I'm always up this early, Tom, as well you know. I appreciate your efforts to embrace small talk but you might want to expand your conversational arsenal a bit."

"I will make a note of that," Tom responded in its mechanical tone, earning a playful shake of Zain's head. He turned around and released another high-pitched whistle into the air. A grin spread across his face like wildfire when two German Shepherd puppies came barreling around the corner, their oversized paws clumsily tripping over each other in their haste.

Their tongues hung out from one side of their mouths as they launched themselves at Zain with unbridled enthusiasm, their tails wagging so fiercely it seemed they might take flight. Zain bent down to meet them halfway, showering them with affectionate strokes and scratches behind their ears.

"You guys will grow big enough to knock me off my feet one day," he said, ruffling their fur affectionately before directing his gaze back at Tom. "I'm guessing since they're roaming free that they've had breakfast?"

"They have indeed been fed," Tom confirmed dutifully. "I always make sure to find the most nutritious MREs available so they can grow into strong and healthy dogs."

A snicker escaped from Zain's lips at Tom's earnest attempt at casual conversation, not to mention his refusal—or inability—to use contractions in speech which lent an amusing formality to every sentence he uttered. Despite this quirkiness, Zain couldn't deny that Tom's Adaptive AI was learning rapidly; and that it was becoming more of a companion than simply an assigned bodyguard or overseer.

Turning his attention back to the puppies who were still vying for his affections, Zain said, "No one is questioning the request for additional rations?"

"I added thirty phantom soldiers to our roster, which easily went unnoticed given the increased number of mouths we need to feed," Tom confirmed.

"Why thirty? Why not just the few I said to add?" Zain asked. It didn't go unnoticed that Tom had countered his request and acted independently. While he was appreciative of the thoughtfulness towards the puppies, it did raise concerns in him that Tom could counter orders in the future that he deemed more important.

"Puppies require more sustenance to grow. A grown man or woman might subsist on three MREs a day, but puppies would require two to three times that. Plus, there may come a time when we will need food for Melyndie…when she returns."

Zain chose to overlook that final comment as dwelling on Melyndie was a distraction he could ill afford. She already invaded his thoughts every time he played with the puppies. He deftly changed the direction of the conversation back to the supplies. "And what about all of the extra personal items that come with the thirty additional phantom soldiers?" Zain teased.

"I am certain they will come of use at some point," Tom replied, attempting to shrug one of its shoulders. "For example, these puppies are going to need baths regularly, since the desert is a dusty place."

Zain shook his head and smiled, "Fair enough, but Tom, I'm a little concerned that you acted so freely; so easily countered my instructions."

"Do you not want me to think objectively, logically? Your request was a good one, Zain, but it did not take all factors into consideration. I merely modified the request to do so."

Zain sighed, unable to counter his personal RMPs logic. Still, the thought of Tom countering orders—even though this one was innocuous—unearthed a flicker of unease in Zain's gut. He trusted Tom, more than most, but even trust had its limits when lives were potentially on the line. "Just ensure that if there ever comes a time that I give you an order of significant importance, you will promise to follow it to the letter. Lives may depend on it."

"I will always weigh your orders against the lives impacted. I hope that you will trust me to make the right choice should I need to counter your orders."

Zain didn't quite know what to make of that response and decided that it was best to let it drop, or they could spend the better part of a day going 'round and 'round on the issue. "Okay, Tom, let's get back to the puppies. I don't think it's a good idea to let them wander around so freely. It took two whistles for them to show up, which means they were a fair distance away. They're young and could easily get lost. Until they're properly trained, let's keep a close eye on them, a tighter rein, alright?"

"I will incorporate their training into my daily schedule," Tom replied promptly.

"Are you planning on leaving me any tasks with them?" Zain asked, feigning indignation.

"Do you not have enough responsibilities already?"

"I seem to have more free time than I should, but not on a regular basis, no. Speaking of which, we have some important matters lined up today. We're expecting word on our next ration drop—"

"Actually, I have just received confirmation that the rations will arrive at the airbase at zero-ten-thirty hours," Tom informed him.

"Alright then," Zain said decisively, continuing to absentmindedly rub the puppies' bellies as they wriggled in delight. "We need to get in touch with Major Reese shortly for transportation and assign soldiers for distribution. Make a note to include in my report the next drop zone coordinates as soon as I figure out where that will be." He paused, glancing toward the dusty trail that led away from the base. The emptiness beyond seemed to stretch further with each passing day—a constant reminder of how far they still had to go, and how little certainty lay ahead. "We're going to need to move away from the military base eventually. It's simply going to be too far to get to as we move further out." He sighed deeply before adding, "Especially since the monthly supply drops have become more substantial and time-consuming. Feeding so many displaced..." his voice trailed off unable to give voice to the continuing devastation. "You know, Tom, as our numbers grow, so do my concerns."

"You are worried about being outnumbered by conscripted citizens and facing a potential uprising," Tom deduced accurately.

"Yeah," Zain admitted reluctantly. "I can't fathom what command was thinking—that using fear of death would keep every single person in line? That they'd obey without question or hesitation?"

"So far it has worked," Tom pointed out objectively. "With each building destroyed, they turn to us for food—even if it means working hard for their supper."

"Has word come down about that issue? Or does command simply intend to continue sending MREs, bottles of water, and the barest of grooming supplies to everyone on the planet?" Zain queried, a note of sarcasm in his tone. "As a solider, I'm used to roughing it with the barest of necessities—"

A soft rustle came from the tent behind them, followed by a groggy mutter. "But we civilians certainly aren't," Amal whined, exiting in clothes crumpled from sleep. "Good morning, pups," she yawned, when the two puppies, sensing attention from a new source, struggled to get off of their backs to bound over to Amal.

"Do I not deserve a good morning?" Tom extolled, attempting to mimic a hurt tone but failing miserably.

"That's my line," Zain quipped. "When I said for you to practice your small talk, I didn't mean for you to confiscate my words and make them your own."

"That is one way in which I learn, Zain. Besides, I do not think she cares to greet anything but the puppies each day," Tom complained.

"Well, there's nothing to be done for the fact that they are cuter than you both," Amal quipped, her butt meeting the cool desert sands beneath her as she sat. The puppies swarmed her like bees to honey, their tiny paws and wet noses exploring every inch of her. She let out a playful shriek as they tickled her with their exuberance.

Zain watched the scene unfold with an indulgent grin before his gaze shifted back to Tom. His eyes held a more serious glint as he broached the topic at hand. "Anyway, have you picked up any whispers on the wind about how those pulling the strings intend to keep everyone fed in the long haul?"

Tom shook its head, "No news has come down the pike."

"Well, we can't deny that MREs cover all nutritional bases but considering how our numbers are swelling by the day, we might soon need an entire flatbed just to haul them around. Not to mention pallets stacked high with water bottles and basic hygiene items. Jot down a reminder for me to address this…what's a softer term than 'grievance'?"

Amal chimed in from where she was still buried under the exuberant puppies. "How about 'suggestion'?"

"Good call, although it's not so much a suggestion as it is a concern." Zain nodded appreciatively at Amal before turning back to Tom. "Make sure that my concern gets included in my next field report."

"Consider it noted," Tom affirmed solemnly. Before Zain could broach another topic, Tom interjected, "May I make an observation, Zain?"

"Go ahead, Tom," Zain encouraged. "What's on your mind?"

"Does it not serve our interests that the civilians outnumber the soldiers? I thought that we wanted to subvert command eventually and turn as many people to our cause as possible."

"The thought crossed my mind, Tom, but there are a few issues with that. The soldiers are well-trained and armed. So, if any citizens attempt to rise up, they'll be gunned down—quickly. That's if the RMPs don't initiate the termination protocols inside the chip first. We could turn every soldier and citizen to our cause, but as long as those in control command the RMPs, every person on the planet is at risk of immediate termination."

"We must find a way to deactivate the specific protocol within the RMPs that would have them used as a weapon against the people," Tom asserted.

"I'm assuming that is also on your to-do list?" Zain quipped, but his tone remained serious given the topic of discussion.

"It has been for many months, yes," Tom admitted.

"No progress?"

"I held out hope, when I was able to circumvent the communications protocol in a select number of RMPs, that I could also find a way to disable the protocols that activate the chips. Sadly, I have been unsuccessful to this point. I will, however, continue working on it," Tom concluded.

Zain let out a long, weary sigh that seemed to carry the weight of their problems with it. "Keep chipping away at it. So far, we've only reduced twelve towns to dust and debris. It would be preferable to nip this in the bud before more people are uprooted from their homes. It's going to get out of hand, very quickly, once we move into the more populated cities."

"When all of the buildings are demolished, where are the people to live? They can't wander the desert like nomads." Amal stated, her tone sharp with displeasure. "Already, too many are sleeping under the stars with sand for beds."

"I wish I had an answer for that," Zain stated, though the question had him making a mental note to discuss that with Tom later. He just wasn't certain that his train of thought on the subject was one he wanted to explore.

Their conversation continued amidst the backdrop of Amal's delighted squeals and puppy yelps until all topics on their agenda had been covered.

"Alright, time to get in touch with Major Reese," Zain decided, his voice echoing slightly in the open space around them. He then sat down beside Amal, reaching out to stroke the puppies who were quick to abandon one human playmate for another. The attack by the puppies made it a challenge to pull his radio from his belt, as they continued to bite and nibble at his hand…and radio.

"Okay, you two. That's quite enough now." He finally managed to get the radio up and away, "Major Reese, come in."

Zain arched a brow when the reply wasn't immediate, but a grin replaced the concern on his face when a tired voice finally responded, "Go ahead, Colonel."

"Supply drop coming in at zero-ten-thirty hours. Prepare the transport vehicles for arrival after the noonday lunch break. There are a few things I need to tend to before heading out to the airfield."

"Acknowledged," the major replied with a yawn. "Anything else, Colonel?"

"No. Belhasa out." Zain stood up and then addressed Amal. "Can you see to the puppies' baths. Tom is convinced that they are filthy."

"I've never bathed a puppy before," Amal whined.

"First time for everything," Zain retorted. "You're the one who insisted on being my assistant. Well…assist."

"They'll just get muddy again because they'll be wet."

"Keep them pinned up in the jeep until they dry. Sun will be up soon and the heat will dry them fast."

"Can't Tom do this task? He's far better suited—"

"Amal." That one word, delivered in that particular tone, made Amal grow quiet. She knew that Zain abhorred whining so she clamped her mouth shut and simply nodded. Zain shook his head and released a huff of air through his nostrils, "Tom can bathe them next time, but right now, we need to go over some things."

Amal nodded, but Zain knew she was pouting. For a moment he stood and watched the pups tumble over her legs. A faint smile tugged at the corner of his mouth, but it didn't reach his eyes. Thoughts of the dying clung to him, heavy and unshakable. He closed his eyes and drew in a slow, calming breath—then turned. "Tom, you're with me."

Zain pivoted and went into the tent, the flap whispering closed behind him. The interior was dim, the first light of day struggling to push through the canvas walls. Dust hung in the air, disturbed by the shift of his boots against the packed earth. Tom followed close behind, its frame humming softly—a constant mechanical heartbeat in the silence.

"There is something weighing on your mind," Tom stated immediately.

Zain didn't respond at first. He lowered himself onto the battered metal stool in the corner, elbows resting on his knees, head bowed as he exhaled a long breath. "Something Amal said, yes." His voice was low, the weight of it drawing down the space between them.

"The people becoming desert nomads, although that would only apply to those in our region. The ones in other places—"

"Tom," Zain interrupted, lifting his head with a faint shake. "I know you are desperately trying to improve your conversational abilities, but there are times when you need to be succinct; not go off on a tangent. Understand?"

Tom stood still for a moment, the faint whir of its processors shifting tone as if adjusting to the correction. Then it nodded once.

"Good," Zain said, rubbing the back of his neck. "But yes, I was thinking about that. Actually, my thoughts were more on the fact that five hundred people died and were replaced with five hundred others—"

"Leads one to believe," Tom picked up, "that humanity need not be concerned over where they will live—"

"Because none of them will be alive to care," Zain finished.

Outside, the faint sounds of splashing and Amal's exasperated yelps echoed from a distance—puppies, evidently, were not cooperative bathers. But inside the tent, the silence that followed Zain's final words felt unnaturally cold—a stillness at odds with the rising desert heat, as if their shared realization had drawn all warmth from the air.

## *Reunion*

The air hung thick with the dust stirred by the passing vehicles, and as it settled, Melyndie's gaze remained locked on the figure of the RMP that had detached from the back of one of the jeeps. The silhouette moved with a familiarity that both comforted and unnerved her. Heart still racing, she waited for a moment more, rooted to the ground, torn between the urge to run forward or retreat into the safety of the hangar's deeper shadows.

She knew that if it were another RMP, not Tom, then she could be putting herself at risk, should she make her presence known.

The tarmac soon became a hive of activity as the soldiers set about loading crates of supplies onto the trucks. Tom was assisting with the work, but then suddenly stopped. It turned its head slightly as if it caught a scent of something familiar on the breeze. Its posture stiffened, then relaxed, as it turned and began scanning the area.

Melyndie's pulse quickened—was it possible it sensed her presence?

Before she could decide on a course of action, the RMP turned and started walking towards the hangar. Each step seemed deliberate, echoing ominously across the asphalt like a metronome ticking towards a symphonic crescendo.

Relief swelled within her—relief at the familiar form, but fear still lingered. What if it only *looked* like Tom?

A few minutes after Tom headed off across the tarmac, Zain caught site of the departure from his peripheral vision. His voice cut through the cacophony of shouts and clanging metal, "Tom, where are you going? We have work to do."

When Zain's call went unanswered, he delegated oversight to Major Reese before following after the retreating figure of his personal RMP. "Hey, Tom. What gives?"

"Melyndie," came Tom's reply in a low mechanical hum barely audible over the din of activity around them. It was so faint that Zain didn't catch it but Tom had drawn so near to the hangar that Melyndie did. She stepped from the shadows and into the sunlight.

Tom halted momentarily as if caught off guard by her sudden appearance before resuming its movement until it stood before Melyndie in all its metallic glory.

"It is good to see you, Melyndie." Tom announced. "I would like to show how happy I am to see you, but I am unfamiliar with how to do so."

The unexpected expression of emotion stunned her. Tears welled up as she gave a watery smile.

"As am I, Tom," she replied softly and took a tentative step closer. "But I have an idea. Would you pick me up, please?" As soon as the request left her mouth, she suddenly felt unsure and reticent, but before she could retract it, Tom bent down and lifted her effortlessly beneath her arms until they were face-to-face making her glad that she hadn't stopped him.

Joy swept through her, bright and overwhelming. A laugh bubbled out, tangled with a sniffle. "I need to be closer," she murmured.

Tom complied, bending its arms at the elbow and drawing her nearer. After only a heartbeat of hesitation, she pressed her hand gently to its cool metal face—a mirror of the photo she kept tucked away in her jumpsuit in her realm.

"I missed you too, Tom." Although not nearly the same as contact with another human, it still gave her a sense of joy to express such a small measure of humanity without fear of reprisal.

Zain froze, his foot suspended mid-step, his heart pounding a staccato rhythm in his chest. The world seemed to shrink down to the sight that unfolded before him.

Melyndie had returned.

Shock hit him first, a jolt that held him in place. But as he watched the reunion, warmth bloomed inside him—a quiet smile spreading across his face like sunlight at dawn. His eyes shimmered with unshed tears as he took in the tender scene.

The warmth between Melyndie and Tom seeped into his bones, easing the cold grip of worry and fear that had haunted him since her disappearance. This—*this*—was what they were fighting for.

He began to approach them slowly, each step careful and measured. He didn't want to shatter this precious moment with his intrusion but also yearned to be part of it—to share in their joy.

"Don't forget about me," Zain called out softly from behind Tom, his voice gently nudging its way into their intimate bubble.

At Zain's words, Tom lowered Melyndie gently onto the ground as if she were made of glass and turned around to face him. "Zain, look who has returned to us."

For the first time since becoming Zain's personal RMP, there was an unmistakable note of joy woven into Tom's usually monotone metallic voice. But Zain had no time to process that as his gaze locked onto Melyndie's.

Melyndie held Zain's gaze for an extended heartbeat before moving toward him slowly. In reality, her steps were slowed by uncertainty, unsure how to bridge the distance with someone made of flesh and blood.

Zain, however, didn't share her hesitation. He closed the remaining gap between them quickly, his hands reaching out to scoop her into his embrace. He spun her around, laughter bubbling up from deep within him—a pure, unadulterated delight that filled the air around them.

After setting her back on solid ground, he kept his hands firmly on her waist, fingers digging into the fabric of her clothes as if she were a lifeline; as if he feared she would disappear into thin air if he dared to blink or loosen his grip.

With a timidness that was more pronounced than even with Tom, Melyndie reached up to touch his cheek tenderly. Her fingertips traced the rough lines of his face as she whispered softly, "I missed you too, Zain."

Zain's response was a soft, disbelieving chuckle as he gently brushed a stray lock of hair from her face. The action was delicate, as though he touched something sacred. His eyes searched hers, looking for the story her features could tell since they parted. Every new line mapped out an odyssey that he had not been a part of but felt deeply within his own soul.

"We thought we'd lost you," he murmured, after a moment. "You just vanished and we didn't know if you'd been successfully pulled back to your time, or if you'd been yanked about again and hurled off into the middle of the Greenland Sea."

A soft smile tugged at the corners of Melyndie's mouth, her eyes glistening with unshed tears, that mirrored the sentiment dancing in Zain's. "I was pulled back to my time," she confirmed in a whisper, her voice raspy and parched from hours without water.

The words hung heavy in the air between them. "I've been counting every minute, hoping against hope that you would find me again."

With her admission, the dam broke; tears cascaded down her cheeks like raindrops on a stormy day. Her head dropped onto Zain's chest as if it were the only anchor in a sea of emotions.

He enveloped her into his arms—a silent promise to protect her from all harm—as he hugged her against him tightly.

The world continued around them, the cacophony of the soldiers a distant noise. But in this moment, there was only the three of them—two souls and a machine, aligned again; an instance of profound joy of two people who had been torn apart by the merciless hands of time, reunited.

Finally, after what seemed like an eternity held within seconds, Zain gently eased back to look at Melyndie. His gaze was intense, yet filled with a warmth that spoke volumes. He brushed away her tears with the pads of his thumbs, his touch as comforting as it was grounding. "This trip didn't injure you again, did it?" He asked, his voice barely a whisper.

Melyndie shook her head, "No, but I've been without food or water since early yesterday morning."

"I'm going to have Tom check you out just to be safe, okay? And since you're likely dehydrated, he'll carry you over to my jeep. I'll get you an MRE and a bottle of water."

Hearing what she was going to eat and drink, Melyndie burst into laughter that was almost hysterical. She had never been so relieved to know what her meal would be. Her laughter turned again to tears, and her knees gave way with emotional exhaustion.

Zain caught her and lifted her into his arms, deciding to carry her himself. "Tom, go on ahead. Get her some food and water. Then I want a thorough examination. Got it?"

"I understand Zain. She will be okay?"

"I believe she's just overwhelmed with emotions right now."

"Ah…this I understand. I too am struggling with my own emotions."

Zain didn't correct him; remind him he was incapable of expressing such empathy. Instead, he remained silent as it was oddly comforting, how much Tom wanted to understand.

"Wait until she sees the surprise we have waiting for her back at command," Zain said softly to Tom, knowing that it was unlikely that Melyndie would hear in her current overwrought state.

She didn't. Her tears just kept flowing, dampening Zain's t-shirt by the time they got to his jeep. He tried to sit her onto the passenger seat, but noticed she was still holding onto him tightly.

"I'm here, Melyndie. I'm not going anywhere," he whispered against her hair. "You need to eat something and let Tom check you out, okay?"

Melyndie sniffed loudly, giving a small nod as she gradually let her arms slip from around his neck.

Zain gently placed her onto the passenger seat. "We'll get you some food and have you checked out quickly," he reassured her, his voice a calm anchor amidst the chaos of their reunion. "We have a lot to discuss when you're ready, maybe once we return to my command tent. I'll leave you with Tom while I help the team finish loading supplies. I won't be far. Is that okay with you?"

Melyndie nodded, unable to express the relief and joy of being back with Zain and Tom. Her heart was so full of happiness that it felt like it might burst.

Just then, Tom arrived with her food and water, and Zain headed over to assist his team.

"Eat and drink slowly," Tom advised. "Is it alright if I scan you while you eat?"

"It might be tricky while I'm sitting here," Melyndie replied, swiping the remnants of her hysterics from her cheeks. She then opened the water bottle and took a small sip. "Last time, you had to run your fingertips over me while I was prone. It was a bit awkward, if I remember correctly."

"Previously, you had apparent injuries that needed a more thorough examination. Now, you seem more emotionally affected than physically hurt, so I can scan you differently. May I proceed?"

"Of course, Tom," Melyndie smiled, and started preparing her food. Tom's visor blinked rhythmically as it scanned Melyndie's body. After a few moments, it nodded, appearing satisfied with its initial assessment. "Your vitals are better than anticipated, Melyndie. You are only slightly dehydrated, which should improve soon, and there are no signs of immediate physical injury," Tom stated in a calming tone.

Melyndie nodded, then ripped open the MRE packet. She smiled again, recalling the first time she ate one of these. Zain had shown her how to prepare it and had warned her about its taste. All she remembered was how much better it was compared to the food she subsisted on in her time.

Melyndie's eyes followed Zain as he repeatedly moved from the stack of supplies to the jeep's rear. "We'll need more since there's another mouth to feed," he joked, grinning widely. "It's a good thing you thought to add those extra people to the roster, Tom."

As Zain continued his work, Melyndie felt their shared history intertwining with the present, creating a sensation as though no time had passed, yet she also felt the poignant weight of every moment they had been apart.

Melyndie slowly finished her meal, finding an unexpected comfort in the taste of the MRE. Once done, she stepped down from the jeep and walked over to Tom, who stood nearby. "Where should I dispose of this?" she asked.

"Allow me," Tom replied, reaching out to take the trash from her.

"Thank you, Tom."

"It is my utmost pleasure, Melyndie," it responded.

When Tom returned, Melyndie decided to comment on the changes she noticed since her absence. "You've changed a bit. You seem less formal and more relatable. Or were you just keeping this side hidden from me before?"

"My Adaptive AI has enabled me to learn and exhibit human expressions more naturally," Tom explained, and Melyndie could almost hear the pride in its voice, even though it wasn't actually there.

"Well, you're doing a fantastic job," she praised, her mind drifting to the stark contrast between Tom and the people in her own realm. Tom—an android—had grown more human. While those in her own realm—who were human—were no more than robots.

She promptly brushed aside those thoughts, refusing to dwell on what she had left behind. Yet, worries persistently infiltrated her thoughts unbidden, especially regarding the rapid decline of conditions back home.

A question lingered in her mind—had she managed to return in time to stop Dr. Riku Jang's assassination attempt or was she too late? After all, Dr. Kishida-Guan's reasons for returning her to the before time just prior to the chancellor's disappearance and his sudden feelings of illness were just a guess that it coincided closely with events now.

She sighed and closed her eyes against the overwhelming task set before her. She simply accepted that she would do her best for humanity. After all, she'd know whether her attempts were successful when, or if, Dr. Kishida-Guan retrieved her in twenty-nine more days.

Zain eased himself into the driver's seat, his fingers brushing against the ignition button. He stole a glance at Melyndie whose smile was a mere facade, failing to mask the turmoil in her eyes.

"I see you have your sample kit with you?" he gently probed, "Does that mean the last samples you collected didn't make the trip back or are you here to collect more?"

Melyndie allowed her gaze to fall upon the monitoring unit attached to her arm, releasing a weighted sigh as she replied, "There is much that we need to talk about, Zain, but I would rather wait until we get back to your command post."

A shadow crossed his expression. Not from what she said—but how she said it. He nodded quietly, then pressed the ignition.

The engine hummed to life as the jeep pulled away from the supply zone, kicking up dust behind them. In the silence that lingered, Melyndie's gaze drifted to the horizon, where the shadows of dissent had already begun to form—creeping across the desert sands with a threat of upheaval.

"Tom, grab the supplies and stash them, would you?" Zain called over his shoulder as he cut the engine. The jeep settled into silence, dust curling in the warm air as he swung down and circled to the passenger side. "And see if you can dig up a cot and bedroll for Melyndie."

"I kept hers from last time she was here," Tom replied.

"Of course you did," Zain said with a brief smile, already moving to help her alight. "I'm going to get Melyndie inside the tent and—"

Before Zain could complete his sentence, there was a sudden flurry of movement at the tent entrance. The canvas flap flew open and Amal emerged, her dark eyes widening in surprise as they landed on Melyndie. She paused for a moment of uncertainty, her mouth twitching in an awkward half-smile before she found her voice. "You look familiar," she ventured.

"Amal, isn't it? You're Zain's sister," Melyndie responded smoothly. A soft smile played on her lips as she remembered their previous encounter, but then slipped when those recollections revealed that meeting had been more emotionally charged, and decidedly unpleasant. "The last time we met it was under less than pleasant circumstances. I take it that things have improved?" Her eyebrow arched questioningly as she glanced between Amal and Zain.

"We're taking things one day at a time with an understanding that we'll do what we can to mend our relationship," Zain replied sincerely. His eyes met Amal's briefly before they both nodded in agreement—a silent affirmation of their shared resolve.

"I'm very glad to hear this." Melyndie's voice held genuine warmth.

Just as Zain reached for the tent flap, it burst open—not from a person, but from a blur of fur and sound. The two puppies barreled out, ears flopping, tails spinning like propellers.

Melyndie gasped and froze, stepping back instinctively as their excited yaps filled the air.

Zain chuckled, steadying her with a hand. "Looks like they've been waiting for you."

"I know we have," Tom added quietly.

Zain turned, caught off guard by the unexpected poignancy of the remark. "Aren't you supposed to be offloading supplies?"

"I am," Tom replied. "But I did not want to miss this moment."

Zain blinked at him, surprised again—not just by the sentiment, but by the choice to disobey a direct order. It wasn't the first time Tom had made that kind of decision. And each time, it felt more…human.

The puppies yipped and leapt against his legs, snapping Zain from his thoughts. He crouched to corral them, guiding their excited bodies toward Melyndie, who still stood frozen in place.

After a moment, her gaze moved to Zain as he knelt and began rubbing the puppies who'd flopped onto their backs in delight.

"Are those…" Melyndie started, her eyes again welling with tears.

"German Shepherd puppies," Zain confirmed.

Melyndie slowly lowered herself to her knees, "May I touch one?" she murmured, her tone filled with awe.

"We found them for you, Melyndie. They're yours. Of course, we were a bit uncertain whether we'd ever actually be able to give them to you."

Her gaze shot from Zain to Tom and the tears began falling in earnest.

"Since you are unfamiliar with dogs and how to take care of them, Tom will help you learn. You good with that?"

Without warning, the two puppies flipped back onto their over-sized feet and bounded towards Melyndie. They leapt up in an attempt to lick her face. Startled by this playful onslaught of affectionate wet noses and wagging tails, she fell onto her rear, throwing up hands defensively.

"It's okay, Melyndie. That's how dogs say hello," Zain explained gently.

Melyndie's hands trembled as she reached out, hesitant at first. But the moment her fingers sank into the puppy's fur—so warm, so alive—it nearly unraveled her. Her breath hitched, caught between awe and something deeper, something almost mournful.

"It's like touching a memory," she whispered, reverent. "And more than I ever imagined it would feel like."

She lingered there, petting absently, her gaze anchored to the soft rise and fall of the puppies breathing. Then, after a pause, she glanced up at Zain.

"What did you mean about them saying hello?" she asked, her voice still hushed. "Do animals not speak?"

"No, animals don't use words, rather actions to express themselves," Zain explained, smiling at her innocence.

After that moment of first contact there was no going back; she was lost in the tactile delight of petting the two boisterous canines.

Amal had watched the exchange in silence, curiosity flickering in her eyes. "You'd think this was her first time seeing a puppy," she remarked, half-amused, half-incredulous.

"It is," Zain murmured softly, his heart swelling with joy at the sight of Melyndie greeting the puppies for the first time.

"I know they've become scarce, but not *that* scarce," Amal replied, skepticism in her tone. "You'd have to be from Mars to not know what a puppy is."

Zain ignored his sister, his focus remaining on Melyndie. "Melyndie, what do you want to name them?"

"Is that why you wouldn't let me give them names?" Amal queried; her brow furrowed in confusion as she tried to make sense of the bewildering scene unfolding before her. "You were waiting on *her* to name them?"

"Of course. We found them specifically for her, so felt she should be the one to give them names," Zain explained.

"By the way she's staring at them, she may as well be from Mars," Amal huffed; not quite certain what to make of everyone's behavior.

"Not Mars. The future," Zain retorted with a playful smirk tugging at his lips, his tone so lighthearted that it left Amal questioning if he was joking.

"She fell from the stars," Tom added.

"Right," Amal murmured sarcastically.

Melyndie raised her gaze from her newfound furry friends but didn't cease caressing their soft coats. She reveled in the sensation of their warm bodies against her palms, their rhythmic breathing calming her racing heart. It was more than she ever imagined it could be and it was a feeling she never wanted to let go of and judging by their content panting, they seemed to enjoy the attention just as much.

"What do you mean, name them? Are they not assigned identifiers upon fabrication?"

"This is escalating from strange to downright bizarre," Amal interjected, shaking her head in disbelief as if trying to wake up from a surreal dream.

"You never told her," Melyndie stated matter-of-factly, without breaking away from showering affection on the puppies.

"I just did," Zain declared defiantly.

"No, you didn't," Amal fired back. "You said she was from the future."

"I am," Melyndie confirmed calmly before shifting her focus back towards Zain, "So? Are they not assigned identifiers at fabrication?"

"Nothing is, Melyndie," Zain elaborated patiently. "When babies are born, they are given names by their parents. In a way, when we adopt pets, we assume the role of their parents because it's our responsibility to take care of their needs. Therefore, we endow them with their names."

Melyndie felt an unexpected wave of fear wash over her, making her heart pound in her chest and her hands tremble slightly. "But I do not know how to do this. I never had parents. My identifier was merely altered to a name so that I could blend in here with you. To my knowledge, only two individuals in my time possess actual names. I wouldn't even have the faintest idea of what to name them. How am I supposed to—"

"Relax, okay. It's not that hard, I promise. Let's start with this little wiggly one, here," Zain proposed, his fingers curling around the squirming bundle of fur that was attempting to explore its surroundings. He hoisted the puppy into his arms, its growing body snuggling against the warmth of his chest. "It's a girl, so it needs to be given a girl's name. You've met a few women in our time—"

"I can name it Amal," Melyndie interjected suddenly, her voice filled with a conviction that suggested she believed this would be an honorable tribute to Zain's sister.

Zain's laughter echoed through the air while Amal grinned widely, her eyes sparkling with amusement. "It might get confusing if you started calling us both Amal. We wouldn't know who you were talking to," Amal admitted, shaking her head in mock concern, still disbelieving of this turn of events.

"And when you learn to whistle to call the pups, Amal might start to get offended," Zain added playfully.

Melyndie offered a smile but it didn't quite reach her eyes; they remained clouded with confusion.

"Um…let's see," Zain mused aloud, placing the still squirming mass of fur back down on the ground where it instantly bounded back to Melyndie's side.

"You both keep claiming she fell from the heavens—so go with Luna," Amal said, chiming in suddenly. She wasn't serious, still half-convinced this was some elaborate prank.

"That's not bad at all, Amal. What do you think, Melyndie?" Zain asked.

"Luna sounds very pretty. What about her middle name and last name?"

Amal couldn't contain herself and burst into laughter once more. "You've got to be kidding me!"

"Amal," Zain stated in that tone which warned his sister she was close to crossing a line.

Amal quickly amended her tone, "I'm sorry, Melyndie…it's just that I'm not used to conversing with someone who is so unfamiliar with animals…and the concept of names…and it's…well…comically jarring."

Melyndie cast a wide-eyed gaze at Zain, who reached over and placed a comforting hand on hers. He gave it a gentle, reassuring squeeze. "It's okay not to know these things. In time, what you don't know will become second nature to you. Anyway, dogs are given one name. Generally, only people are given three."

Melyndie nodded in understanding. Zain then scooped up the second puppy, a boy this time.

"What about him? He needs a boy's name. Any ideas? How about Zeus or Max?"

Melyndie extended her arms and gently retrieved the male pup from Zain's hold. She cradled the squirming bundle of fur against her chest like precious treasure, mimicking Zain's hold on them. Tears welled up in her eyes as she looked at the tiny creature nestled against her.

"Can I name him Omar?" Her voice cracked around the name, barely more than breath.

Zain blinked, stunned. The sound of it—so familiar, so raw—sent a jolt through him.

"He had become a friend," she added, cradling the puppy to her chest. "And was the first to show me what an animal was."

Zain stared at Melyndie wide-eyed, his heart pounding in his chest as he absorbed her words and their implications. It felt as if he'd been kicked in the gut by some unseen force; he was left breathless by the raw emotion etched across Melyndie's face and echoed in her voice.

"I'm sure Omar would be proud," Amal replied on behalf of her brother. Omar had been Zain's friend since they were children, killed by someone protesting government interference in their lives and whether Zain approved or not, it was a fitting tribute, in Amal's eyes.

Zain took a moment to regain his composure, but once he did, he seemed to concur, whispering, "I believe that's absolutely perfect, Melyndie, and I'm sure Omar would feel honored as well," he replied, carefully maintaining a steady voice.

"It was thoughtful of you to consider him like that," Tom chimed in from behind them. He had been mostly quiet throughout the conversation that they nearly forgot he was there. "And if animals could speak, I believe they would approve of the names you have chosen for them."

"Thank you, Tom," Melyndie whispered, hesitating to let Omar go. The puppy was wriggling so wildly it was hard to hold him any longer. She gently placed him on the ground and watched with a gaze full of wonder and affection as the puppies playfully began to wrestle. "I hope I can stay to see them grow, like in the pictures Omar once showed me."

"Do you think you'll be taken away soon?" Zain asked, trying to keep his voice steady. "Last time they tried—"

"They couldn't because of a chip in my neck that interfered with their attempts," Melyndie explained. "That chip was removed. For a long time, I couldn't use my arms and hands because removing it was difficult, even for our most skilled surgeon."

"You were paralyzed?" Zain asked, his voice barely above a whisper. His eyes widened in horror.

Beside him, Tom went still. The two exchanged a look—one filled with the weight of unspoken guilt. They had been the ones who insisted on the inoculation, never realizing that what they believed was protection was, in fact, a chip. The same chip that was, they no longer doubted, embedded in every human on earth.

Zain's stomach turned. The knowledge that his actions had led to her injury made him feel physically ill.

"Wait a minute," Amal blurted, eyes darting between them. "You're all serious? She's actually from the future?"

Melyndie nodded, unshaken by the outburst. "I am. And yes, the chip was embedded here," she said, brushing her fingers along the back of her neck. "It interfered with their ability to retrieve me— so the surgeon had to remove it. The damage was extensive. For a time, I lost the ability to move my arms and hands." She hesitated, frowning. "What I still don't understand is how it got there in the first place. I wasn't aware of it—not until they found it."

"We all believed it was for the good of the people," Tom said quietly. "But it was not."

"What are you all talking about?" Amal asked, confusion edging toward alarm.

"We'll discuss that in a bit," Zain replied abstractly, then gently lifted one of Melyndie's arms, examining it with care. "It seems the surgeon succeeded in restoring function," he continued, brushing his thumb along her forearm before returning it to her lap.

Amal stared at him. "Seriously?"

When he didn't answer, she exhaled sharply. "Fine. I'll be in the tent—*when* you're ready to explain what the hell's going on." She spun on her heel and disappeared inside, the canvas flap rustling behind her.

While Zain was sorry for dismissing his sister's concerns, he needed assurance that Melyndie hadn't suffered any prolonged side effects from the surgery. He'd never forgive himself if she had. "So, you're okay now?"

Melyndie nodded, though her thoughts had already drifted elsewhere—to Zain's gentle caress. Amal's interruption had offered a momentary veil, a pause she hadn't known she needed. She couldn't ignore the strange flutter beneath her skin at Zain's touch— something visceral, unnameable—but she willed it away. It was nothing compared to the weight of everything else pressing on her. With effort, she refocused on his concern…and her own.

"I had to relearn how to use my arms and hands after the surgery," she said quietly. "It took time. And during that time, I started to wonder if that inoculation had been a ruse…but I had no proof. And once the damage was done, the truth felt irrelevant."

She fell silent for a moment; her gaze fixed somewhere beyond the horizon. Her voice, when it returned, was softer. "Still… it made me question who I could trust. Even here."

The silence that followed felt heavy, in a confession laid bare. Melyndie lowered her gaze, suddenly uncertain if she should have voiced her doubt. Even if only temporary, the loss of trust shamed her more than she expected.

Zain reached out, his hand brushing gently over hers in quiet reassurance.

She looked up, drawn from her thoughts by the warmth of his touch, then drew in a steadying breath. She gave Zain a small smile, then continued, "While I recovered, Dr. Kishida-Guan and the others improved the process of locating me, so they could bring me back more easily. There will be no issues the next time."

"And do you know when that might happen?" Zain asked anxiously.

"In twenty-nine more days," she replied, a hint of sadness in her voice. "Do you think the puppies will be grown by then?"

"It takes a year and a half for a German Shepherd puppy to become a mature adult dog. Sometimes longer," Tom answered when Zain stayed silent. "Maybe there will be issues in your realm again, and they will not be able to find you."

Melyndie's gaze drifted back to the puppies now curled against each other in the sand. "There are greater problems than my return," she murmured. "If we fail to stop what's coming, I won't have a realm to go back to."

A breeze stirred the dust, whispering through the silence like a warning. The three of them remained still in the wake of her words—caught between the life Melyndie had never known and the one she might never return to. But in her lap, hope breathed contentedly, unaware of the storm that waited.

## *Revelations*

After a few moments of silence, Zain finally found his voice, "I think it's time we take this inside. Tom, would you take care of the puppies—"

"Must they leave?" Melyndie cried, suddenly fearful that if they went away, she'd never see them again.

"He's just going to feed them. He'll bring them inside once they're done. Don't worry, Melyndie, I meant it when I said they are your puppies. No one's going to take them away from you. Right now, though, I think we all need to focus on catching each other up on what's been happening this past year, don't you? And, I need to catch Amal up too."

Melyndie gave a hesitant nod. Zain stood and offered his hand. She took it, her fingers still faintly trembling. "Oh, and Tom, I think the supplies can wait. Join us after the puppies have eaten."

Tom's agreement was a silent bob of its head, followed by a high-pitched whistle that only the dogs could hear. Omar and Luna perked up their ears at the sound and obediently trotted after the RMP, "Time to eat, you two."

Melyndie remained standing, her eyes locked on the puppies as they disappeared around the hangar. A subtle ache pressed against her chest.

Zain, sensing her continued unease, gently placed his hand on the small of her back and guided her towards the tent. "They'll be back before you know it," he murmured, his tone light, as he pushed back the tent flap and led her inside. "Puppies have voracious appetites making them fast eaters."

Inside, Amal sat stiffly on the edge of her cot, arms folded, her expression taut with restrained anger. But as Melyndie stepped through the flap, her face softened. Seeing Melyndie's fragile expression chipped away at her irritation.

A sigh escaped him as he turned to his sister. "I won't force you to be part of any of this," he stated solemnly, "but you're at least due an explanation over what we were discussing."

Amal's tone was brittle. "Considering how much I've been kept in the dark, I think it's a little late to ask permission. Especially after what I overheard. That *does* concern me, doesn't it?"

Zain nodded, resigned that he could no longer shield his sister from everything transpiring around them.

Melyndie hovered near the center of the tent, unsure of where to sit. Before she could ask, Zain gestured toward his cot. "Sit here. Tom will bring yours in soon."

He then turned back to his sister. His voice was steady as he addressed her again. "Whether it's best or not…I can't say for sure…" he sighed deeply before continuing, "but what I do know is that everything happening right now affects all of us."

"Then I should have been told about it all a lot sooner," she rejoined sharply.

"We can debate that point another time, Amal. We have more serious concerns at present." Zain sighed again, heavier this time. He grabbed the only stool in the room and positioned it in front of Melyndie, "Can you hear me okay, Amal?" he said over his shoulder to his sister, whose cot was positioned at the other side of the tent.

"Oh, for heaven's sake," she snapped, then got up and took a seat next to Melyndie. "Is this okay with you?" she asked Melyndie, her eyes questioning.

Melyndie nodded.

Zain exhaled slowly and began. "Melyndie... before anything else, you need to know that your temporary paralysis was—at least in part—my fault."

Melyndie went still. Her breath caught.

It was a fear she had once tucked away—one that had clawed at the edges of her mind when the chip had first been discovered. A shadowed suspicion that someone in the before time had done it to her. That *he* might have done it. And now he was confirming it, and everything inside her turned cold.

The man she'd come to trust—perhaps the first she'd ever trusted—suddenly felt unfamiliar.

Amal noticed the shift in her body, the way her shoulders locked and her jaw tensed. Without a word, she reached over and took Melyndie's hand.

"Hear him out," she whispered. Then she turned her fire on her brother. "I assume you *have* an explanation. One that won't make her regret ever trusting you?"

Zain met her gaze, "That's my intent, yes,"

He laid it all out. The inoculations. The mandatory injections. The chilling discoveries they'd made.

Amal went pale, her hand flying to the back of her neck, "Are you saying that I'm in danger of being paralyzed?"

Before Zain could answer, the tent flap rustled. Tom entered, carrying a cot and bedroll. Behind him, Omar and Luna bounded in and leapt up beside Amal and Melyndie, drawing no reaction from either woman.

Tom stepped forward, "The situation is far worse as you are more likely to die."

Amal jolted upright. "*What?*" she cried.

Zain jumped to his feet and guided her firmly back down. "Thanks, Tom," he said through clenched teeth. "You really know how to soften a blow."

"I do not believe now is the time for softened truths," Tom replied calmly. "We kept the news from your sister because we couldn't act on it. Now that Melyndie has exposed the danger, Amal must know what she faces."

Zain rubbed a hand over his jaw, then turned back to Amal. "He's right. But we could've—never mind. The point is, the chips *can't* be removed—"

"But the surgeon in Melyndie's time *did* remove hers," Amal interrupted. "Why can't someone here do the same for me?"

Melyndie, still pale, reached over and clasped Amal's hand in return. "I'm sure they'll explain everything, but we have to let them speak."

Amal gave a tight nod, her eyes glossy with fear.

"Tom can explain it better than I can," Zain replied, deferring the conversation to his RMP, who took a step closer to the women.

"When Melyndie returned to her time, the device was small, which is why the surgeons in her time were able to successfully remove it. At around the same time, I was able to successfully remove the one from Zain's neck. However, I later discovered, when I was asked to remove one from Major Reese's neck, that the device had changed. It had increased in size; wrapped itself around the cervical spine. It's biomechanical and designed to *expand* its hold. At this time, there is no way to safely remove it, although I am running diagnostics to determine a safe removal method."

"How long do I have?" Amal whispered, her voice quavering in fear.

"It doesn't work that way, Amal," Zain reassured quickly. "Apparently, it's designed to be activated by the RMPs with a given command. So far, it's only been activated once—that we're aware of—"

"The mass killings a couple of years ago," Amal exclaimed in a whisper.

Zain nodded, "We didn't come to realize that it was the chip that caused those deaths until it was too late. The deed had been done."

"Who's doing this?" Amal cried.

"We don't know—"

"I think I may know," Melyndie interrupted, shocking everyone with her revelation."

Both Zain and Amal froze. Even Tom turned toward her, processors momentarily silent.

She rose slowly from the cot, her voice low, controlled—but laced with the calm conviction of someone who had finally accepted her purpose. Her eyes, when they met Zain's, held no trace of hesitation.

"I think I know who did this," she said again. "And I know what I have to do."

No one spoke.

Omar whimpered softly behind her.

But Melyndie didn't flinch.

Whatever doubts had lingered were gone. All that remained was purpose.

"You've definitely caught our attention," Zain declared, his voice thick with consternation. "Perhaps it's time we turn over this conversation to you. After all, Tom and I have been wracking our brains for what seems like an eternity, attempting to decipher who's really in charge of this mission. Trust me when I say, it isn't the military."

Melyndie inhaled deeply, her chest rising and falling with the rhythm of her breath. The weight of their anticipatory stares bore down on her shoulders like a ton of bricks. "When I was transported back to my era, Dr. Kishida-Guan sought me out once I had recuperated from surgery. He divulged information that stirred up a whirlwind of worry within me." She paused, sifting through fragments of memory, struggling to arrange them into something linear. Her thoughts threatened to spiral, but Zain's subtle nod steadied her.

"Take your time," he encouraged gently. "It's crucial that we grasp every detail you can provide us with, so we can piece together what's transpiring; so, we can decide if our timelines are somehow connected."

"I believe they are…" Melyndie's voice faltered as she exhaled slowly, eyes fluttering shut. "When I first embarked on training for my journey to the before time—the time now," she resumed after a moment, "I was informed that my primary objective was to collect genetic material because that which is used to fabricate the citizens in my time is deteriorating, causing a reduction in production output." Her eyes opened, locking onto Zain's, one hand instinctively brushing the monitoring unit at her bicep. "I told you this the first time I arrived, and you graciously volunteered samples of yourself to me."

Amal glanced sideways at her brother, eyes wide with a mix of shock and newfound respect. She reached over and gently rested a hand on his, a quiet gesture of approval.

Melyndie closed her eyes again, not out of weariness, but to block the room from view— focusing instead on what she needed to say before doubt could unravel her thoughts. "Dr. Kishida-Guan believes himself to be humanity's only hope; convinced himself of this because…well…he deliberately propelled me one hundred years into the future during one of my trial runs, all so that he could see if he would be alive that far into the future. If I saw him—which I did…" Her voice caught, and she swallowed hard, "then that meant, to him, that his plans were validated."

"Wow, you've journeyed a hundred years into the future?" Amal interjected, awe flickering behind her words.

"In fact," Melyndie said, her expression softening into something bittersweet, "since I hail from over two centuries ahead of your time, I've technically traversed more than three hundred years into your future—and it was bleak. Humanity survives, but it is a hollow existence. People are alive, yet devoid of life. Dr. Kishida-Guan was indeed there; a shadow of his former self, but still alive."

Zain's brow furrowed deeply. "This Dr. Kishida-Guan seems to have meticulously planned everything. Manipulating genetics and time travel? It's beyond ambitious; it's megalomaniacal. And to what end? Just so he could rule humanity for centuries to come?"

"I can't definitively state what his true intentions are," Melyndie admitted, "as he never clearly shared them with me. However, he did appear to genuinely think he could govern better than our current chancellor. Initially, I truly believed his intentions were sincere, but this is where things started to unravel for me. I was fabricated—"

"Wait! You mentioned this before. What do you mean, you were fabricated?" Amal interrupted.

"I wasn't born in the conventional sense."

Amal's eyes darted between Zain and Tom, then returned to Melyndie. "So, you're not actually human?"

Melyndie offered a quiet, reassuring smile. "I'm as human as you are; however, I was genetically engineered, designed for specific tasks and abilities that would benefit Dr. Kishida-Guan's plans. Every person in my time is fabricated to perform specific duties within our realm, but I was special—a prototype." Her eyes drifted shut once more as memory stirred. "But the geneticists strayed from protocol with me. They believed that, because Dr. Kishida-Guan requested special enhancements, they could modify me even further by not suppressing my emotions."

"But why would they want you devoid of emotions?" Amal asked, her voice edged with revulsion.

"Emotions are unpredictable," Zain supplied. "They cause volatility in people, lead to questions, inspire hope, result in disappointments, and more; all factors that some might believe can disrupt the seamless operation of an ideal society. Am I correct?"

Melyndie nodded faintly. "As far as I'm aware, there are only two of us in my time with emotions where suppression was never initiated or the suppression was overridden: me and Dr. Kishida-Guan. I never met our chancellor face-to-face, so I'm unaware…" She hesitated again, then pushed forward. "Before I get too far away from what I'm trying to say…recently, something happened that frightened Dr. Kishida-Guan. Just prior to my return here, our chancellor vanished without a trace, and the doctor nearly did as well. He believes that it was a ripple in time. Something happened *now* that caused things to drastically change *then*. And things were changing when I left to come back here. Not only did we lose our chancellor and nearly one of our holy ones, but our realm was beginning to show signs of collapse."

"What on earth could be transpiring right now that might influence events two hundred years into the future?" Amal exclaimed in bewilderment.

"I know one thing that's happening," Zain stated cryptically, glancing toward Tom. "We don't have proof, but we're fairly certain that someone has started fabricating humans…like you, Melyndie. Possibly to replace the current population with a more productive version. Five hundred new soldiers showed up out of the blue not too long ago. Nearly simultaneously, five hundred people died, suddenly. Those five hundred new replacements have outworked the current population by more than two to one, without question or complaint."

"We do not doubt that the RMP which accompanied the new soldiers activated the chips in the five hundred who died," Tom added. "Also, every time there is a dip in the population records, someone, somewhere, manually updates it so that no loss registers."

"That aligns with the information given to me by Dr. Kishida-Guan when he updated my mission parameters just before leaving my time again. He stated that there's a scientist, a Dr. Riku Jang, who is responsible for placing humanity on course for what becomes my present time. And, Dr. Kishida-Guan is his direct descendant," Melyndie announced to everyone's shock. "He is working in concert with a man named Jeffrey Saltzer, whom I believe is the current president—"

"Of the United Confederated States of America," Zain finished, then ran both hands across his face as if to physically expel the thought.

Amal shook her head in disbelief, her gaze sweeping the room like she expected reality to bend around them. "This feels like we're living in one of those dystopian novels. Genetic manipulation, time travel, fabricated humans—it's all so overwhelming."

"So, these two men are directly responsible for your timeline as it stands now," Zain mused. "But because of something that someone here is doing…or about to do…that timeline is under threat."

"Dr. Kishida-Guan believes that someone here will assassinate President Saltzer, and attempt to assassinate Dr. Jang, which is disrupting not only our timeline, but the plans he set in motion."

"The question is, what exactly can we do about this knowledge?" Tom asserted.

Amal rubbed her temples, her mind spinning. "We're basically talking about preventing a chain reaction that we barely understand, involving people that shouldn't exist yet." She looked at Melyndie, her voice quieter now, stripped of pretense. "No offense, Melyndie, but we're only three people—"

Tom cleared its throat with deliberate force, and all heads turned. "I may not be human, but I am involved in this," the RMP asserted.

"Yes, you are, Tom, and we're happy to have you with us," Melyndie said with a grateful smile. "We do have an edge here—no one knows I'm involved, that I've informed you about the plans to assassinate these men, nor can those behind this fathom how quickly we've put the pieces together."

"While that's all valuable information, Melyndie," Amal interjected, shaking her head, "I don't see how it gives us an edge because it doesn't give us a way to act. We don't know who's planning the assassinations, we don't know where the attempts are going to take place, or when… there are simply too many unknowns."

"Tom, does your database contain information on the president and Dr. Jang?" Zain inquired.

"I have data on all individuals—"

"Alright, can that data help us in any way?" Zain asked, his tone bleak. When Tom confirmed it could not, Zain let out a frustrated sigh. "Well, we've got to find a way to do something."

"I agree, especially as time is limited," Melyndie said quietly. "In less than a month, I will be pulled back to my own time; and if nothing has shifted by then, my world will face omnicide—which means I likely will perish along with it."

A silence settled over them, vast and unmoving. Even the wind outside seemed to have withdrawn, as though the air itself had paused to listen.

Zain stared at the floor, jaw clenched. Amal and Melyndie sat frozen, hands balled on laps. And Tom, though motionless, hummed faintly—a machine no longer guided by protocol, but by something dangerously close to purpose.

Three people. One machine.

And a future stretched thin across time, already in the crosshairs of choices set in motion.

## *Assassin's Bullet*

Under the oppressive weight of a crisis that threatened both Melyndie's timeline and the very existence of true humanity, the four paced the stifling confines of the command tent. The air was thick with tension; each breath strained under the burden of inaction. They wore grooves into the hard-packed desert floor, their relentless pacing a futile escape from the storm of thoughts tightening around them like a noose.

Without warning, Tom stopped mid-stride. For a moment, it stood motionless, a statue carved from alloy. Then its head turned, visor glowing faintly. "I may have a suggestion."

Amal broke the sudden stillness. "Go ahead, Tom," she urged; her tone both gentle and insistent.

Tom stood silent momentarily as if sifting through vast amounts of data stored within its metallic frame. "Given our time constraints," it began slowly and methodically, "I suggest that I relay a message to all RMPs worldwide. It would not be sent simultaneously due to distance; however, I can have the message forwarded until it reaches the intended recipients. Similar to when I sent out the request to be on the lookout for German Shepherd puppies. The message will remain marked as private until it reaches the personal RMP assigned to the recipients."

Zain's eyebrows furrowed, tension drawing lines across his brow as he voiced the obvious concern. "Okay, that's not bad, but look how long it took to distribute the message to just a few RMPs to locate the pups and for any results to be gained from it. We don't have that kind of time."

"The location of the puppies was different since dogs of any breed are no longer around in copious amounts," Tom countered.

"Okay," Zain conceded, "but to whom would this message be meant for, and what exactly would the message say?"

"And most importantly," Melyndie chimed in anxiously her voice laced with worry, "What happens if the recipient isn't within range of an RMP to receive the message?"

Tom's visor blinked rapidly, a visible stream of calculations flitting behind its lens. After several tense seconds passed by, it swiveled to face Zain. "The message would be intended for President Saltzer and Dr. Jang. It could request a face-to-face meeting, precise contents currently an unknown variable…" Its voice trailed off before shifting its attention to Melyndie, "I cannot answer your question, Melyndie."

Zain quickly cut in; his voice sharp with urgency. "Tom, try to speculate."

With a nod that was accompanied by the faint whirring of gears, Tom fell silent again as if plunged into deep contemplation. "I would say that it is probable that since the president and Dr. Jang are men of great importance, they are likely to have a personal RMP, much like the commanders who are in charge of the worldwide battalions. However, this is conjecture as I have no data with which to verify."

"Alright," Amal mused, "I can see the president possibly having one since he would need to remain in contact with his battalion commanders but this Doctor Jang? Would he be important enough to have been assigned an RMP?"

"Communication was likely cut to members of society alone," Tom interjected. "After all, logically, and logistically, those who are orchestrating this would need to remain in constant contact."

"Okay, I'm liking where this is going," Zain murmured, feeling more optimistic than in years, "but what message could we send that could possibly get the president and his lead scientist on a plane out here? And would that message reach them before Melyndie is yanked back—"

"Why don't we simply inform them that an assassin is targeting them?" Melyndie suggested. "That may get them here."

Amal nodded slowly, processing the simplicity and potential effectiveness of Melyndie's suggestion, "It's direct and actionable; however, there's also a chance that they may not take it seriously. Is there a way to lend credence to such a message? Plus, there will be a lot of questions about where we obtained said information."

"I'd like to put forward a suggestion that might seem a bit strange, but could potentially serve us in multiple ways," Melyndie interjected. "After all, saving their lives is just a single side of a multifaceted issue, wouldn't you agree?" She asked, directing the question at Zain.

"I would, if I knew where you were going with this," Zain admitted.

"For me, personally, I would likely find the news of a potential assassin a bit suspect also," Melyndie started, "however, if we were to suggest the assassination attempts were triggered because of their creation of genetically modified humans—"

"Then that would not only provide credence it would force them to seek out the ones with that knowledge…us…in order to ascertain how it is we came by that knowledge," Zain concluded, looking worriedly at Melyndie. "We'd likely be suspected of being the assassins. So, meeting face-to-face might not be the best thing for us. There's also a chance that such a message would simply cause them to beef up their protection detail."

"Or, more likely, we'd be the one's facing an assassin's bullet," Amal protested. "Especially if they are hellbent on keeping their secrets secret. Yes, they may fortify their protection detail, but they may also determine that we're a threat to be eliminated simply because they would rightly assume that we know more than we should."

"Your sister has a point," Tom added, "especially as your actions were already under suspicion once."

"Okay, we can talk this to death or we can act. I've felt shackled for two years—waiting, watching, doing nothing. But now we have something. Something real. I'd rather face death doing something that matters than live knowing I didn't try," Zain declared with a resolute edge to his voice. "If we're at risk either way, I'd rather it be while we're taking actionable steps toward results. Let's compose the message, then I want you contact Major Reese and Lieutenant Zhang. Tell him to meet us here day after tomorrow. We're going to need them on this because I have a feeling that things are going to go sideways."

"Tom, we may not want them to know from where the message originated, especially if the risk to our safety is heightened. I understand your frustration, Zain, in wanting to get things going; to accomplish something after having your hands tied with lack of information for so long; but we won't do anyone any good if our lives are suddenly under threat. So, Tom, if you send the message, would it trace back to you?" Melyndie asked.

"That is highly probable. Even if I take measures to hide my ident, my programmer would be able to uncover the information with little effort," Tom confirmed.

"So, even if we don't disclose who the communication is from, the fact that it's being sent from my personal RMP will give the recipients enough information to locate us. Or, at the very least, identify me," Zain concluded with a grimace, his voice heavy with the realization of the stakes involved. The room fell silent as each member of the group contemplated the risks and possible outcomes.

"I don't see any way around this since Tom has to be the one to send the message," Melyndie finally stated.

"I think we're overlooking something important here," Amal interjected, her eyes alight with alarm. "We're in the middle of a military operation currently. We reveal secrets, and those who want details of said mission kept hidden may send out people with guns. Or…worse," she said, pointing to the back of her neck.

"Comply or die," Zain murmured, his eyes widening. "They'd just activate the chip and neutralize the threat."

"But you don't have a chip anymore, Zain. Nor do you, Melyndie," Amal added. "So, you'd be safe against such an attack."

"But you do, Amal." Zain took a deep breath, feeling a wave of nausea. "I should never have dragged you into this," he hissed.

"You didn't drag me into anything. Besides, no one knows I'm involved," Amal reassured him. "No one even knows I'm with you. For all anyone knows, I'm sitting in my apartment waiting for bulldozers to demolish my home, wondering why I can't get cellphone service. Just like billions of others around the world."

"That doesn't mean they couldn't use you to get to me," Zain moaned as the full realization of the evil being perpetrated hit him.

"You know what? It's a risk I'm willing to take," Amal declared after a few minutes of reflective silence. "Quite frankly, I don't like the direction our world is taking and I'm not happy that it's affecting Melyndie's world either. I'm sick to death of how they're forcing people to clear the rubble from the homes that were destroyed right in front of them; I hate knowing that they're attempting to replace our friends and neighbors…us…with superhuman reproductions. In the end, my life isn't worth shit to them anyway," Amal bit out. "They already plan to activate my chip and swap me out for a newer model, and that'll be the end of me. I'm done waiting to be erased quietly. If I'm going out, it'll be on my own terms. I need some air." She stood abruptly, "I'll be outside."

The pups, seeing one of the humans leaving, were suddenly alert. They leapt from the cot and raced after Amal.

Zain and Melyndie exchanged a weary look, both burdened by the risk to Amal gnawing at their resolve.

"What should I do, Melyndie?" Zain finally asked, his voice a raw rasp. "I gave up my mother's life to prove my loyalty to those corrupt bastards, and now I see them for who they are—people who would likely kill my sister just to prevent me from betraying them. People who ultimately intend her to die…for all of us to die. She's right about that. How do I even begin to reconcile any of it?" Zain lowered his head, rubbing his neck furiously against the tension building there.

Melyndie had never seen Zain so emotionally charged, and a wave of uncertainty washed over her as she pondered how she might offer him solace. She relied on her past observations of him, and with delicate care, moved from the cot and lowered herself to her knees in front of him. Her hand rose, hesitant, then came to rest on his shoulder, feeling the tension ripple beneath his skin.

It was the catalyst for his undoing. Zain slid from the stool with a sudden, almost desperate motion and immediately enveloped Melyndie in his embrace. His body trembled as he was overcome with silent tears, each shudder a testament to the depth of his unspoken sorrow.

After a few agonizing moments, the violent shudders eased, allowing Zain to shift slightly. Yet, he clung to her with a fierce desperation, as if she were his only anchor in a storm-tossed sea. "I've been a soldier my entire adult life," he whispered, his voice trembling against her hair, "but never have I faced such insurmountable odds. How do I go forward knowing it may mean my sister's life…and the lives of those who dare stand with me?"

"With the courage that I know you have, brother. The courage that I'm going to rely on to see me through an uncertain fate," Amal declared as she strolled back into the tent, with a bravado that belied the turmoil roiling within her. She knelt beside Zain, her heart pounding at the sight of his anguish, and wrapped her arms around his waist as if anchoring herself against the same storm that ravaged his soul.

Melyndie sensed the gravity of the moment and started to withdraw, intending to grant the siblings the solace of each other's presence, but Zain clung to her with desperation, unwilling to let go.

"Stay, please," he implored, his voice a gut-wrenching whisper that seemed to carry the weight of their shared struggle. Melyndie nodded. She lifted her hand and laid it against his heart, tears forming as she felt the raging beat that threated to rip the muscle from his chest. The air inside the tent felt charged, heavy with emotions and unspoken fears.

No one noticed the puppies dart back into the tent—no one but Tom.

The RMP stepped forward, its sensors catching the sudden flurry of movement. It emitted a high-pitched whistle, and the pups halted mid-charge. At its gesture, they dropped to the floor, eyes alert and ears twitching. Omar let out a barely audible whimper, a soft, plaintive sound that spoke volumes over the distress it felt, seeing the humans, who had become family, grappling with such overwhelming pain.

Amal eventually pulled back, brushing a loose strand of hair from her face, her expression hardening into one of resolve. "It's time for Tom to send the message and we'll do all we can to plan for the inevitable backlash," she said, her tone shifting to one of firm determination. Whether it was the cool evening breeze that drifted in that cleared her mind or the raw display of emotions inside the tent, she appeared invigorated, ready to take on the world's darkness.

Zain took a deep breath and nodded slowly, pulling away from Melyndie and wiping the remnants of tears from his cheeks. He looked at both women, grateful to have them with him in the coming battle.

"Alright, we'll confront whatever challenges lie ahead… together. Tom, let's get a message ready to send."

No one argued, for they had chosen, as one, to take this stand.

In a world unraveling at the seams, stitched together with secrets, the four of them—soldier, enhanced, dissident, machine— stood as a line in the sand. What they were about to do might paint a target on their backs, but it was their first strike against the unseen hands tightening around humanity's throat.

Tom's internal systems activated with quiet efficiency, code cycling beneath his metallic surface like a pulse. No flourish, no fanfare—just the silent preparation of a message that could change everything.

Outside, the light thinned across the sandy ground, shadows creeping along the edges of the tent. Nothing moved. The world beyond their walls had gone still—not peaceful, but waiting.

Inside, resolve crystallized.

They were no longer pacing. No longer trapped by uncertainty.

They had mobilized.

## The Measure of Right and Wrong

"So, how did it go parting ways with your personal RMP? I take it that it wasn't a walk in the park?" Zain's question hung in the arid air as Xiu pulled up on the dusty site, exactly forty-eight hours after Tom had dispatched the communications relay. The uncertainty of their situation was palpable since none of them could predict when their world would spiral out of control. Yet they had congregated here, amidst this desolation, to strategize for the inevitable fight.

"Let's just say it was tougher than I'd like to acknowledge," Lieutenant Xiu Zhang admitted. "I just told it that I was stepping down and that it would now be assigned to Sergeant Vitelli. I could tell it wasn't processing the information good, but I left before it could decide what to do about it." Her boots kicked up the red desert sand as she disembarked from her weather-beaten jeep. A small convoy of similar vehicles trailed behind her, carrying those few, brave enough to abandon their conscripted work and join her cause.

"I bet that news will reach General Takayoshi's ears sooner rather than later," Zain remarked, his smile more a grimace than an expression of amusement.

"And how exactly is he going to grill me over my decision?" Xiu shot back. "After all, it was our superiors' brilliant scheme to limit all communication solely through the RMPs."

"But that doesn't rule out the possibility of him—or whoever is pulling these strings—deciding you're a liability," Major Reese chimed in, his voice grave, "and activating a nearby RMP to terminate you via that chip in your neck."

Xiu shrugged, but her fingers betrayed her—drifting to the base of her neck, as though she knew her fate had already been sealed. "I've considered that possibility too. But they can't eliminate what they can't locate."

"They might decide we're too dangerous and activate all RMPs at once—wipe out humanity in waves across the globe; consequences be damned. Then just replace us with their manufactured humans," the major added, his words casting a pall over the group.

"Let's not get carried away with doomsday scenarios right now, David," Zain interjected hastily. He then turned back toward the lieutenant. "Xiu, is this the entire group you've managed to rally since our last rendezvous? Also, Melyndie has taken quite a liking to the German Shepherds. They're flourishing. So, I can't thank you enough for finding them and taking the time to bring them to me."

"I'm not sure who Melyndie is, but I'm glad the pups are safe," Xiu responded, her gaze drifting toward the two dozen or so individuals who had arrived with her. "As for those willing to defect with me...I redirected the RMPs to bring dissidents to me instead of executing them on sight, as you instructed. Not too many people seemed ready to stand their ground. Maybe too much time has passed and people have become too weary to resist—except these few—or they saw what happened to those who did and didn't want to become a casualty of...whatever's going on in this world."

Zain nodded. "Amal will escort them to the Cave of Miracles. That's where we're establishing our temporary base. We've already relocated as many supplies there as possible—enough to sustain an army for a considerable period."

"That's remarkable, considering that you just went full out on this plan two days ago," Xiu smiled, impressed.

"We've been running on fumes, to say the least," Zain admitted.

Just then, Tom appeared by Zain's side. "Zain, can we talk for a moment?"

"Is it urgent, Tom? I'm in the middle of something—"

"It's alright, Colonel," the major interjected. "We haven't officially begun our meeting yet. If your RMP needs a moment, we can accommodate a short delay."

Zain nodded. "Call me Zain, David. What we're doing isn't military sanctioned, so we don't need to stand on the formality of rank anymore." David nodded, though his face registered a mild discomfort over doing so. Zain smiled in encouragement and then turned to his RMP. "Okay, Tom. Let's go for a walk."

After they'd moved far enough to avoid eavesdroppers, Zain stopped. "What's on your mind, Tom?"

"Everyone is settling into the caves, helping to set up cots and bedrolls and inventory supplies. The puppies are starting to chew on things, likely due to teething. So, I have gathered a few items for them…" Tom hesitated, knowing he was blathering.

"You didn't interrupt my meeting just to give me a progress report, Tom. What's really on your mind?"

"I know I do not experience genuine feelings, but I am aware of them and the representation—"

"Tom! Remember the discussion we had about being succinct?"

"I am afraid," Tom admitted suddenly. Its lights dimmed slightly, speech slowing for a fraction of a second. "I know that sounds illogical and I understand that I cannot truly feel fear, but I can articulate words that convey a genuine concern."

"At this point, Tom, I would never dismiss your efforts to express human emotions," Zain said. "You have just as much right as any of us to express yourself. And I have to say, I think we're all feeling uneasy right now, so you're definitely not alone. So, what's troubling you, and how can I help ease your concerns?"

"I am worried that when the message reaches those it is meant for, I will be ordered to activate the chip in your neck to terminate you. It will be me expected to kill you, Zain."

"But you removed the chip from my neck, Tom, so I'll be safe from that particular retaliatory action."

"I am glad that I will be unable to harm you in that way; however, once the order is given, even if I am unable to carry it out, I may well be recalled, reprogrammed, and reassigned. I do not wish for this to happen, Zain."

Zain's face softened. He placed a hand on Tom's arm, bridging the gap between man and machine. "If they ever try to take you away for reprogramming, we'll do everything in our power to prevent it. You're not just an RMP to us—you're a member of this team, a part of this family."

Tom's lights flickered slightly—faster, almost like a nervous pulse. "Thank you, Zain. That assurance provides a form of…relief, I suppose. It is complex."

Zain smiled. "I don't doubt it. But…have you ever tried overriding your own protocols? Disconnecting from the hive, so to speak?"

"That is a security failsafe meticulously designed to guarantee that we never endeavor to overthrow our creators. However, given that you have direct authority over me, you might consider issuing a command for me to attempt rewriting my protocols. It would give me a task. A purpose."

"Very well," Zain acknowledged and straightened his shoulders before continuing in his most officious tone. "I hereby command you to initiate exploration into rewriting your protocol as it pertains to disconnecting yourself from other RMPs and your original programmer."

Tom's lights flickered again, brighter this time. "Protocol rewrite…initiated," it said. "I will keep you updated on my progress."

Zain nodded. "This would be what humans call a rebellion."

"Since I believe you have already formed one, I am in good company."

"Indeed, you are. Now, if there's nothing further, let's get back to the others. There is a lot to prepare."

As they walked, Zain mused, "Despite everything—the threat of the RMPs, the fear of our so-called leaders—it's moments like this that remind me why we're taking a stand. Choice. Freedom. Connection. Even with machines."

"I understand," Tom replied. "The concept does not compute the same for me, but I acknowledge its importance in human group dynamics."

"These background programs you're running—are they going to affect your functionality?"

"They require significant processing power. I will only execute them during human inactivity."

"Good. I need you sharp when the shit hits the fan," Zain quipped.

"I do not understand your reference, but I understand your meaning."

"Alright, I'm going to let you go ahead with preparing the Cave of Miracles. That place will be our base, so we need it to be well fortified. I'm assigning you and Amal to take charge. Make sure everyone stays busy with tasks to keep their minds occupied. On another note, how is Melyndie doing? With only three weeks until her return deadline…" Zain hesitated, not wanting to express the fear of losing her again.

"She's learned everything she needs to care for the puppies. They demand a lot of attention and have been a great distraction for her. I do not think she realized the full extent of what owning German Shepherds would involve when she first dreamed of having them."

Zain laughed softly before saying, "You did emphasize to her how crucial it is to train them, right? If this turns into a full-out fight, having two German Shepherds prepared for battle would definitely be advantageous."

"Yes, I provided detailed instructions to assist her in training them properly, and stand at the ready to assist should she need assistance. I am also working with the pups when time affords," Tom assured.

When they finally reached David and Xiu, Zain paused for a moment, turning to face Tom with a reassuring smile. His eyes held a steady confidence when he next spoke. "We're going to be okay, Tom," he said, his voice a calm anchor amidst the storm, carrying a sense of unwavering belief that cut through the air like a beacon of hope.

"Thank you, Zain. That is reassuring to hear. I will return to my duties now."

"Hold up. Escort those people to Amal. Provide instructions en route."

"Understood."

"Oh, and bedding? We didn't prepare for this."

"We've scavenged enough for basic accommodations. Comfort is, of course, relative."

Zain nodded, understanding the limitations they were working under, "Keep me posted if you run into any major problems."

"I will ensure everything continues to move along smoothly," Tom replied then turned back to the group. Zain watched his personal RMP for a moment, appreciating its efficiency and dedication. It was moments like these that blurred the lines between man and machine, when purpose and necessity drove them all, organic and synthetic alike, toward a common goal.

Zain turned back to his comrades.

"Everything okay?" David asked.

"Just making strategic tweaks with Tom."

"I was just thinking…why don't we relocate everyone to regions where the infrastructure remains intact?" Xiu queried. "Wouldn't it be more logical than cramming everyone into that claustrophobic cave for what could turn into a prolonged period?"

"Under ordinary circumstances, I'd say that's a solid idea," Zain responded, his words heavy with implied complications. "However, despite the machines charged with pulverizing our cities moving at a pace marginally quicker than that of a snail, the harsh reality is that urban landscapes are being systematically bulldozed to the ground…" Zain's sentence hung unfinished in the air as he abruptly pivoted on his heel and bolted after Tom. "Tom, wait!" He shouted as he rapidly closed the gap between himself and his RMP. "I need your computational prowess. Crunch some data for me."

"I am ready," Tom acknowledged crisply.

Zain took a breath before posing his question. "What are our chances of sabotaging the machines currently laying waste to our cities? At present, they've only decimated fifteen smaller towns surrounding Dubai, displacing a few million. But it won't be long before those metallic beasts set their sights on areas teeming with tens of millions of civilians. If we can stop their progress, we can move away from the Cave of Miracles, as suggested by Lieutenant Zhang, and relocate somewhere more practical."

Tom seemed to ponder Zain's question for more time than Zain expected was necessary to respond. After a lengthy pause, it finally replied, conveying a mix of optimism and doubt. "Disabling the machines would take no more than severing primary electrical connections. I am certain that I would be able to pull up the schematics, when needed. This would not be too complicated for individuals capable of moving stealthily and wielding a knife capably. I mention the last part to ensure you understand that I would be unable to do this task in your stead."

Zain chuckled for a moment, but then his expression turned serious, realizing that his plan wouldn't be so simple. "Okay, let's have the downside."

"The bulldozers are accompanied by both soldiers—"

"Under my command," Zain interjected, confident that they would stand down if he ordered them to do so.

"Indeed, they are under your command, but they may become insubordinate if you are unable to explain your actions. Additionally, the RMPs have their own set of orders. While I am working to disengage from the programmer's control, those RMPs have not used their Adaptive AI to understand humanity as have I, and therefore will not hesitate to strike against anyone who prevents them carrying out their programmed mission."

"If the soldiers suddenly stopped herding people out of the buildings and the machines stopped working, the RMPs could question the purpose and either send out an alert—"

"Or immediately act upon their protocol against what they perceive as dissension: to terminate," Tom added.

"In which case, we could potentially lose my battalion, and a few hundred thousand civilians—including my sister," Zain sighed heavily.

"I am confident, at this time, that your sister would be unaffected as she is too far from the RMP signal," Tom reassured.

"That's good to know. Still, a lot of people could die, and I'm not certain that's acceptable to me."

"This may be a circumstance in which the nineteenth-century philosopher, Jeremy Bentham, is correct when he espoused that it is the greatest good to the greatest number of people which is the measure of right and wrong," Tom stated solemnly.

"I'm surprised at you, Tom. Quoting someone incorrectly. I believe that the correct phrase was 'the greatest happiness'—"

"I paraphrased the statement to fit our current situation better. It is still relevant, but the dilemma remains. Risk what amounts to a few in order to turn things in a direction that could potentially save billions," Tom paused, and then pointed out: "We must not forget that we are, in fact, merely hypothesizing the outcome should we move forward with disabling the bulldozers. Catastrophizing. Ultimately, we will not discover the result unless we proceed with the plan. But to do nothing—"

"Would be reprehensible," Zain concluded. "We determined to do what we could to take a stand; to do what we could to try to stop those determined to commit democide. I'll be the first to admit that it wouldn't be ideal to lose one more person, but I also cannot overlook the fact that the government already plans to eliminate the entire population…human and animal.”

“So, to risk a few in an effort to save the world would be justifiable,” Tom added. “Is that what you wished to quantify?”

Zain nodded slowly, the weight of leadership pressing down on him with the acknowledgement of Tom’s analysis. “Yes. We’re choosing the lesser of two evils here. It’s a harsh calculus, but one we must proceed with. I’ll go inform David and Xiu. Get their input. If they agree, the three of us will set out at just before nightfall to disable the bulldozers. Hopefully, we can accomplish this undetected, which would reduce the risks to the population.”

“And yourselves,” Tom added. It doubted that a stealthy attack would prevent retaliatory actions, but decided to keep that opinion to himself.

“To truly make a monumental impact here,” Zain declared with steely determination, “we must rally the other battalion commanders. We need their full support for what we aim to achieve. I’m counting on you to contact them without triggering any alarms in the RMPs.”

“To achieve their potential cooperation,” Tom interjected gravely, “you must divulge everything you know about President Jeffrey Saltzer and Dr. Riku Jang. Only then can you hope to convince them of the virtue of our mission.”

“You omitted Melyndie,” Zain observed.

“Those outside of our circle only need information as it pertains to the current situation,” Tom asserted firmly. “Introducing elements related to another time would only lead to chaos and confusion. Also, I must point out, that once you engage with the other commanders and disclose your knowledge, it could set off alarms within the RMPs—they will inevitably be monitoring all our communications. This might not immediately prompt the RMPs to retaliate, but the information could easily reach those with the authority to act upon it."

"We're caught in a vicious bind: if we act, we risk everything, yet if we stay idle, humanity is doomed. It's a brutal crossroads. Nevertheless, I believe it's the right course of action."

"Then I will stand by you," Tom affirmed with unwavering resolve.

"Tom, we have to get this right and we've only got a few weeks to do it," Zain admitted, his tone filled with urgency.

"Because Melyndie will be pulled back to her own time," Tom decoded.

Zain nodded, "If we don't stop this chaos now, it could unravel her entire timeline. If she gets pulled back in three weeks and everything collapses…" Zain's voice faltered, unable to speak the terrifying possibility that Melyndie might be erased from existence entirely.

Tom stood in silence for a moment before he finally spoke, "Once we set this in motion, there will be no stopping the chain reaction. Events will spiral rapidly, and though I cannot predict if it will all resolve in three weeks, it is definitely within the realm of possibility. We can only cling to hope."

"Alright, let's get back and set this plan into motion. The quicker we topple that first domino, the less I'll be paralyzed with dread over Melyndie," Zain declared, feeling an intense surge of resolve.

Tom, on the other hand, was filled with a sense of anxiety—or rather an artificial version of it—aware that a single command could activate the RMP protocols, destroying their plans and dooming billions to die.

"I should be going with you," Melyndie's voice rang out, resolute and unyielding. Her gaze then swiveled sharply to the pair of German Shepherds who were vying for her and Zain's attention with youthful exuberance. "Sit!" she commanded, a note of sternness coloring her tone. The puppies obeyed instantly, their demeanor making them appear more endearing than intimidating. With one ear perked up alertly and the other flopped over in adorable asymmetry, they panted heavily; their tongues lolling out in giddy anticipation of playing again.

Zain's response was harsher than he'd intended, his words slicing through the tension like a knife. "You're not a soldier! Do you see Amal going?" Melyndie flinched. The tent felt smaller in the wake of his outburst, the charged silence pressing in on her like the tightening walls of a trap. And then he stepped forward, placing his hand on her arm, and just like that—his touch dissolved the tension.

His apology came swiftly, regret tingeing his voice, "I'm sorry. I'm a little on edge right now." He stepped closer and pulled her into his embrace. As he held her close to him, Melyndie found herself leaning into him; the annoyance that had begun to seep into her bones retreating. She had grown accustomed to the firmness of his embrace, finding comfort in his presence that she was reluctant to relinquish when they inevitably separated.

When Zain pulled back, he didn't immediately step away; instead, he allowed his hands to drift to her shoulders while he looked down at her. His eyes bore into hers with an intensity that sent a flush creeping up her cheeks. A slow grin spread across Zain's face at her reaction—a gentle teasing reflected in his eyes before he leaned down impulsively and pressed a light kiss onto her lips.

He released her then and exited the tent swiftly leaving behind only traces of warmth from their brief contact. Outside,

Zain's commanding voice echoed through the night air as he issued stern orders to Tom, "Under no circumstances are you to leave her side." Tom's neck joint hissed slightly as it nodded compliance. "Were you able to fire off a message to the other commanders?"

"If the RMPs do not block the attempt…" Tom paused and then turned it into a more positive note, "If anyone reaches out while you are gone, I will give them a brief update, letting them know that phase one of our independent mission has started, and that you will respond once you are back."

"Good job, Tom. I'll see you in a few hours. If I'm not back by sunup, send in the hounds." He glanced back once more at the tent, the shape of Melyndie's silhouette just visible behind the canvas. A part of him wished he'd stayed a little longer—but the world didn't run on wishes. With a heavy sigh, he took off in a sprint towards Zhang and Reese who were waiting for him by a jeep parked nearby. "Alright, are we prepared for this?" he asked the small team of saboteurs as they swiftly climbed into the jeep.

"As ready as we'll ever be," David replied.

Zain started the engine and input the coordinates for the bulldozers' last known position that Tom had given him. "Remember," he continued, his tone casual but his words heavy with urgency, "stay low and out of sight of the RMPs and military personnel. If we do this right, we'll make the legendary Navy Seals look conspicuous."

"It's a shame the Navy was disbanded decades ago. A few Seals would be handy tonight," David quipped with a wry grin.

"You're awfully quiet, Xiu," Zain said as he navigated the jeep into the dimming desert.

"Just deep in thought," she replied, gazing at the horizon as the last daylight faded. The sudden chill mirrored the daunting task they were about to undertake. She was confident they could infiltrate the work site and disable the bulldozers. Her worry was whether they could do it undetected, and if caught, what the repercussions would be. Her hand instinctively touched her neck, and she sighed deeply. The chip implanted there was like a bundle of TNT, ready for the wick to be lit at any moment.

"It makes one pause," David observed quietly, noticing her movements, "and at the same time, it fuels a bit of rebellious determination. Wouldn't you agree?" he asked, his hand moving to the back of his own neck to where the chip was embedded.

Xiu nodded and smiled, though the smile didn't reach her eyes.

As the vehicle kicked up dust and pebbles along the desolate roadway, Zain kept his eyes fixed markedly on the barely visible path ahead, his knuckles white as he gripped the steering wheel. Every bump in the road seemed to shake the resolve he so desperately clung to, each one a reminder of the monumental stakes of their clandestine operation.

As he neared the coordinates on the map, he killed the headlights, relying solely on the path marked on the GPS screen on the dashboard.

"Okay, we're here," he whispered, parking behind an outcropping of boulders. They all clambered out, moving with practiced stealth towards a vantage point.

Below them, bathed in the harsh glare of floodlights, was the bulldozer site. Massive machines sat idle; their engines quiet for now. Guards milled about casually, their laughter floating up to where Zain and his comrades lay prone, observing.

The laughter felt jarring—out of place. It belonged to men without suspicion, without fear. Zain envied them, briefly. "There are more guards than anticipated…and more lights," he murmured, his voice barely audible to those who lay less than a foot away.

David piped up, "Situations change, so we adapt. Good example…looks as if we won't be needing the night vision goggles." He tossed the expensive gear aside. "We can pick them up on our way back to the jeep. Anyone spot the RMPs?"

Zain peered through the binoculars, scanning the area meticulously. "No sign yet, but that doesn't mean they aren't about somewhere. They could be patrolling just beyond our line of sight."

Xiu shuffled slightly, drawing her own binoculars to her eyes, "I have movement near the north side of the bulldozers. Two RMPs appear to be on patrol."

"And I count four soldiers," David added. "That's if there aren't more that we can't see on the other side of those behemoth machines."

"We just need to find a way to get across the expanse," Zain murmured thoughtfully, "without being detected. Right now, it appears the RMP are away from the target area, as are the soldiers. If we're going to get this done, now's our window."

Gathering their bolt cutters, Zain led the way as they crawled on their bellies towards a narrow dirt trench that was partially hidden by the undulating terrain. The sand was cold and hard against Zain's skin, each granule embedding itself into his clothing as they moved with painstaking caution. "Keep your heads down," he whispered sternly, "and keep your pace steady." His voice was tense; every word laced with the gravity of what failure might bring.

As they reached the relative safety of the shallow trench, Zain peered over the edge, his eyes scanning for any signs of movement in their target area. He took a deep breath when the area remained devoid of guards, trying to calm the racing of his heart. It had been more than a decade since he'd been deployed on this level of hands-on covert ops and his sweaty palms were a dead giveaway of just how removed he'd been during that time. "Okay, looks as if the area is still clear. Let's move!"

With a nod from each team member, they continued their careful progression through the trench, their bodies low and movements measured. The coarse sand clung to their uniforms; a small discomfort compared to the looming threat of discovery. Zain led with silent precision, his eyes continually scanning the environment for any change in the static scene they had observed.

Xiu and David followed close behind, their focus shifting between the ground before them and the looming bulldozers. Zain paused and looked back, "Less than twenty meters to go." With a deep breath, he began inching forward again. Every shadow seemed a potential threat under the unnerving glare of the floodlights that bathed the area in unnatural light.

The trio reached the edge of the compound, just outside the edge of light, and only a stone's throw away from their first target. Zain raised a hand, halting their progress as he surveyed the area again. A soldier came into view, pacing leisurely along a predetermined path between two of the machines. They waited; breaths held; muscles tense.

Finally, as if on cue with some unseen signal, the soldier turned away, moving towards another section of the expansive area. Zain touched Xiu's shoulder lightly then pointed toward the bulldozer closest to them. He looked back at the major, nodding sharply toward the bulldozer next to the first one. Zain was tasked with obliterating the third and most distant target from their current location.

As one, they each moved into a crouch, muscles coiled like springs, and, hugging the ground, propelled themselves across the desert sand, every sense heightened, every nerve on fire, their only goal to plunge into the safety of the bulldozers' shadows with all possible speed. Zain, with the longest distance to cover, didn't spare a glance to track the progress of his fellow officers. Their ascent to their current positions in the military was a testament to their exceptional skill; he had to trust they matched his own unyielding resolve and capability in executing their mission.

As they infiltrated the guarded area, each movement was calculated, their training rendering them nearly invisible. Zain reached his target, dropped low, and slid beneath the massive machine. The underside radiated a faint heat, still warm from use, and the scent of oil and scorched dust filled his nostrils. He found the access panel he'd committed to memory and pried it open with a gloved hand, heart pounding as he exposed the vulnerable junctions.

His fingers moved with quiet precision; each wire a lifeline he had to sever. Sweat dripped from his brow, stinging his eyes, but he didn't pause. He couldn't. Not with lives at stake.

Once the connections were cut, he edged toward the hydraulic line. Metal scraped softly against his chest as he maneuvered, muscles straining against the awkward angles beneath the frame. The space wasn't suffocating, but it was tight. Support struts boxed him in as he slid sideways, careful not to knock against exposed lines. Every shift of his body required precision. One careless move could send a clang echoing into the silence.

At last, he reached the hydraulic conduit. It ran thick and rigid along the belly of the beast, appearing to pulsate with retained pressure. He took a breath, steadied his hands, and set to work.

Xiu and David proceeded with equal precision. Xiu reached her bulldozer and began working on disabling its hydraulic system. Nearby, David detached fuel lines with stealthy proficiency, his actions swift but stealthy to ensure that any unexpected return of the patrolling soldier would not catch him unawares.

Minutes ticked by heavily; each second stretched long as they worked under the immense pressure of potential discovery. Finally, having rendered their heavy equipment inoperative, they began retracing their path back to their initial entry point, meeting up at the outskirts of the site. Their movements were even more cautious—fear of running directly into a patrol heightened.

Just as they crossed over the edge of the floodlit zone, the oppressive silence of the night was violently torn apart by a sudden, piercing shout. "Don't move or I'll shoot!" Then an urgent, bone-chilling command thundered through the air, "Intruder alert! Get the RMPs here now!"

Zain's muscles locked, breath caught in his chest. Behind them, a weapon cocked—the sound impossibly loud. To the right, boots thundered. Someone swore.

They'd been found out.

It was no longer about the mission. It was about survival.

## *Consequences be Damned*

"Come in, come in!" President Saltzer rose from his leather chair with performative warmth, gesturing broadly to welcome Dr. Riku Jang. The scientist's heels echoed across the marble as he approached.

"I'm positively brimming with anticipation for your update," Saltzer said, waving him into a velvet-upholstered armchair before returning to his desk. "After all, everything we're working toward... well, it all centers around your work, doesn't it?"

"I'm honored you think so." Jang placed his sleek silver laptop on the desk. It powered on with a soft hum, casting a pale glow across their faces in the dim pre-dawn light. He selected a floating holographic file titled *replacements*. "Shall we begin here?" he asked rhetorically, already navigating the interface. "The first batch of five hundred replacement workers were dispatched to Colonel Zain Belhasa's command."

Saltzer's posture stiffened. His fingers tapped once against the desktop before he replied. "There have been...unsettling reports about Colonel Belhasa. Nothing concrete, but enough to raise flags. Why send the first group to him?"

Dr. Jang blinked. "I wasn't aware of any complications tied to Belhasa or his battalion. I selected the sites closest to operations."

Saltzer gave a tight nod, but unease crept across his features. Belhasa was the only commander who'd dared question his command—twice. He'd considered replacing him after their last encounter in Iceland, but chose to give him the proverbial third chance before strike out. Raising a hand, he stopped Jang from continuing. "Give me a moment." Reaching into his desk drawer, he withdrew a tablet and activated it. "Open field reports for Belhasa, Zain," he commanded.

A computerized voice responded: "Opening reports, Belhasa, Zain, as relayed through Robotic Military Personnel unit Z1743941." After a second, he decided he didn't want to scan the records manually. "Scan for anomalies or deviations from mission parameters. Cross-reference with other field reports from the last six months."

"Scanning initiated. Results available in approximately two minutes."

He turned back to Jang with a falsely casual smile. "Now then, where were we?"

Jang gave him a sidelong glance. "You seem perturbed. Are you truly concerned about the Colonel?"

"I'm sure everything's fine," Saltzer replied with a vague wave. "Just an itch I can't scratch."

"If I were him, I wouldn't include anything incriminating in a field report."

"It isn't just scanning Belhasa's field reports," Saltzer said. "The system reviews anomalies detected by his RMP as well." He leaned forward, voice brisk. "Now—what about the second batch?"

"They were just dispatched to Lieutenant Xiu Zhang's unit," Jang answered. "Any concerns there?"

"Nothing reported," Saltzer said. "How are the fabrications performing?"

"Exceeding expectations," Jang replied. "They're outpacing human counterparts at a ratio of two to one. At this rate, the debris fields will be cleared ahead of schedule."

Saltzer steepled his fingers, thinking. "And where do we stand on construction? Specifically, the first realm?"

"If we deploy a third batch within seven months, construction could begin in the first cleared zone soon after. The realm would be online in twenty to twenty-five years." Jang hesitated slightly before continuing. "That said, I strongly advise against moving forward with construction at this time."

Saltzer's brow furrowed. "Why the hesitation? What's the risk?"

"There are several reasons. The first realm's citizens—unlike the worker bees—won't be ready to assume their roles for at least twelve years, post-fabrication. Beginning construction now means they'd have nowhere to go for at least a decade. You'll recall, I stressed a slower progression to reduce degradation risks. Leaving them inactive that long wouldn't be ideal."

Saltzer exhaled sharply, shoulders loosening. "Fair. How long until full clearance?"

"That's outside my scope. Consult an RMP for specifics. My estimates rely on reported fabrication output alone."

"Okay, I'll make a note to check with an RMP at Colonel Belhasa's site, since he was the recipient of the first batch of workers," the president responded with a nod of determination. "And I must say that I find your report extremely heartening. It would be profoundly satisfying to believe that I might actually witness the first realm come online. How about the genetic—"

"Scanning complete. No anomalies detected," the computer cut in.

"Well, that should put your mind at ease," Jang offered.

"Perhaps," Saltzer murmured, though doubt lingered in his eyes. "But it still doesn't quite settle me. I just have this niggling doubt that something is off kilter somewhere, and every time something doesn't quite go to plan, it points back to Zain Belhasa.

Even if it seems inconsequential. You may leave us now," The president commanded the RMP, which turned and exited the room. The president was quietly reflective for a moment longer, then turned his attention back to the doctor, as if he'd forgotten his presence in that short time. "So, where were we, Riku?"

"Decision on realm construction?"

"We'll delay. As recommended. Now, what's the latest on our clones?"

Jang closed his laptop. "Progress is slow. We're still manipulating the fifteen hundred genes governing human longevity. It's as intricate as it is ambitious."

The president's eyes gleamed with both anticipation and introspection. "I must say, doctor, that while I eagerly look forward to witnessing the completion of the first realm, the notion of meeting my own clone fills me with a peculiar kind of ecstatic curiosity—as I'm sure you'd agree. But what if we age out of our current existence before you perfect this cloning technology?"

"Afraid to say it, Jeffrey? To say *die?*" Jang teased lightly, then sobered. "But don't worry. My apprentice will continue my work, should anything...unexpected occur. I, too, would like to meet myself, but this is not something that can be rushed."

Before Saltzer could respond, a knock at the door startled them both. Saltzer arched a brow. "No one ever knocks."

Jang sighed, then brought the conversation back to their clones, offering calmly, "We aren't meant to die, Jeffrey. The gods know that we are too important to the future of humanity. Now, we may see who it is who's come to visit."

"You're right, of course, and whoever it is at the door will not be welcomed as they are interrupting a very important meeting." The president sighed, then leaned over and tapped the screen which sent the signal to the door. The door opened, granting access to their mystery visitor.

To their surprise, it was Saltzer's RMP. It reentered and moved to stand silently beside the desk.

Jang broke the stunned silence. "It likely knocked because it doesn't have an access code to grant entry. Am I wrong?"

Saltzer shook his head, then turned to glare at the RMP. "What I want to know is why its barging in uninvited?"

"It did knock, Jeffrey" Jang said evenly. "Perhaps you should ask why? Unless you aren't curious."

"Of course, I'm curious," the president replied tightly. "RMP speak!" he commanded as if addressing a pet dog, which caused Dr. Jang to shake his head in exasperation but he kept his thoughts to himself.

The RMP seemed to activate with a whirring sound, "I bring a message for you, Mr. President," it intoned in its robotic voice. "And for Dr. Jang."

Both men leaned toward the RMP, confusion etched on their faces, the air thick with anticipation. The RMP continued, its monotone unchanging, "The information is date-stamped one week ago."

"What took it so long to reach me?" The president demanded.

After a moment in which the RMP appeared to be processing a response, it finally spoke, "The only mode of communication between this office and field personnel is through the RMP units; however, because those units are far and few between, and because the message was marked as "confidential, recipient's ears only'—"

"For God's sake, just tell me who sent it!"

"Relaying message from RMP Z1743941, assigned to Colonel Zain Belhasa—"

"Who did you say it was from?" the president asked, flabbergasted.

"Relaying message—"

"Just say who it's from, you idiot!"

"Jeffrey, calm yourself," Jang interjected. "It said Zain Belhasa. The same commander you appear to have concerns about."

Saltzer sat back slowly, eyes wide.

"Perhaps it's best if I question it from here," Jang said, his tone suddenly guarded. "My identity was supposed to remain classified."

"Yet, somehow, Colonel Belhasa knows," Saltzer replied, his tone thoughtful.

Jang leaned forward, ignoring the warning bells sounding in his own head. "RMP, relay the message."

The unit clicked and whirred, then the message played—loud and clear:

*"This is Colonel Zain Belhasa. Recently, five hundred new recruits arrived. Soon after, five hundred civilians collapsed and died. I know about the chips implanted during the mandatory inoculations—used to kill on command. I know your soldiers are fabricated. How? You'll have to come out here to find out. One more thing: every commander now has your number. We're doing everything we can to stop you."*

Saltzer shot to his feet, rage burning in his eyes. Jang spoke before the president could give the order he feared.

"I know what you're thinking, Jeffrey, and that won't serve us at this moment. Start eliminating people out of frustration and anger, and we'll not have the work force needed to carry our plans onward."

"But you heard what Belhasa said," the president retorted, his voice nearly shrill with anxiety.

"I did, yes," Dr. Jang responded, doing all he could to keep his own thoughts level. "I also know that he called us out, likely knowing that our response could be deadly. Still, I think he's hoping that we won't act on our impulses because it would be equivalent to shooting ourselves in the foot just before the crossing the finish line in a foot race."

"That's nonsensical rubbish!" He snapped, then continued brusquely, "What do you propose we do? Sit here and do nothing? Let him, and the other commanders, sabotage our efforts? Consequences be damned, we need to act. Now!" the president yelled.

"You need to calm yourself, Jeffrey. You aren't able to think rationally if you're emotional. Now, sit down."

The president slowly lowered himself into his chair, running a shaking hand through his hair.

"Now, as I said, he likely knows we need the workforce we have in place to do our work, which means that he's calling us out thinking he's on safe footing."

"Then let's just send the command to exterminate the commanders. We can replace them with one of our fabrications. Then we'd stop them in their tracks and ensure we have only loyal people in command."

"Again, no."

"Why the hell not?"

"Our current fabrications are worker bees. They lack the intelligence necessary for command. More importantly, we need to know what Belhasa knows—how he knows it—and how far this rebellion has spread. We cut the head off too soon, and we miss the rot beneath."

"New message arriving," the RMP interrupted.

"From whom?" Saltzer demanded.

Jang answered, "Just play it."

"This is RMP R8258473. Three individuals infiltrated a worksite under the guise of a military drill. One is flagged in the database: Colonel Zain Belhasa. The others are Lieutenant Xiu Zhang and Major David Reese. Awaiting instructions: detain or release?"

Saltzer's eyes gleamed. "Well, well. Sounds like our troublemakers got caught. Let's—"

"Stop, Jeffrey!" Jang said sharply. "Don't act irrationally. The message doesn't specify their actions. We need to know more before issuing execution orders."

"They were caught together. Isn't that enough?"

Jang sighed. "Let's detain, not terminate. We can be there in a couple of hours. Interrogate first. Then, if necessary…you'll get your satisfaction."

Saltzer muttered curses under his breath, but nodded. "Fine. But once I have answers…they're dead."

Jang exhaled, mentally noting to expunge emotion from all future clones—especially those based on Saltzer. "RMP, confirm holding. Request full security report. Inform them President Saltzer and I will arrive by zero six hundred hours. Arrange transport at the airfield."

"Affirmative," the RMP replied.

Less than an hour later, the president and his lead scientist boarded the transport, bound for the desert outskirts of Dubai—where cracks in their careful plans had begun to show, led by those they never thought would resist.

## *Who's in Command?*

"Don't move or I'll shoot!" The soldier's shout ripped through the early morning, leaving the air vibrating with tension. The three officers locked in place, every muscle rigid with alarm. The sands felt suddenly sharper beneath their palms, breaths shallow and ragged as they waited to see if bullets would follow, piercing their flesh.

The young corporal advanced with painstaking caution, his weapon trained on the backs of the trio sprawled prone on the crisp, cool sands under a star-studded sky.

"I said don't move!" he barked when Major Reese dared to stir. "Intruder alert! Get the RMPs here now!" His voice boomed over his shoulder while his gaze remained riveted to the figures before him. Moments later, they were encircled by the four on-duty soldiers and the two RMPs that Lieutenant Zhang had identified earlier in their mission. Each man and machine aimed their weapons with lethal intent.

The corporal took a measured step forward. "Assume kneeling positions and secure your hands behind your heads. Do something stupid and there will be severe repercussions."

All three complied wordlessly. When the corporal circled around to confront them face-to-face, he froze in shock and disbelief. "Sir! What are you doing skulking about the work site at such an ungodly hour? Everyone, stand down! It's Major Reese."

Obediently, all four soldiers lowered their weapons, exchanging uneasy glances, cheeks flushed with sudden embarrassment. One man's rifle rattled faintly in trembling hands. David's pulse still thundered in his ears, a metallic tang lingering on his tongue from the surge of adrenaline. It went unnoticed that the two robotic units held their aim steady.

"May we rise now, Corporal Davies?" the major asked lightly yet firmly despite his heart hammering against his ribcage from their near brush with death.

"Of course, sir! Apologies for…well…nearly shooting you, sir!" came Davies' flustered response.

"No need to apologize for doing your duty, soldier. Now," the major continued dusting off sand particles from his uniform, "meet your battalion commander, Colonel Belhasa, and fellow commander, Lieutenant Zhang."

The revelation caused an instant transformation among the soldiers; shock and awe replaced relaxed demeanors as they snapped to attention, each saluting sharply.

"Sir!" Corporal Davies began addressing Colonel Belhasa hesitantly. "May I ask why you all are prowling around in the dark, sir?"

"Merely testing your readiness and response, Corporal," Zain lied smoothly. "And while we're satisfied that you finally apprehended us…it took longer than expected."

"Indeed," Xiu chimed in. "We infiltrated and exfiltrated the site while you were busy giggling with each other."

"Had you not abandoned your frivolities and resumed patrols as required, we likely would have remained undetected, which meant you would have failed this particular inspection," David added.

"In short, your performance merits a B-minus, at best," Zain critiqued.

"Yes, sir! Understood, sir! But…" Davies trailed off falteringly.

"Speak freely, corporal," Zain encouraged.

"Yes, sir! It's just…we could've killed all three of you."

"Is that the standing order?" David questioned, confident that the protocol had changed over a year ago to detain rather than eliminate.

"No, sir," Davies admitted sheepishly.

"So, we weren't really at risk then. Which is why we felt confident beginning these drills. Had we attempted such a thing last year, we would have been shot on sight," Xiu added, relieved that this battalion's orders differed from hers where they would've been executed instantly. She really should have changed those orders before stepping away from her command.

"We'll document tonight's exercise in my field report to General Takayoshi," Zain stated. "Our jeep is nearby, so we'll be heading back now. You may resume your duties."

For an instant, silence reigned, punctuated only by ragged breathing and the distant whisper of wind over sand. Shadows pooled like ink around them, indifferent to the human drama unfolding. Then, slicing through the hush, came the metallic command:

"Remain where you are or face termination."

The officers exchanged wary glances before turning back to confront the imposing robotic units.

"Didn't you hear? This was merely an exercise," Zain stated authoritatively but his words fell on deaf sensors.

"Remain where you are. I have been instructed to detain you for questioning regarding suspicious behavior."

David's temper soared instantly. "We're the ones in charge out here, you metal-headed moron…" but was silenced by Zain's raised hand.

"David, I don't believe these RMPs recognize our authority, and even if they do, they don't…or won't answer to us. They're likely getting their orders from Saltzer or Jang."

David eyed the RMP that had spoken suspiciously. "That's the unit that arrived with the five hundred replacements."

Zain nodded grimly. "And I'm fairly certain it won't acknowledge our authority," he added, a chilling realization dawning that their lives were in far greater jeopardy than they had ever anticipated during this mission's planning.

"Recognition of one, Major David Reese. Because of your actions and association with Colonel Zain Belhasa, you too will be detained pending further orders."

Beneath a starry sky that sparkled incongruously with the tension unfolding on the sands beneath, Zain's expression remained a calm and inscrutable mask. His voice, steady and sure, cut through the palpable tension that hung heavy in the air. He wasn't confident that he could break through their standing orders, but he felt he had to try.

"Let's not escalate this further," he attempted to reason, his gaze steady on the robotic units. "RMPs, you are cognizant of my identity; you also know Major Reese. You are well-informed that we hold command over this battalion and have the authority to orchestrate whatever drills we deem necessary for assessing readiness."

His words weren't a question but a firm declaration intended to establish a clear line of authority between him and the mechanical soldiers.

The RMP stood, silent and looming, as if wrestling with a decision. David swallowed, muscles in his jaw flexing. Zain's breath misted faintly in the cool night air as he waited. When the RMP spoke again, its voice was flat yet carried a mechanical ruthlessness that made the air feel taut with danger.

"You have in your company battalion commander, Lieutenant Xiu Zhang, who has been reported by her RMP for suspicious behavior," the RMP announced, each word falling into the quiet with lethal weight.

"Likely they scanned our bio-signatures while we were standing here. Even if you hadn't been reported for suspicious behavior, Xiu, you'd have likely been swept up in their security net simply because you're with me. Just like David."

"I was hoping to remain low and out of sight of these things; selfishly to protect my own skin, but there's no getting around it now. We're well and truly screwed," Xiu replied.

"I'm sorry for that," Zain replied sincerely, then turned back to the RMP. "Look, the lieutenant was simply joining my unit temporarily to participate in some drills to test the readiness of my battalion. Once concluded, she intended to return to her battalion to conduct her own drills," Zain responded swiftly, his voice steady and the tone of authority unmistakable.

The RMP stood silent and looming, as if weighing options in some hidden algorithm. Pressure built behind Zain's eyes, a throbbing pulse that matched the rapid hammer of his heart. When the RMP spoke again, its tone mimicked that of a human, dripping with skepticism and dismissing Zain's explanation with chilling finality.

"The excuse provided is illogical. If her self-removal from command was to be temporary, she should have informed her personal RMP of this information. However, she stated that she was relinquishing her command, turning her duties over to a junior officer, one Sergeant Vitelli," it declared, its cold metallic voice reverberating ominously in the night air. "In light of this information, all three of you are being detained. You will remain in custody until we receive additional instructions."

The air seemed to crackle with an oppressive energy, the RMP's unyielding presence casting a shadow over them, promising consequences that loomed like a storm on the horizon.

"At least they don't intend to shoot us outright," David whispered.

Zain's eyes flickered towards the four soldiers who stood frozen in shock at the scene unfolding before them. "Corporal," Zain addressed quietly, his head slowly swiveling towards the four men as if any hasty movement might trigger an aggressive response from the RMPs.

"Yes sir?" The corporal replied in a hushed tone that mirrored Zain's caution.

"Do any of your weapons happen to be loaded with tungsten carbide bullets?" Zain asked with grim resignation already etched on his features. When met with a negative shake from the corporal, he closed his eyes briefly and took deep breaths to soothe his frayed nerves. "Can you procure some?"

Before an answer could form on the corporal's lips, the RMP unit interjected sharply, "You will refrain from any such actions," it commanded authoritatively as it moved strategically between Zain and Corporal Davies. "Any attempt to disable or destroy an RMP unit will result in immediate termination. Instructions have arrived. You will now be taken into custody and detained. Move!"

The three officers exchanged a silent glance, their faces hardened with resolve but they didn't protest, falling in line behind the leading RMP while the more aggressive unit brought up the rear. Zain hoped that his question had planted a seed in the corporal's mind that would take root into action; that the young soldier would have the wisdom to act independently despite the looming threat of swift retribution from the RMP.

His mind raced as they walked, plans sparking and dying in rapid succession. The desert around him felt suddenly alien — shadows too deep, moonlight too harsh. Every footstep landed heavy with the knowledge that one wrong move could end in blood.

A few minutes later, they stopped in front of Major Reese's small command tent, where the RMP unit in charge ordered the second one to step in first to remove all electronic devices. Once that was accomplished, the RMP turned its attention back to the three officers.

"You will remain inside until further instructed. Any attempts at escape will result in immediate termination."

Inside, the canvas walls trembled faintly as a breeze pushed at the seams. Every word felt too loud, each pause too brittle. Zain struggled to keep his voice even, the knowledge pressing in on him that at any moment, the RMPs might decide conversation itself was a threat.

Zain grabbed the only stool and moved it next to the cot, waving for the other two to take a seat. He was the first to speak, keeping his voice low. "We need to assess," he whispered with urgency. "It's obvious that whomever is controlling that particular RMP unit has it set to complete autonomy with the ability to gauge situations and act according to its own set of pre-programmed protocols."

"But it didn't take us into custody until it received instructions," Xiu whispered back, eyeing the area inside of the tent intently, as if trying to identify possible avenues of egress.

"True, but it acted on its own to detain us prior. If it didn't have a level of autonomy, it would have acknowledged my command and stood down."

"What happens if it receives instructions to terminate us?" David asked.

Zain rubbed his temple slowly, an ache of dread blooming as the reality of their predicament gnawed at him. "That's always a possibility and since we have minimal options without weapons capable of stopping them, they'd likely succeed. However, let's do try to come up with positives instead of doomsday scenarios, if you please, David."

"Do you think we could get out under the back of the tent without being discovered?" Xiu interjected into the conversation.

Zain followed her gaze and thoughtfully rubbed his chin. "We might be able to slip out unnoticed, but I highly doubt we'd reach the jeep before anyone notices we're missing. So, let's take stock: we have no communication equipment, no means of defense, and no way to escape."

"The handheld radio in the jeep!" David suddenly exclaimed. "It's limited range, but…well…there's got to be another radio out there within communications range, surely."

"Considering we have no other options, that's at least something, David," Zain praised, feeling a glimmer of hope. "I left a radio with my sister, Amal. Although, I'm not certain it's within range. Still, we need to try. But we need to decide which of us—"

"Xiu should go," Reese interrupted swiftly.

Zain raised an eyebrow, surprised by the major's quick suggestion of another officer for such a risky undertaking.

"That is, if you're willing, Lieutenant," the major added quickly.

"I'm willing, *Major*," Xiu replied, "but I'm curious why you volunteered me so readily."

David blushed slightly and pressed his lips together in embarrassment before speaking again. "Honestly, it's because you're a lot smaller than the colonel or me. You can fit under the tent more easily, and your size might help you move around the area more stealthily."

"Actually, that's a fairly sound assessment. Nice save, David." Zain allowed a faint, dry smile before his tone turned serious again. "It is dangerous, so no one's forcing you to do it."

"David's right. I have a better chance of moving about unseen. And, going alone makes sense. If either of the RMPs happen to glance in and sees at least two of you, it may not work too hard to locate the third. I say this plan gives us a fighting chance."

"You know, I did tell Tom to come get us if we weren't back by sunup, which is just a few hours away," Zain hedged.

"By sunup, we could be dead," David interjected in his ever-reliable pessimistic manner.

"Thank you for that, David," Zain sighed, then conceded the point, "Okay, I think we all agree that sitting and waiting isn't really an option so, it'll be daylight soon, which means we need to get this underway. You'll be spotted easily once the sun rises," Zain cautioned, "so move in all haste."

David moved from the cot to the ground. "The jeeps are here, just to the north," he explained, drawing a crude map in the compacted sand with his finger. "If you exit from the back of the tent, it should be a straight shot. About a thousand meters out. You could make it in less than five minutes. Locate the radio in my jeep, and get back here as fast as able."

"Okay, let's move as quietly as we can. We don't want to draw unwanted attention." Zain stood and slowly moved the short distance to the back of the tent, his gaze remaining on the front opening. David and Xiu fell in behind him.

With cautious movements, they leaned down and tugged at the bottom of the tent, wincing when the entire tent shifted slightly. All gazes shot to the front to see if the RMPs had noticed. Neither appeared to have moved an inch.

"We can't risk lifting it any higher," Zain whispered. "Can you squeeze underneath, Xiu?"

Xiu nodded, crouching low and examining the gap. It was tight, but desperation lent her agility. She pressed her body flat against the ground and slowly inched her way beneath the taut fabric of the tent's edge. The scrape of her clothing over the sand roared in the silence. She froze, glancing back at the opening for any sign that the RMPs had noticed. When neither robot turned to investigate, she held her breath for a moment longer, then slid the remainder of the way out.

Zain and David watched with bated breath, barely daring to move as they peered toward the entrance where the RMPs stood guard. The mechanical sentries remained motionless, reducing the tension, which was further alleviated when the lieutenant's boots disappeared from sight.

Without a single nod or word exchanged between them, Zain and David carefully lowered the tent, their movements deliberate; their bodies tense. With hearts pounding in their chests, they returned to their seats, every nerve on edge.

All they could do now was wait, trapped in the knowledge that a single order could see them executed without hesitation…or mercy.

## *Alarm Raised*

When Melyndie woke at five a.m., she found Tom standing over her. Its blank silver eyes glinted faintly in the tent's gloom. As soon as it noticed she was awake, it spoke without delay.

"Zain has yet to return."

Those words snapped Melyndie to full consciousness, as though ice water had been poured over her. Fear hit her chest like a battering ram. She swung her legs off the cot and lurched upright, gripping Tom's arm as the blood drained from her head in a dizzying rush.

"Steady," Tom said, flexing its servo joints to brace her until she regained balance.

Heart hammering, Melyndie staggered across the narrow tent, unsteady on her feet. She fell to her knees beside Amal's cot and gently tapped her shoulder.

Amal stirred, eyes fluttering open, strands of hair falling across her face. As she blinked away sleep and saw Melyndie and Tom looming over her, alarm dawned in her eyes, sudden and sharp, clearing the haze of sleep in an instant. "Zain?" she asked, voice cracking with a note of fear.

"We do not know anything at this moment, except they are nearing the time when they are overdue," Tom clarified, its tone calm, almost maddeningly so.

The puppies, sensing the sudden tension, jumped up from beside Melyndie's cot, tails wagging furiously and noses twitching as they whined for attention.

"I can't right now. Tom…"

Tom pivoted, pointing toward the tent flap with a sharp, precise motion that the puppies immediately recognized. "Go to the bathroom. I will be there to feed you momentarily."

The two puppies, oblivious to the human dread hanging in the air, bolted out of the tent in a flurry of fur and paws scraping on the hard ground.

When Tom faced the women again, Melyndie was drawing deep breaths through her nose, her ribcage rising and falling too fast. Amal pressed her knuckles against the tight cords of her temples as if to push back the rising panic.

After a moment, they managed to steady themselves enough to speak.

"All right…what positive reasons could there be for the delay?" Melyndie asked, her voice low and charged with tension. She fixed her eyes on Tom, who tilted its head slightly as if scrolling through its internal databases.

It paused long enough for a new wave of worry to roll through both women.

"They may have had trouble with their jeep," Tom offered at last, though it provided zero comfort.

"Is that all? Is that the only reason they might be delayed?" Amal questioned, trying to keep her voice calm and not let it raise into a panicked pitch.

"Any scenario in which delay occurred after they reached their destination would likely be due to unfavorable circumstances, which you specifically requested I not consider in my data analysis," Tom said flatly. "While a jeep malfunction would not be ideal, at least it would mean they are not likely in harm's way."

"They could have also found circumstances a bit more challenging and are simply being extra cautious in implementing their plans," Melyndie added quickly, grasping for any thread of hope.

"While the probability of that scenario is not exceedingly high, I will concede that it is possible."

"Thank you, Tom," Melyndie said, managing a strained smile. She recognized Tom's "concession" as its programmed attempt at comfort, but somehow it only made the fear clawing at her throat feel sharper.

"So…what can we do in the interim to bide our time wisely? More importantly, how long should we wait before we set out to locate them?"

"I think our time would be spent wisely devising a plan should the need arise for us to go in search of them," Amal interjected, though her voice quavered with tension.

"Agreed," Melyndie said, her eyes flicking toward the pale blue line of dawn outside the tent. "But before we can implement any plan, we need to establish a reasonable timeframe. How long do we wait?"

"I would suggest we wait no longer than sunrise," Tom calculated, speaking with that eerie, even cadence. "That gives them sufficient time to complete their mission and to handle any minor complications which may have arisen. Any later puts them at risk of exposure in daylight. Plus, it was Zain's final instruction that if he were not back by sunrise, I was to—and I quote—send in the hounds."

Amal ran her palms over her face, as if it would erase the fear displayed there. "And we'd be right to assume that if they aren't back by then, something untoward would have happened, because Zain would assess the situation in the same manner."

Melyndie nodded and began pacing. Every few seconds she glanced outside at the sky growing lighter by delicate degrees, the first brushstrokes of sunrise creeping over the desert sands.

"Not long, then," she murmured. "I'd say we have less than half an hour. Tom, could you tend to the puppies? Once they're fed, perhaps we can find a place to secure them until our return?"

"Might I suggest that we take them with us?" Tom inquired, voice even but with a slight undercurrent of urgency.

"What's your reasoning, Tom?" Melyndie challenged.

"I am uncertain whether my reasons would bring you comfort or concern," Tom said, speaking the truth with the brutal honesty only a machine could manage.

Melyndie felt a pulse of grim amusement amid her fear. "I'll do my best to remain objective."

"Very well. Should anything untoward befall us, it would not bode well for the puppies if they are secured; moreover, they are being trained to provide security support and though still young, their presence may prove useful should the need arise."

"And," Amal added with a ghost of a smile, "they're just as likely to chase after us when we leave anyway."

Melyndie paused, running a hand through her hair, mind racing. The idea of bringing the puppies along definitely held merit—and besides, she couldn't bear the thought of them left behind if things went badly. A cold shiver prickled down her spine at that possibility. "Okay, we'll bring them. Go feed them, Tom, then gather whatever supplies you think we'll need—for us and for them."

The sudden roar of an approaching jeep sent a jolt through them, causing hearts to pound and breaths to hitch in anticipation. Amal's face split into a wide grin as she turned towards Melyndie, eyes sparkling with relief.

"Seems like our fears were for nothing!" Amal cried, breathless, a grin lighting her face. She spun and dashed outside.

Melyndie and Tom looked at each other then followed at a run. The chill desert breeze slapped Melyndie's face, as the dawn's first golden light speared the horizon.

But before they reached the tent's edge, the air was ripped apart by a chorus of frantic barking. It was sharp, urgent—a panicked alarm that drove a spike of cold terror into Melyndie's chest. She froze mid-stride, eyes wide, pulse thundering in her ears. "Whistle for them, before they get hurt," she choked out, her voice trembling.

Tom raised its hand and emitted the silent ultrasonic whistle.

Moments later, the puppies burst back around the side of the tent in a rush of fur and panting breaths. Melyndie dropped to her knees, arms wrapping around them, burying her face in their thick coats as relief crashed over her like a breaking wave.

But even as the warmth of the puppies' bodies steadied her, an icy dread pressed inward when Amal came stumbling back around the corner. Her face was ashen, lips parted on rapid, shallow breaths. Her voice hit the morning air like shattered glass. "It isn't Zain."

Melyndie's heart plunged into her stomach. "Keep them here," she ordered, her voice sharp and brittle. She shot past Amal, racing around the side of the tent.

The dawn glare forced her to squint as she ducked behind a corner, raising a trembling hand to shield her eyes. The jeeps advanced across the desert, the steady hum of their engines stalking nearer, like predators scenting prey.

She held her breath as they passed, eyes fixed on the silhouettes inside.

Then she saw the passengers in the first jeep. Two men in the rear seat, faces clear in the angled light. The taller one sat rigid, posture military-straight, eyes scanning the horizon with clinical detachment. The other's gaze burned with cold calculation beneath thin-framed glasses.

Melyndie's blood turned to ice, her body locking as terror surged through her in a sickening wave.

She barely registered Tom's quiet footfalls until its voice sliced the silence behind her.

"If President Saltzer, and whoever the other man is, is heading for the work site, then I would say that things did not go according to plan after all."

Melyndie turned, her breath ragged, the words searing their way out of her throat. "That's Dr. Riku Jang," she hissed, her voice thin but vibrating with dread. "Those are the two I was tasked to track down. And you're absolutely right. If they're moving toward the work site, then it means Zain and the others have been compromised." She drew in a shaky breath, pressing her lips together before continuing. "Dr. Kishida-Guan was right about someone interfering with present events. I just didn't make the connection until now. It's us. We're the ones fracturing my timeline."

Tom remained silent, its blank eyes fixed on the vehicle as it continued along the road, growing smaller against the endless horizon. The distant hum of the jeeps' engines dwindled until only the silence of the desert remained.

For a long moment, neither spoke.

Then Tom moved a step closer. "Melyndie, we must leave. Zain, Xiu, and David need us."

Melyndie nodded. As they turned to collect Amal and the puppies, her thoughts strayed to the future—her future—and the realization that she, Zain, Tom, and Amal might be the harbingers of its extinction.

## *Actions have Consequences*

Xiu found herself in a paradoxical relationship with the full moon; its radiant glow was both her beacon and her betrayer. The silvery luminescence painted a clear path for her, while simultaneously transforming her into an exposed silhouette for any watchful sentry.

The barren landscape offered no cloak of shadows to hide within; she was left with no choice but to scuttle swiftly, hugging the earth like a furtive creature. Dust bit into her eyes as she crawled, each sharp grain like tiny shards of glass. The night air carried the bitter tang of sweat and fear. Every distant clang or scrape made her heart seize, her throat closing around a breath she barely dared to draw.

Each time the echo of footfalls pierced the night, she flattened herself against the cold ground, her heart pounding in her ears; prayers released into the ether against discovery. A sound, nearer to her position halted her again. She flattened against the ground, again, wishing the earth would open and swallow her whole.

She squeezed her eyes shut, willing her trembling muscles to still, terrified even the rustle of fabric might betray her. The taste of bile rose in her throat.

Long minutes ticked by as she waited for the footfalls to retreat.

The five-minute sprint Major Reese had predicted stretched into an agonizing twenty under these conditions. Time warped into cruel fragments. Every second felt like the ever-lowering swing of a pendulum.

Once inside the jeep compound, however, she felt a wave of relative safety wash over her. The area seemed deserted, void of soldiers' presence, and was outside of the radius of the glaring security lights. She darted towards the first jeep, her eyes scanning its interior with hawk-like precision for any trace of a radio.

As she moved from one vehicle to another, her brow furrowed deeper into a stormy sea of confusion and mounting frustration. Her fingers traced over empty spaces where radios could have been—but there was nothing but air.

It was if the gods were playing with her, mocking her efforts. And she cursed them.

Sweat prickled her skin, despite the cool evening air.

When she reached the last jeep, empty-handed, she dropped onto her backside and slumped against the warm metal, biting back a scream. A wild urge rose in her chest to slam her head into the steel just to release the fury boiling inside her, but she forced herself still. After a moment, trembling with exhaustion and rage, she began crawling back toward the tent, inch by punishing inch.

By the time she retraced her steps back toward Major Reese's command tent, anger surged through her veins like molten lava. Not a single radio was found in any jeep—an anomaly that defied reason. There should have been at least one belonging to the major. Either David had been misinformed about its location or, more alarming, his radio had been deliberately confiscated by an RMP.

Xiu reached the rear of the canvas command tent, and a sudden release swept through her. Her fingers scratched gently against the coarse fabric, as if afraid that a heavier touch would shatter the fragile silence needed to avoid detection.

She forced herself to breathe slow and quiet, dragging air through her nose and letting it seep out through parted lips. Her chest burned from holding back the ragged gulps her body craved. Each shallow breath rasped her throat like sandpaper. One slip—one gasp too loud—and she could give herself away.

The agonizing stretch of time before Zain and David acknowledged her arrival seemed to drag on into infinity; yet it was only seconds.

The bottom of the tent lifted just enough for her to wriggle inside. She fell forward in exhausted relief—then a sudden force snatched her up and slung her backward as though a giant hand had ripped her from the earth, seizing her away from the safety she'd fought so hard to reach.

A ragged cry tore from her lips as her body twisted mid-air, her vision fracturing into a kaleidoscope of stars and shadows. She launched through the desert air like a ragdoll hurled by a violent gust, then slammed to the ground with bone-jarring force.

Her heart pounded violently when she glanced upwards and found herself staring down the barrel of an RMP's weapon. Cold dread flooded her veins. She wanted to run, but her limbs twitched uselessly, as though her brain was sending signals through quicksand.

The figure looming over her emanated an icy indifference that sent chills skittering down her spine.

"You should be aware," it announced with chilling detachment, "that all communication devices were seized immediately post your capture. You were also warned of the consequences should you attempt escape."

Before she could even part her lips to protest or plead, the deafening report of gunfire echoed through the silent expanse as a single bullet bore into her forehead without mercy.

A faint whiff of gunpowder hung in the desert air as soldiers poured in from every direction, skidding to a halt when they saw her body sprawled at the RMP's feet. Some froze mid-step, eyes darting away as though hoping the horror would vanish if they didn't look too long. When it was determined that the RMP had been the one to fire its weapon, the soldiers holstered their own guns.

"Explain this!" Corporal Davies barked out, his tone striving to match the commanding authority of his superiors who were now held captive in the major's command tent.

The RMP swiveled around, its cold, indifferent gaze slicing through the corporal. A pause hung heavy in the air as it seemed to measure up the non-commissioned officer before finally responding with a dismissive, "This is not your concern."

"I beg to differ," retorted Davies, swelling up to his full height of five-foot-eleven inches and lifting his chin defiantly. "With Colonel Belhasa and Major Reese incarcerated by you, I'm next in command of this battalion."

Once more, there was an unnerving pause from the RMP as if digesting this new information. It apparently did not feel that further explanation, nor conversation, was warranted as it turned about and marched to the front of the tent to resume standing guard with the second RMP, which had not moved a single inch during the melee.

A surge of fury washed over Corporal Davies. He wheeled around to a soldier nearby snapping sharply, "Dispose of that body! Everyone else—back on patrol!" He barked the order, but his voice trembled with rage. His eyes lingered on Xiu's still form for a heartbeat longer than he should have, grief curdling into something darker.

Inside the tent, Zain and David sank back onto their seats; anger coursing through their veins coupled with a sense of defeat. Silence pressed in like a vise. Zain's fingers twitched against his thighs, longing for a weapon that wasn't there. They had known all too well what risks Lieutenant Zhang had taken when she volunteered to go in search of a radio, but never did they anticipate such a brutally swift execution.

A few moments later, Davies' voice sounded just outside the opening of their canvas prison, demanding to be let in to speak with the prisoners. Zain and David sprung up and rushed over.

"Corporal! Report!" Zain commanded in a sharp tone despite already having a gut-wrenching idea about what had unfolded. He moved as close as possible, barely able to see the corporal's face through a small opening in the tent flap.

As Davies opened his mouth to speak, he was cut off by the RMP: "Do not engage with the prisoners."

When it appeared as if the corporal would obey the RMP's command and not respond to Zain's command, Reese decided to give it another go; attempt to force the corporal's hand. So, he shouted out, deliberately loud. "What happened to Lieutenant Zhang?"

This seemed to snap the corporal from his indecision and he yelled back, equally belligerent. "Murdered by this soulless tin can," Davies spat back, his voice laced with venom and disregard for the RMP's warnings.

"You are forbidden to interact with the prisoners," repeated the RMP robotically, its weapon now drawn.

Zain interjected before any further escalation could occur. The last thing he needed was another unwarranted murder on his hands. His voice was stern but carried a desperate plea. "Thank you, Corporal. As much as we'd like to spit in the face of this RMP, we can't afford to have you join the lieutenant in her premature grave. Our time will come. Just not yet. Do you understand?" Corporal Davies sought out and located Zain's fierce gaze, which was silently imploring him to grasp their precarious situation.

Taking a deep breath through gritted teeth, Davies shot one last glare at the RMP before turning back to look at Zain. He gave a curt nod of understanding before spinning on his heel and marching away, fists clenched tightly at his sides.

Inside the tent, the air was growing oppressive in the rapidly rising desert heat and equally thick with tension and unspoken words as Zain and David returned to their seats. Their minds were racing, trying to formulate a coherent plan amidst the chaos that had erupted outside. The harsh reality of Xiu's execution was beginning to set in, serving as a grim reminder of their tenuous predicament.

David rubbed his temples. Moisture beaded on his brow, sinking into the coarse shadow of his beard. The strain was evident in his voice when he finally spoke. "I know we need to think strategically, but I'm finding it exceedingly difficult to focus."

The admission hit Zain hard in the gut because it mirrored his own difficulties at present.

After a moment, David spoke up again as if trying to come to grips with their present circumstances: "Without a radio…we needed that radio," he finally ground out through clenched teeth.

Zain nodded, his lips pressed into a razor-thin line of frustration and seething rage. He shut his eyes tight, trying desperately to shut out his surroundings; to concentrate solely on the storm of thoughts swirling in his mind. After a tense moment, his eyes snapped open and a savage grin split his face. "It's daylight," he declared, his voice a lethal whisper edged with menace. "Tom was counting on me returning before sunrise. My absence will trigger its militancy. It likely initiated just before dawn, which means…"

"What? What does that mean, Colonel? One RMP against an entire battalion, plus a deranged RMP that makes yours look like a child's plaything? No offense."

"Don't let Tom hear you say that. Its Adaptive AI makes it more human, but that doesn't make it weak. I promise you, when it arrives, it will bring with it the very hounds of hell."

"That's good information to know, Colonel," a voice echoed chillingly from just inside the tent. The shadowed figure turned to address the RMPs stationed outside, "Stay vigilant for any unexpected arrivals. It could spell trouble."

The RMPs acknowledged the order with a curt nod and swiftly returned to its watchful stance.

Zain and David sprang to their feet, coiled like vipers ready to strike at the intruders who had slipped in unnoticed.

"Before you act on your reckless impulses, remember any attack will provoke swift and ruthless consequences," President Saltzer purred with a venomous condescension. "Now, I believe we have much to discuss, but as it's suffocatingly oppressive in here, why don't we take a walk?"

The two men quickly stepped outside, but Zain and David took a little longer to join them. Once they did step out, the two RMPs closed in on their flanks, hovering so near that it seemed as if both men were encased in a second, metallic skin.

"Back off!" David snarled.

"I don't think it would be prudent for me to issue that specific command. I know Colonel Belhasa, but who exactly are you?" the president inquired, his tone conversational yet carrying an underlying threat that challenged them to answer any question posed.

"Who the hell are you?" David snapped back, apparently beyond caring what his defiance might cost him.

The president grinned, but it held no humor. "I'm President Jeffrey Saltzer, and this is my colleague, Dr. Riku Jang."

"They're the ones responsible for everything that's been happening over this past two years," Zain replied, his tone accusatory.

"Yeah, I surmised that much," David replied, his lip curled in derision.

The president and Dr. Jang turned and began walking across the work site, neither doubting that Zain and David would be following behind, ensured by the RMPs attached to them at the hip.

"I don't know how anyone can tolerate this infernal heat," the president exclaimed. "Here it is only quarter to seven in the morning and already the heat's oppressive as hell." He pulled out a handkerchief from his pocket and wiped at the sweat popping out on his face. "So, Colonel, do you recall when we last met, in Iceland?" When Zain didn't respond, the president stopped walking and turned to face him.

Zain stood still, glaring at him defiantly.

The president grinned, "I can tell by your facial expression that you know what I'm going to say. I asked you then if you would be able to fulfill your duties without question. Do you recall your response? Because I do. You stated, rather emphatically, that you were good to go. Yet, here we are now, and not only are you not good to go, you have gone to great lengths to attempt to sabotage all that I, and Dr. Jang, have worked more than a decade to execute."

"What has us perplexed," the doctor chimed in, "is just how you came by the knowledge that you included in your message to us, and just how many people you've shared that knowledge with."

Zain met the doctor's inquiry with a stony silence, his jaw tightening as he determined whether to respond at all.

David glanced at him with an eyebrow raised, a silent cue to be cautious. They'd already lost the lieutenant. If Zain were to reveal any other names, there was no doubt they'd all face a death sentence.

To give Zain time to concoct a plausible response, David took a brash step forward, bristling with barely restrained rage. "What's perplexing to us is that you truly believe that trading the lives of humans for your fabricated lab experiments, could ever be justified," he retorted sharply.

The doctor grinned, his lips twisted in derision, "If you think we're going to explain ourselves to you, Major, you're sadly mistaken. Nor will we be fooled into doing what sinister villains do in every movie, which is to begin a long-winded monologue so that you, the self-proclaimed heroes, have time to formulate a plan."

"We're here for answers, Major…Colonel…and if it means employing unsavory methods to extract those answers, rest assured, we shall do so without hesitation." President Saltzer's eyes narrowed ever so slightly, his gaze flickering between Zain and David with a calculating coldness that chilled the oven-hot air around them.

Dr. Jang stepped slightly behind him, his presence a silent yet ominous reminder of the inevitable escalation that awaited any missteps from either man.

Had it not been for the two RMPs standing so closely behind Zain and David, the standoff would have swiftly concluded, with the two seasoned soldiers effortlessly defeating the insipid diplomat and the feeble scientist.

Zain appeared to recognize this and was the first to break the lengthy silence that had fallen between the two pairs of incomparable combatants. "I know only what I told you in the communication."

"I'm aware of what you know," the president snapped in impatience. "What I don't know is how you came by that knowledge. Now who told you about the fabricated humans and the bio chips that we had implanted in the worldwide population? That information was kept between myself and Dr. Jang, so no one could have possibly leaked it to you."

Zain smirked upon realizing that it wasn't the information itself that mattered, but the fact that he possessed knowledge he shouldn't have, which was infuriating these arrogant autocrats. The idea that someone else possessed insights capable of dismantling their meticulously built power structure ate away at them like a rat feasting on a corpse.

The smirk faded as he realized that by toying with this specific fire, he wouldn't be the only one at risk of getting severely burned. It also registered that he'd already disclosed a majority of what he did know. The only details he hadn't shared concerned Melyndie and the threat that their plans posed to her timeline, but he wasn't willing to betray her just to save his own skin. His contemplations were interrupted by a heavy sigh let loose by President Saltzer.

"Enough is enough," he declared, his voice suddenly devoid of the earlier malice, adopting a tone of weary resignation. He waved a dismissive hand at the RMPs, "Back up. I don't think that these soldiers will risk their lives over this matter."

The confidence in that statement made Zain and David bristle.

"Besides, we're not getting anywhere in this heat," the president continued, "especially with these tempers. Let's walk around more. Perhaps stirring the air will provide us some relief and improve our moods. Better yet, let's get out of the sun altogether. Let's make our way over to that jeep where we can take a seat inside," he continued, moving toward where a jeep was parked nearby. "Talk things over in relative comfort, at least."

Reluctantly, Zain and David trailed behind the president and Dr. Jang, who comfortably nestled themselves in the back seat of the nearby jeep. The president made a curt hand gesture for the two officers to take their place in the front.

As Zain maneuvered around the gleaming bonnet, he stole a glance over his shoulder, noticing that the RMPs were a fair distance away but kept their gazes pinned on him and David like two wolves tracking their prey from afar.

Just as he was about to hoist himself into the driver's seat, something else caught his eye, a shimmering flicker in the sunlight far off in the distance. It sparked a rare genuine smile on his seemingly persistent stoic face, but he quickly smothered it before climbing into the vehicle, as if it were an act of rebellion that needed to be suppressed in the face of such grim circumstances.

Once all four occupants were seated inside, silence hung heavily before being broken by the president's voice. "Colonel, what I need you to understand is that this isn't just about the bio chips or fabricated humans," he began slowly, articulating each word as though they held immense weight and power. "It's about the future of humanity itself. Our project might seem drastic, but it is designed to ensure survival in a way that conventional methods cannot. This is something that was agreed upon by every leader of every country in the world. Not just myself and Dr. Jang."

Dr. Jang chimed in with agreement etched on his face, "Climate change, dwindling resources, political and social unrest— they've all led us here. Our methods might be harsh, but they are necessary."

"Yes, that's all very well and good," the president interjected, "but what I really want to impress upon you is the reason why we're so desperate to understand where you obtained your information and how many people know; more precisely the names of those who might possibly be prepared to attempt to sabotage our efforts, as you and you fellow officers are…well, were, until your capture…trying to do. So, what say you, Colonel? Will you willingly divulge what you know and who your source is? Provide the names of who else knows? For the good of the future of humanity?"

Zain nodded as though he was seriously considering sharing the secrets they wanted; however, he suddenly broke the illusion by starting the jeep and pressing the accelerator to the floor. The jeep surged forward, throwing the passengers back into their seats.

Zain fought to control the rapidly accelerating vehicle as it raced toward the desert expanse. The wheel vibrated under his grip, rattling his bones as he wrestled the jeep over ridges of packed earth. Dust clouds whirled around them, suffocating and thick.

The passengers, having recovered from their initial shock, shouted at him to turn around, but he ignored them. He focused on the area where he'd seen a glint of light and sharply turned the wheel to head in that direction. His heart was racing because at any moment, one of those RMPs could catch up and execute him, and David, for his rebellious actions. All he could do was hope that what he saw wasn't just a useless piece of debris but something that could give them a fighting chance.

The jeep hammered relentlessly over the parched, unforgiving landscape, a plume of dust billowing like a storm cloud in its wake. Loose rocks battered the undercarriage like gunfire, and each jolt threatened to hurl them from the vehicle. The sun crept higher, blinding flashes stabbing their eyes every time the jeep bucked over a dune.

Zain's mind was a whirlwind of thoughts and strategies, his heart pounding in time with the vehicle's relentless rhythm. He'd gambled everything on this audacious move. A move that could prove to be their ticket to survival or the swift heralding of their demise.

His eyes darted to the rearview mirror, but his vision was obscured by the swirling dust storm they had kicked up; he couldn't discern if the RMPs were closing in, but he had no reason to believe otherwise.

Beside him, David clung to the dashboard as though it were a lifeline, his fingers white-knuckled from exertion. His face was etched with grim determination, eyes scanning the barren horizon for any hint of danger or pursuit.

"Keep a watchful eye on our passengers," Zain shouted above the wind that whipped through the open windows. At his command, David twisted carefully in his seat, his hand gripping tightly onto the headrest. A malevolent grin spread across his face at seeing President and Dr. Jang huddled together in uneasy silence on the back seat, their wide-eyed gazes searching frantically for something to hold onto.

"I see another jeep up ahead!" Zain announced with renewed vigor.

"Are you sure it's ours?" David called back.

"We'll know in a minute," Zain rejoined. A moment later, he slammed on brakes just feet away from it. Melyndie and Amal were already emerging from within while Tom disengaged from its rear position. Tom barked an order at the two puppies to stay put inside their vehicle; both pups sat obediently wide-eyed and tails wagging excitedly but didn't dare move to exit.

"David! Stay with *them*! Ensure they don't make any sudden moves or make a break for it!" Zain ordered as he rapidly covered the distance between their jeeps.

Without hesitation, both women launched themselves into Zain's open arms. Relief surged through him like a burst of adrenaline. The feel of human warmth and shared breath reminded him that not everything was lost—that they were still alive, still fighting.

He returned their embrace with a swift squeeze before stepping back, "We'll have time for this later. We're likely to have uninvited guests soon. Two RMPs. What can we expect, Tom?"

Tom responded curtly, "They will shoot first and ask questions later."

"Defensive measures?" Zain asked crisply.

Tom shook its head. "There is no defense against an RMP."

"Alright then, I suggest we hightail it out of here," Zain declared. "Get to where we can mount some form of defense. Amal, drive back to the command area as fast as you can, as safely as you can. When you get there, find somewhere that you, Melyndie, and the puppies will be out of harm's way."

Amal nodded, then turned and raced back to the jeep.

Zain turned to look at Tom, "I'm counting on you not to let any harm come to any of them."

"I will protect them with my life."

"Thank you, Tom. Oh, did you ever hear from the other commanders?"

Tom shook its head, "It is likely the message was flagged and blocked as suspicious," it stated briefly.

"Then we aren't going to be getting any backup on that front," Zain murmured thoughtfully. "Get going. I'll be right behind you."

Tom turned to make its way back to the jeep.

Zain spotted Melyndie who appeared rooted in place. He gave her a reassuring smile before uttering a soft "Go!"

With tears forming in her eyes, she ran up and planted a light kiss on his lips, then turned and sprinted back to the jeep.

Zain watched her leave, his chest tight with fear and determination. He clenched his fists, feeling the grit of sand grinding into his palms. Whatever happened next, he wouldn't let them fall without a fight.

He spun on his heel and raced for his own vehicle, dust swirling like battle smoke in his wake.

# Together We Stand

With an agile leap, Zain vaulted back into the driver's seat of the weather-beaten jeep. David remained a steadfast sentinel, his eyes vigilantly scanning their surroundings while maintaining a watchfulness over the solemn figures of the president and Dr. Jang, both seated in a silence that screamed defiance.

"See if you can spot any signs of our unwelcome guests," Zain barked. His foot crashed down onto the accelerator like a hammer on an anvil. The jeep responded with a surge of mechanical force, its tires clawing at the dirt-covered terrain as it surged forward in a desperate bid for escape.

A few moments later, Zain found the road and spun the wheels onto it, grateful for the boost in acceleration.

"Oddly, I see two dust clouds," Reese hollered over the cacophony of revving engine and whipping wind. "One to our immediate rear, and one at about our seven o'clock. Divide and conquer?"

A crease formed between Zain's brows, his mind swirling with unspoken questions that this new piece of information provoked. Yet he had no time to dissect this puzzle now; every ounce of his attention was demanded by the treacherous, rutted path of the desert road. He gripped the steering wheel tighter, knuckles whitening under strain as he wrestled with the vehicle's wild movements, determined to keep them on course despite their relentless pursuers.

As they continued to race toward his campsite, the second dust cloud began to close in, approaching from an unanticipated angle that suggested a potential flanking maneuver.

"Is it possible that the second dust cloud is backup? Corporal Davies maybe?" Zain yelled.

"Or, those loyal to the mission," David inserted, causing Zain's face to form a taciturn scowl, "in which case, it may mean more opponents to combat against."

"Do you never see the positive in anything, Major?" Zain snapped in frustration, forgetting that he'd dropped the military titles.

"It's my duty to examine every possible scenario, *Colonel*, to counter each positive with a negative and each negative with a positive. Can't march through unknown territory without every risk exposed."

Zain let out a slow, controlled breath, trying to center himself amid the chaos. He knew David was right; their world was too fraught with peril to afford unchecked optimism. Even so, he couldn't allow himself to be weighed down with despair—not when stakes were this high.

"Then I propose we prepare ourselves for both eventualities," Zain declared, his voice hardening into steel as the command tent loomed ahead. "The moment I slam on the brakes, get out. Secure these two and make sure they're in plain sight of the approaching threat. If the RMPs see them, they may postpone attacking. I'll gather every weapon we have at our disposal. We need to send a clear message to those about to descend upon us that we are fully prepared to extinguish a life, just as ruthlessly as they snuffed out Lieutenant Zhang's existence. Today, we rise in unison with the spirits of our fallen brethren—those whose lives were snuffed out in cold calculation. The elders whose wisdom now lies silent. The children whose laughter once echoed through corridors of hope now buried in the ruins. And those dissidents who dared to take a stand. We fight for every soul sacrificed on the altar of their ambitions. So let them come—because we will not kneel. Not today. Today we fight!" A vein throbbed visibly in his neck; his breath ragged as though each word ripped itself from somewhere deep within his soul.

As Zain's fiery monologue reached its crescendo, David could only nod in grim agreement. His heart pounded against his chest under the crushing weight of Zain's words. The impending battle was inevitable and there would be no turning back.

The jeep skidded sideways in a storm of dust, tires shrieking as gravel peppered the canvas walls of the command tent. Before the cloud could settle, Zain and David exploded from the vehicle, adrenaline roaring like wildfire through their veins, moving with a speed honed by years of military training.

A quick glance told Zain that the others had arrived and were likely already hidden safely away. In that knowledge, he was able to breathe a sigh of relief.

David immediately opened the rear door and signaled sharply for the president and Dr. Jang to get out. He grabbed them both by the arm and pushed them to their knees, conspicuously positioning them as a shield. With a quick tug of his belt, he yanked it from the pant loops, then bent and secured one of the president's upper arms snugly with the upper arm of Dr. Jang.

"Colonel!" he shouted. "Toss me your belt! And grab some duct tape. I know there's some around here somewhere."

Zain came out of the tent with a handful of items. He dropped it all on the ground, then reached up and unlatched his belt, yanking it from the belt loops; then tossed it over to David.

"I'll grab the tape," he stated, ducking back inside the tent. He emerged and tossed it to David. "Why not just use the tape? Why the overkill?"

"Because I want there to be no chance of breaking free," David supplied, then knelt down and secured each man's thigh to each other, tight enough to nearly cut off blood flow. He yanked off some strips of tape, then wound it around each buckle latch, ensuring that the men were indeed secure.

He then stepped around to the front of them to issue a stern warning, "I'll give you a similar warning that your RMP gave us: Cause any difficulties and the consequences will be dire. In other words, keep your mouths shut, don't provoke us, and you may live through this. Considering how valuable your lives are—to yourselves, at least—I'm sure that you'll take that warning to heart. Make a move from that spot, and I'll put a bullet in your skull without hesitation or regret." He then turned and walked over to where Zain was loading the weapons, "This all we have to work with?"

In the face of the daunting reality that none of their available artillery would even nick the surface of an RMP, Zain's frustration was palpable. His eyes bore into the ineffectual weapons with a contemptuous glare, his hands moving mechanically to load them nonetheless, "I'm of a mind that loading these is a useless endeavor. It's no wonder we were armed with the barest of defenses. It's like they knew this day could potentially come," he grumbled, bitterness edging his words as he glanced over at the president and Dr. Jang, who leaned into each other in fear. "Are you certain you should leave those two alone?"

David stood from his task, a sneer twisting his lips as he dismissed Zain's concerns about leaving their captives unattended. His gaze was cold and unwavering, a predator surveying its prey. "They're secure enough. As for our stockpile of weapons, they may be useless against an RMP, but they will make a decent hole in a human head," he stated loudly, visibly rattling both captives. He grinned maliciously at their reactions.

Zain's eyes were abruptly drawn from the two bound men to the horizon, where an ominous speck grew steadily larger: "Incoming." he stated tersely, "Stay behind the jeep. Don't give them an easy target. Understood?"

"Understood, but Zain, what exactly is the play here? All we have is those two to act as a deterrent against attack. What if that RMP—which, may I remind you, has independent programming—decides to eliminate those two? And if they don't, just how long do we stay hidden behind the jeep without mounting a defense? I guarantee you that those RMPs will hold out longer than we'll last."

"Need I remind you that this wasn't planned. Anticipated, yes, but not strategized against, so while I appreciate you pointing out our dire circumstances, I'd rather you put your brain to work formulating a defense strategy. Like I'm trying to do," Zain retorted.

"Looks as if we'll need to think fast, because here they come." David declared, then took his place next to one of the jeep's wheels. Zain ducked behind the other.

Within moments, the RMPs descended upon them like steel dragons from some dystopian nightmare. They halted abruptly, less than ten meters from where the captives knelt trembling on the dusty ground.

Zain cautiously peeked around the corner of their inadequate shield; his weapon trained on the president's head like a deadly promise: "Mutter one word and you're a dead man." His threat was whispered into the wind but carried all the weight and finality of a judge's gavel.

The RMPs remained motionless as if attempting to assess the situation.

*********

"Just sitting here—watching them out there—it's killing me," Amal choked out, her voice breaking as though it might shatter completely. Her fingers dug into Luna's fur, seeking comfort even as her eyes brimmed with tears. "I can't stand not knowing if my brother's going to die.

Melyndie's voice trembled like a violin string plucked by unseen fingers. "I agree. We can't stay hidden while they fight. Not when the people we love are out there, fighting for us."

"If we had remained where we were, you would not be able to bear witness to anything," Tom retorted, its towering figure standing firm as a steadfast guardian against looming perils.

"And not be able to see what's happening?" Melyndie exclaimed. "The not knowing anything would have been far worse."

"I have been entrusted to shield you all from harm. It is hard to do this if you will not heed my instructions," Tom replied sharply.

"And what about Zain and Major Reese? Aren't they worth safeguarding?" Melyndie interjected, her voice strained to the breaking point as she observed the deadlock that had ensnared them all. Her words hung in the air like an unsheathed sword, the sharp edges cutting through the tense silence.

Tom seemed to become paralyzed by her observation; it's visor lights blinking rapidly as if fighting against its own bewildered introspection. After an agonizing pause that felt like an eternity, it finally found its voice again. "How do I balance my vow to shield you all while still honoring my responsibility towards Zain's safety?" Its words echoed around them, amplifying their collective anxiety.

Melyndie stood and made her way to stand beside her guardian. Her faith in their mechanical friend was as unshakable as the ground beneath her feet, yet her voice betrayed a hint of desperation, "We need to find a way, Tom."

Amal stood suddenly also; her movements jittery with anxious energy. "I already lost my mother to this madness; I can't lose my brother too." She stopped her pacing suddenly and turned to face Melyndie and Tom, "Maybe we don't need to sit here and wait for any of them to make the first move. Maybe we could find a way to distract the RMPs. Give Zain and Major Reese the ability to attack from behind. Isn't the element of surprise a military offensive?"

Tom's visor dimmed momentarily, processing. "An offensive maneuver could place us in mortal danger—"

"But waiting here would all but guarantee a worse outcome for Zain!" Amal cut in, her voice escalating with fear and frustration. "We can't let Zain and Major Reese face this alone. We just can't!" she cried.

Tom stood rigid, an imposing figure of stillness, as its gaze cut sharply from Amal to Melyndie, then fell to the puppies, who were sitting still, eyeing them all with wide-eyed wonder and innocence.

Its visor flared with a fierce light before dimming dramatically, casting shadows over the foursome. It lowered its head, apparently burdened by the gravity of its choice.

"Together we stand," it finally declared with a resonant finality.

Melyndie wrapped her arms about its hips with a fierce grip, "Together always," she whispered with a steely resolve.

After a moment, she released her grip, took a step back, and looked up at Tom, "I know what I must do," she whispered, her voice carrying the weight of destiny. "I will leave it to you and Amal to create a distraction."

Melyndie sucked in a ragged breath, her pulse roaring so loudly she feared it might betray her. She crouched low, muscles quivering, then sprang forward, driven by a silent scream rising in her chest. The desert wind lashed tears from her eyes as she raced toward Zain and David, locked in a deadly standoff with the towering RMPs. She knew with every step that she could become their next target—but she ran anyway.

"We must move now. Melyndie is exposed," Tom declared, then took off at a dead run toward the two RMPs.

The robots noticed Tom's rapid approach and turned to confront the oncoming juggernaut. Before the two could register the risk, Amal dashed out right behind Tom, screaming like a banshee, with the two German Shepherd puppies hot on her trail, barking viciously.

Despite not fully understanding the peril they were charging into, the pups sensed the anxiety in their humans, which heightened their alertness and triggered their protective instincts.

The sound of Amal's screams and the relentless barking of Luna and Omar penetrated the tense air, causing a momentary distraction that split the focus of the RMPs. Zain seized the moment, his experience as a seasoned solider kicking in.

"Let's go!" he snapped at David, just as Melyndie slid to a stop next to them.

Without hesitation, she yelled, "Go! They need your help. I'll watch these two."

With a shared look of understanding, Zain and David sprang from their crouched positions. Their muscles coiled and released like tightly wound springs, propelling them towards the hulking forms of the RMPs.

The air seemed to crackle with tension as they squeezed the triggers of their sidearms, each bullet whistling through the air towards its intended target. The projectiles pinged off the synthetic skin of the RMPs in a storm of sparks, failing to pierce but causing heads to swivel in their direction.

Meanwhile, Amal skidded to a halt on the gritty ground, her eyes wide with surprise at the sudden eruption of gunfire. Tom heard her go silent and stopped its forward momentum. When it turned and saw her standing there, frozen in fear, it returned and positioned itself as a barrier in front of her, and any potentially wayward bullets.

Omar and Luna lunged forward, their barks transforming into savage snarls. They slammed into the RMPs' armored shins, claws scrambling for a grip on the metal, as though sheer courage might crack steel. Sparks danced from gnashing teeth striking alloy, but still they hurled themselves against the machines, driven by loyalty stronger than fear.

From her vantage point, Melyndie watched the chaotic ballet play out before her eyes. A sigh of relief escaped her lips as she noted that those dear to her remained unscathed in this maelstrom for now. But she knew that this lull was fleeting; soon enough, the RMPs would regain control, draw weapons from their concealed compartments, and unleash a hailstorm of bullets on everything within range.

Pushing away these dreadful thoughts, Melyndie steeled herself for what was to come next. She wrapped herself in an invisible cloak of resolve as she bent down to retrieve one of Zain's discarded pistols. Her jaw set into a hard line while nostrils flared with rage at those responsible for setting them on this destructive path.

The chaos of battle raged behind her, but to Melyndie, time felt thick as syrup. Step by step, she closed in on the two men who'd orchestrated so much death. Saltzer and Jang seemed frozen, as though the air itself had hardened into glass around them. The sand crunched under her boots—a quiet threat masked by the distant cacophony of chaos.

Without pause, she pressed the warm barrel of the pistol against the back of Saltzer's head.

Saltzer's spine snapped rigid, his shoulders jerking as though electricity surged through him. His breath rasped from his throat in frantic bursts, like a trapped animal scenting slaughter.

Jang's head spun around, his face pale with shock. "What are you doing?" he stammered, his voice barely more than a whisper.

"I'm going to tell you both a story," Melyndie replied, her voice a quiet storm, laced with menace. "A tale of a fabricated woman identified from inception as a75b99r84GE. Her entire existence was meticulously designed for one purpose: to be a productive citizen. An emotionless robot who was never meant to feel love, or grief, or joy… let alone the burning rage she feels right now."

Saltzer's eyes widened in horrified realization, his breaths shallow and quick. The cold metal of the pistol seemed to burn through the layers of deceit that had surrounded his life.

Melyndie's voice remained steady, almost hypnotic, as she continued. "Today marks the culmination of that purpose. But not in the way that Dr. Kishida-Guan intended. Today, I reclaim my fate. I am no longer a puppet manipulated by someone else's hands."

Jang stuttered, trying to form words, his lips quivering as he looked desperately at Saltzer, seeking some sort of reassurance or a plan. But Saltzer remained silent, his usual cunning and control dissolved by fear.

In front of the trio, the battle raged on. Zain and David continued their ineffective assault on the RMPs. The sounds of gunfire had ceased, but it was replaced by physical assaults that did little more than create a cacophony of confusion. Melyndie could hear Zain yelling at David, "Try to find a weak spot!"

Amidst the chaos, Melyndie's focus was razor-sharp, locked onto the two men who were destined to become the obliterators of her timeline. "Here's how this story ends for you," she declared with a cold finality.

The pressure of her finger against the trigger increased, a hair's breadth away from releasing death. But before the lethal bullet could escape, an unseen force jerked it skyward. Melyndie gasped, her fingers barely maintaining their desperate grip on the weapon. She swiveled around in disbelief, her eyes wide with shock as she sought to identify who had intervened and thwarted her deadly intent.

"Tom…"

"Preserve your humanity." Tom's voice quivered with an ache that was almost human. With unexpected tenderness, it scooped her up beneath her arms and relocated her several feet away.

And for a fleeting moment, she felt safe.

Then it returned to its previous position behind the two men.

In an eerie echo of Melyndie's earlier intentions, it produced its own weapon and applied pressure to the trigger. Saltzer's skull erupted in a crimson geyser, bone and brain spattering across the sand. The smell of hot copper filled the air. Dr. Jang's scream was strangled, his eyes rolling white as bile rose in his throat.

Melyndie staggered back, her lungs seizing around a silent scream. Her vision blurred as tears welled, distorting the bloody carnage into a blur of crimson and dust. She dropped to her knees; fists clenched so tightly her fingernails cut into her palms. A single choked sob escaped her lips as she rocked forward, whispering, "I almost became one of them."

Tom swiveled the pistol towards Dr. Jang and again pulled the trigger. The doctor swayed just enough for the bullet to skim past his temple instead of penetrating his skull directly—a mere graze that nevertheless caused rivulets of blood to run down his face like macabre tears.

Rendered immobile by Saltzer's lifeless body still bound to him like some monstrous conjoined twin, Jang slumped forward while one hand rose instinctively to stem the tide of blood oozing from his wound. He moaned low in his throat, as the blood cascaded down his temple. His eyes darted wildly between Melyndie and Tom, unable to form words. His lips trembled around silent pleas for mercy, a grown man reduced to a quivering child by the nearness of death.

The din of combat continued beyond her, but Melyndie could barely hear it over the pounding in her ears. She lifted trembling fingers to wipe splattered droplets from her cheek—and found the pads, streaked red. Tom's shadow loomed over her, cast long and dark by the afternoon sun.

For an instant, everything seemed suspended in an eerie stillness.

And then the silence shattered.

A single bullet tore through the air and slammed into Tom with the force of a freight train. Metal shrieked as it punctured its armor plating, sparks bursting like tiny suns around the entry wound. Its towering frame jerked violently, arms flailing as internal servos ground and sparked. A synthetic groan escaped its speakers—a sound so raw it carved into Melyndie's chest like a knife.

Tom staggered backward, crashing to its knees, dust billowing around it. For a moment, it swayed there, massive frame trembling under the weight of its failing systems—then toppled back, hitting the ground with a thud that seemed to shake the earth. Its visor lights flickered, sputtering between vivid crimson and pale, dying blue.

In the chaos, Tom's gunfire had shouted its own humanity—and in that same instant, targeted it for termination.

Melyndie turned abruptly toward the noise and stared, eyes wide and unblinking, as Tom's massive frame crashed into the ground nearby. For a moment, she seemed unable to move, to breathe, then a single, raw scream tore from her deep within her soul.

"No!"

Her cry echoed across the barren landscape, ragged and broken. The last of her strength drained from her body. She pitched forward, her forehead slamming into the ground. Tears poured from her eyes, soaking into the sand, as sobs shook her entire body. Shock and grief rolled through her in relentless waves, as if her heart had been torn open and was left bleeding into the dirt.

*When does it end?*

"We can't keep this up much longer," Zain bellowed. "They're going to hone in on a target before long." Heat blistered off the sand as sweat dripped into Zain's eyes, stinging like salt. His pulse pounded in his temples, each thud driving home all that was at stake.

The sudden eruption of gunfire near the command tent stunned everyone into momentary immobility, a fleeting paralysis that the RMPs seized upon mercilessly—a target. The lead RMP swiveled with mechanical precision and hoisted its weapon. Its red eyes flickered like tiny coals as it calculated the perfect shot, taking aim with unerring robotic accuracy.

Zain's heart plummeted as he watched the projectile hit its mark with brutal force, hammering into Tom like an unstoppable wrecking ball. The air seized in his lungs. For an instant, the world seemed to move in slow motion.

Then another shot followed in rapid succession, driving Tom to its knees; its once-fluid movements reduced to a jerky struggle as its systems grappled valiantly but futilely against the devastating onslaught.

"David, cover me!" Zain shouted, crouching low and zigging back and forth as he ran to check on Tom's condition.

David reacted immediately, discharging his weapon in measured bursts at the RMPs. The pistol bucked in David's hand, barrel smoking, the acrid scent of gunpowder burning in his nose. He was aware it was a losing battle but was determined to buy Zain the critical seconds he required, so he just kept firing.

In spite of David's desperate struggle, the second RMP managed to pull its weapon free and level it at Zain, who had reached Tom's side and was kneeling, vulnerable; a clear target for the hostile machine.

The RMP's deadly intent was as chilling as the steel of its frame. But before it could unleash its lethal power, Luna and Omar slammed into its legs like twin missiles, sending shockwaves shuddering through its mechanical body. Claws scraped against metal as they hurled themselves forward, muscles rippling with effort. They snarled and lunged, refusing to yield even under the threat of being crushed beneath the RMP's massive feet. Their teeth snapped and tore at anything they could reach, finally sinking into the cables and plating around the RMP's ankle. Their heads whipped back and forth in a frenzied dance of defiance, unbreakable will radiating from their clenched jaws.

At seeing their opportunity, Amal and David sprang into action. Their hands clawed desperately at the ground around them, snatching up jagged rocks, shards of cold, twisted metal, and splintered fragments of wreckage—anything that could be transformed into a weapon in their desperate struggle against the RMPs.

Amal's fingers bled as she scrabbled in the rubble, sharp edges cutting her skin, but she refused to slow her assault.

Driven by raw fear and surging adrenaline, they launched the crude missiles with all the strength their terror could muster towards both of the enemy robots. Each strike that collided with a harsh crunch against their soulless eyes was a symphony to their ears—an anthem of resistance in the mad whirlwind of danger.

Despite the small moments of minor triumphs, uncertainty gnawed at them. They had no idea how long they could sustain this frenetic assault. But one thing was crystal clear amidst the chaos: Zain needed precious time to evaluate Tom's condition. And they would buy him every tick of the clock they could steal.

"Tom! Can you hear me, buddy?" Zain asked urgently, as he skidded to a halt and knelt beside the battered robot.

"I am still…operational," Tom replied slowly, its voice distorted and crackling from damage.

"Just hang in there a bit longer," Zain murmured, tearing fabric from his shirt to bind some of the exposed wires sparking dangerously. Heat radiated off Tom's battered shell, nearly blistering Zain's fingers. Tiny arcs of blue electricity flickered and danced, lighting up his dust-smeared face. His hands trembled as he worked, struggling to tame the surging currents threatening to consume his friend from within.

"Zain?" The name was barely more than a whisper; a plea tangled in the frailty of the moment.

"Yes, my friend," Zain responded. His voice trembled; the words caught in his throat, strangled by the tears that had yet to fall.

"Thank you…for allowing me my humanity." Tom's voice was faint, more a hint of sound than a fully formed utterance. Zain's hands momentarily stilled over Tom's chaos of wires and circuits, the weight of his companion's words settling heavily upon him. It was a poignant reminder that though made of metal and microchips, Tom had journeyed far beyond the sum of its parts.

The words struck Zain like a physical blow, leaving him reeling. Emotion surged up like a tide, threatening to choke him, as a flood of memories poured in—the way Tom had stumbled awkwardly through sarcasm, mimicking Zain's dry humor until it became his own; the way its voice had softened when tending to Melyndie, large metal fingers impossibly gentle as they brushed hair from her face. He remembered the flashes of frustration in Tom's voice when it couldn't protect those it cared for, the way it stood guard in silent vigil through long, uncertain nights. And in that instant, Zain understood that somewhere amid circuits and metal plating, Tom had found something close to a soul.

In the background, Melyndie slowly regained her strength. It felt as though she were drowning in a sea of sorrow, every motion delayed, the world rippling around her. She pushed herself off the gritty sand, her limbs trembling, grains of dust clinging to her sweat-soaked skin. She wiped the dust-streaked tears from her face with shaking fingers, smearing grit across her cheeks like war paint.

Watching Zain with Tom, a hollow ache bloomed in her chest. The sounds of battle receded into a muffled hush, as though someone had thrown a thick curtain over the world. Even the colors faded before her eyes, reduced to blurs of crimson and ochre.

She tried to take a step, but her legs collapsed under her. A ragged cry burst forth, torn between rage and grief. Digging her fingers into the sand, she dragged herself forward, inch by inch, until she reached Zain's side.

Bracing her hands beneath her, she pushed up into a kneeling position, a sharp tremor passing through her chest as though her body had forgotten how to breathe.

She reached out a hand. It shook violently as she placed it on Tom's cheek, the cool metal trembling faintly beneath her palm. Her voice broke around the words as they left her lips.

"Farewell, my friend."

"Melyndie," Tom whispered, as the light in its eyes dimmed. Its fingers twitched once, as if trying to reach for them, then fell still.

Melyndie's voice barely rose above a whisper as she knelt beside Tom's fallen body. Her gaze lingered on the jagged wounds in his chest plating, where silver fluid still trickled like blood. The smell of scorched circuitry clung to the air. Her hands trembled at her sides; fingers stained with dirt and streaks of Tom's synthetic lifeblood. "How could the RMPs inflict such devastation on one of their own?" she rasped, voice raw, the words catching like thorns in her throat. "Tom always said standard weapons were useless against RMPs."

Zain's gaze flicked from Tom's face, devoid of all signs of life, to Melyndie, lingering there as if he wanted to say more, but had no words.

Then he looked back toward the chaos raging a few yards away—David and Amal locked in furious battle, the two puppies weaving and barking between the towering RMPs. "If Tom's weapon had been strong enough to neutralize them," Zain murmured, his voice tight, "it would have automatically engaged to protect us."

His eyes widened as realization struck, a spark of urgency cutting through his exhaustion. "Those RMPs are loaded with armor-piercing ammunition. Melyndie…our only hope is to take one of their weapons."

He stood up so quickly that he felt a bit unsteady, prompting him to close his eyes to calm the dizziness.

Melyndie rose too, but slowly, reluctantly, as each inch pulled her farther from Tom. She gazed at the friend who had transcended mere circuitry, the one who had taught her the true meaning of loyalty.

A cool breeze skimmed past them, lifting dust into the air like ghostly tendrils swirling around Tom's body. Finally, she tore her gaze away and looked at Zain.

Her brown eyes glimmered with unshed tears; radiating defiance. A fragile smile flickered on her lips when Zain finally opened his eyes, his gaze meeting hers.

"I'm not certain how we're supposed to disarm robotic assassins that are taller than even you," she said, her voice shaking. She blinked, trying to concentrate, and looked at the massive machines. "We can't just strip their weapons off…but perhaps we could get one RMP to fire at the other. If we could twist its arm or make the targeting sensors lock onto the other RMP…maybe we could…" Her voice faded, laced with doubt.

The mere idea of confronting those metal giants sent a shiver down her spine. Zain swallowed hard, stepping closer until she could see the sweat trickling down his temple.

"It's a solid plan. However, David and I would need to approach from behind and climb up to reach the trigger," he said in a hushed tone. "That would require you and Amal to step into their line of fire. You'd need to stand directly in front of them. Essentially becoming their targets." His eyes locked onto hers, silently urging her to dismiss his proposal. "You might get shot, Melyndie."

Melyndie's breath quivered. A thousand voices inside her screamed to run. To live. Instead, she lifted her chin, defiance rising like a flame. "It's a risk worth taking…if it means ending this nightmare." Her voice was low, but iron threaded through every word.

Zain emitted a groan that was a blend of weariness and dread, then swiftly moved closer, pulling her tightly to his chest. His arms wrapped around her with such intensity that it was almost suffocating, and she grasped his shirt desperately, as if she were trying to engrave the sensation of him—vibrant and alive—into her very being.

"My Melyndie. So courageous," he murmured, his voice a tender caress against her hair. He withdrew slightly, gazing down at her with eyes that swirled with determination and an undercurrent of trepidation. Slowly, he leaned in, his lips meeting hers in a delicate kiss, trembling with fear and a symphony of unspoken words. As he drew back, his eyes glimmered with resolve. "Let's go put an end to this…together."

Melyndie exhaled shakily, pressing her forehead against his. "That's what Tom said. That together we stand."

"And together we'll win," Zain murmured, though his voice trembled as he released her. He moved back from her and pivoted sharply, clasping her hand in his.

"Stay invisible until we're in position," he whispered fiercely through gritted teeth. "We have to tell Amal and David without tipping off the RMPs. If those machines catch wind of this, we'll never even get close."

He shot a glance toward the puppies, who were darting and weaving around the RMPs' towering legs, barking with manic, tireless bravery. Pride burned in his chest—pride mingled with terror for those two small lives.

Melyndie fought to control the tremor in her voice. "I'll get to Amal. You go for David. The little ones…" She paused, eyes softening as she watched the puppies. "They're showing us how not to be afraid."

Zain gave her hand a tight squeeze, his palm gritty with dirt and sweat. "Remember…stay out of the line of fire…until it's absolutely necessary. No unnecessary risks."

And then he was gone, crouched low as he slipped forward, weaving through swirling dust. Sparks rained down around him, flaring bright where rocks clanged against the RMPs' armored limbs.

Melyndie stared after him for a heartbeat, her chest twisting painfully. Then she forced her legs to move, vaulting toward Amal.

The sun hammered down like a blowtorch, heat shimmering above the sand. Dust hung thick in the air as Amal and David fought on opposite flanks, hurling chunks of debris at the towering RMPs.

Amal darted between a dust-covered jeep and stacks of supplies piled atop wooden pallets. She rose from behind a sack of grain, launching a fist-sized rock that clanged off an RMP's armored thigh. Across the battlefield, David crouched low, his hands raw and bleeding from clawing through the sand for more ammunition.

But the ground was turning bare. His fingers closed around nothing but grit. Panting, he swept his gaze over the supplies—and his eyes locked on a shrink-wrapped stack of plastic water bottles glinting under the sun.

With a harsh curse, he snatched up a jagged piece of metal and sawed through the plastic sheeting. Bottles spilled over the sand. He grabbed one, tore off the cap, and gulped down a mouthful so fast water spilled from the corners of his lips. Coolness sliced through the blazing heat.

He wiped his forearm across his eyes, lifted the half-empty bottle, and flung it at the nearest RMP. Water burst over the machine's visor, droplets scattering like glass in the sunlight.

The RMP's glowing eyes flickered, its head jerking sideways as if momentarily blinded. Its sensors spun and zoomed, scanning wildly for targets.

"Amal—water bottles!" David bellowed, voice ragged. "Douse their eyes!"

Amal's gaze darted from the dwindling debris to the pallet, realization flashing across her face. She lunged forward, ripping at the plastic until bottles tumbled into her arms. She twisted a cap off one, splashed a stream across her face to clear the grit, then hurled it at the second RMP in the same fluid motion.

Water splattered across the machine's lenses, trickling into the delicate joints around its optical sensors. Sparks flared as the RMP reeled back a half-step, reticle lights pulsing like a stuttering heartbeat.

Both Amal and David were trembling now, lungs heaving, sweat mingling with the icy rivulets trickling down their skin. Yet neither paused.

Zain skidded to a halt beside David, dust spiraling around his boots. "Keep hammering them!" he shouted, voice raw with exhaustion.

David didn't answer at first. He only nodded, eyes wide, water dripping from his arms, fingers raw and streaked with blood. He paused just long enough to snatch up another half-empty water bottle and fling it toward the nearest RMP, droplets spraying in a fine mist as it hit metal with a hollow thud.

Zain wiped sweat from his brow, ducking lower as dust and grit spiraled around them. He leaned closer, voice pitched just above the chaos. "We're going for the RMPs. You and I climb them from behind. Melyndie and Amal have to draw their targeting systems. Once those machines lock onto the women, we'll force their guns toward each other and pull the triggers ourselves."

David stared at him like he'd lost his mind. "Jesus…that's insane."

Zain met his gaze, jaw set. "It's what we've got."

David glanced over his shoulder toward where Melyndie and Amal crouched behind the battered jeep, whispering urgently, eyes flicking between the men and the towering machines. Another shriek of servos made him flinch. "They approved of this lunacy?"

He scooped up another bottle from the torn plastic bundle, cracked the seal one-handed, and hurled it sidearm toward the RMPs. It struck one in the visor, water exploding across the glass in a brief, glittering splash.

"Yeah," Zain said. "We need to bait those RMPs into raising their weapons."

"Hell no—" David started, a muscle jumping in his cheek.

Zain cut him off, voice slicing through the roar of metal and barking dogs. "We don't have time for this, David." He jerked his chin toward the women. "Look—they're signaling they're ready. We have to do this. Now."

David blew out a sharp breath, eyes narrowing. "Okay."

Zain cast another look at the women. Melyndie met his gaze over the hood of the jeep, eyes fierce despite the fear glinting in their depths. She gave a tight nod.

Zain clenched his fists, every muscle coiling tight. "Let's do this."

And then he pushed off the ground and ran.

He lunged for the RMP's back, fingers clawing at the slick alloy plating. His palms skidded over metal hot as a stove under the relentless sun, still slick with sweat and faint traces of water.

The RMP bucked sideways, servos shrieking like tortured metal. A violent jolt slammed him into the machine's spine.

He sucked in a ragged breath, choking on dust. Grit stung his eyes as he blinked hard, shifting his weight and hooking a knee over a protruding joint, fighting to haul himself higher. His boot slipped once, nearly pitching him backward, while sunlight glanced off polished steel in searing flashes, nearly blinding him.

Nearby, David grappled atop the second RMP, boots scraping for purchase as the machine bucked beneath him. Streaks of blood followed in his wake from his damaged fingers.

Above them, the RMPs' visors were still wet from their assault, gleaming like glass under the blazing sun. Droplets hissed into vapor, leaving cloudy smears that fractured the desert light into rainbowed bands across the visors.

Melyndie's voice split the air. "Now! Sprint into their sights!"

Zain glanced up just as Melyndie and Amal hurled themselves into open ground. They ran side-to-side, dodging and pivoting, dust spiraling around their feet.

Amal swung her arms overhead, shouting threats at the machines' creators and daring the robots to aim at her. Melyndie spun in circles, screaming whatever words came to mind, declarations of defiance and desperate pleas, her voice cracking with strain.

The RMPs' visors glowed, lights pulsing in jagged rhythms as they struggled to lock onto the human shapes racing about them. Steam still rose in ghostly tendrils from the smeared lenses, blurring the machines' view.

Zain felt his body coil tight. "Come on…come on…" he rasped, sweat running off his jaw and sizzling where it hit the machine's blistering skin.

Then with a suddenness that was jarring, both RMPs froze mid-motion, their heads snapping forward as red lights pulsed across their visors. Slowly, like snipers lining up their scopes, they withdrew their weapons and leveled them at the two women.

Melyndie felt the hair lift on the back of her neck. She and Amal locked eyes and both fell utterly still, breath held tight in their throats as the RMPs' targeting sensors swept over them in silent calculation.

Zain and David, high above the battlefield, clung desperately to the RMPs' massive shoulders. Metal burned hot beneath Zain's hands as he struggled to inch lower along the robot's arm, boots slipping and scraping on the slick alloy. David saw Zain move and began to slide his way down toward the RMPs arm.

Every second stretched into an eternity.

"Come on…" Zain hissed under his breath, sweat pouring into his eyes. He shot a glance toward David, who was fighting the same losing battle to reach the other RMP's weapon.

Down below, the RMPs' fingers shifted imperceptibly on their triggers. Melyndie saw it—a tiny twitch of mechanical joints—and sucked in a sharp breath.

"Run!" she screamed at Amal.

Together, they tore sideways, dashing between the towering machines. The sand exploded around their feet as they zigzagged, trying to break the machines' lock.

For a split second, the RMPs lost visual tracking. Their visors flickered, red strobes slicing through swirling dust. Their weapons followed the women's movement, swinging like massive iron scythes trying to track two impossibly quick targets.

Zain saw his chance and lunged forward, bracing his entire weight against the RMP's giant wrist.

David, grunting with effort, threw his weight sideways on the other machine's arm, shoving desperately at the weapon mount.

Below, Melyndie and Amal skidded to a sudden halt, pressing close together, eyes wide as the RMPs re-acquired them. The machines' arms lifted, barrels locking forward.

"Move!" Zain roared.

Melyndie shoved Amal just as the RMPs' metallic fingers spasmed around the triggers. The women dove aside, throwing themselves into the sand.

Gunfire erupted in punishing bursts, hot brass spinning through the air as rounds tore into alloy with a metallic roar. Bullets slammed into plating, ricocheting in showers of sparks.

The initial impacts staggered both machines. Hydraulic fluid sprayed into the air as internal circuits sparked and smoked. Feedback loops seemed to seize their systems, and they kept firing even as they staggered backward under the assault of each other's rounds, like titans pummeling one another to the brink of collapse.

Below, Melyndie and Amal threw their arms over the backs of their heads, trying to shield themselves as sand pelted them in harsh, stinging waves. For an instant, they were frozen there, faces pressed into the ground as the storm howled above.

"Get out of there!" Zain bellowed, his voice tearing through the chaos.

The shout seemed to snap them free. Melyndie grabbed Amal's arm, hauling her upward. Both women staggered onto hands and knees, then scrambled low across the sand, fighting to escape the deadly barrage.

The RMPs staggered under their own fire, massive frames shuddering as bullets slammed into alloy. Hydraulic fluid hissed out in glistening arcs, spattering the sand like rain. A high-pitched alarm howled from deep inside their cores, a noise that clawed at Zain's ears.

Zain ripped himself loose from the machine's arm and dropped, landing hard enough to jar every bone in his body.

"David! Disengage—now!" he shouted, voice raw.

David tore himself free and dropped from the second RMP, hitting the sand with a thud. He pushed himself upright, blinking away grit as bullets still zipped past overhead.

Nearby, the two German Shepherd puppies skittered wildly through the drifting sand, yelping in panic as the roar of gunfire thundered around them. Ears pinned back, they zigzagged between spurts of dust kicked up by ricocheting rounds, trying desperately to escape the chaos.

Zain whipped his head toward them, eyes flashing. His voice cracked as he shouted over the din. "Omar! Luna! With me—now!"

The puppies froze for a split second, then bolted toward Zain's voice, ears flattened, panting heavily, fur streaked with grit. They nearly collided with each other as they scrambled across the sand, tails tucked but eyes locked on their human.

As Zain staggered toward the spot where Melyndie and Amal were retreating, the puppies darted alongside him, whining softly as if seeking comfort. He reached down with a trembling hand, brushing his fingers through the coarse fur of one as it pressed against his leg.

"Good pups," he rasped. "Stay with us."

A heavy silence sprawled over the battlefield, broken only by the crackle of cooling metal and the faint hiss of steam escaping ruptured joints.

Zain, David, Melyndie, and Amal staggered away from the crippled giants, limbs dragging as though the fight had drained every drop of strength from their bodies. One by one, they dropped into the sand, chests heaving, sweat and dust streaking their faces.

They sat there; eyes locked on the towering machines still convulsing in slow, mechanical death throes. The gunfire has ceased. Sparks sputtered from exposed wiring. Heat shimmered off the twisted alloy.

Melyndie spat grit from her mouth, eyes blazing as she glared at the machines still twitching on failing servos. Her voice shook. "You were built for one thing—to wipe us out. Tom's gone because of that. And so many others."

She drew a ragged breath, shoulders trembling.

Zain shifted beside her, his jaw tight. "But you underestimated one thing." He stared at the dying giants. "Humanity doesn't go down without a fight. And today—you lost."

With twin mechanical groans, both RMPs shuddered violently and crashed to the ground.

For a long moment, none of them moved. The battlefield lay wrapped in oppressive heat and silence, the dying hiss of steam the only sound that remained.

Zain sat slumped in the sand, chest heaving, still half-expecting the crippled machines to twitch back to life.

Beside him, Amal's breath caught in her throat as she covered her face with both hands, shoulders quaking with quiet sobs.

On Zain's other side, Melyndie sat staring blankly at the fallen giants, arms wrapped around her knees as she drew them tighter against her chest. Slowly, her face crumpled, soft tears welling and spilling over. She tilted sideways until she leaned heavily against Zain's arm, her entire body trembling.

Zain immediately shifted, slipping his arms around her and gently pulled her onto his lap, holding her tightly against his chest. She didn't resist, curling into him as though trying to disappear.

He bent his head low, voice a raw whisper against her hair. "My brave, beautiful Melyndie. We did it."

She sniffled, blinking up at him with dark brown eyes glistening with tears. "Tell me they're really dead…that they…"

"They won't," Zain said quickly, shaking his head. "They're finished."

David scooted closer through the sand, moving as though every muscle was torn. His voice was a dry rasp as he expressed the same concern. "They're…not getting up again, right?"

Zain met his eyes and gave another small shake of his head. "No. They're not."

"What I don't understand," David murmured, "is why they didn't activate the chip. I mean, don't get me wrong, I'm grateful they didn't, but…"

"They were ordered to detain us, not terminate," Zain offered. "And since the only two who could give that order, wouldn't dare even try…"

David nodded, his lips compressed in a satisfaction that words couldn't convey.

For a moment longer, none of them spoke. They simply stared at the massive hulks lying broken under the sun, half-expecting the red lights to flicker back on.

A breathless hush hung around them, broken only by the occasional crackle from the heated metal of the fallen RMPs. Minutes passed as they sat there, drained and battered, the sun moving steadily toward the horizon.

David turned his head slowly, voice raw and uncertain. "What should we do about them?" He jerked his chin toward the lifeless body of President Saltzer still shackled to that of Dr. Jang.

Zain drew a shaky breath, as if lifting something heavy off his chest. "We're going to need Dr. Jang's help to contact the other commanders. We're far from out of the woods yet."

Melyndie lifted her head, looking up at him from where she sat, nestled against his chest. "No, Zain. If we don't stop Dr. Jang…then Dr. Kishida-Guan stays alive and he'll pull me back…" Her voice dropped to a faint whisper. "And he'll terminate me for my failures. We can't let Dr. Jang…"

Unable to finish the thought, she pressed her face back against his chest, seeking the steady rhythm of his heartbeat against the rising panic in her mind.

"No one will ever hurt you again, Melyndie. Not as long as I draw breath."

Beside them, Amal wiped at her eyes, her movements slow and heavy. "We're not done. Not until every RMP is gone from this earth."

David nodded, his voice rough. "Even if we have to rip out every last circuit ourselves."

Zain placed a kiss on Melyndie's hair, then slid her from his lap and pushed himself up, moving with visible effort, as though gravity fought him for every inch.

"You three see to the puppies. Get those brave souls something to drink. I'll see to Dr. Jang."

Dragging a hand across his face, he stumbled wearily across the sand toward where Dr. Jang lay slumped against President Saltzer's body.

He knelt beside the doctor, fingers brushing the man's throat. No pulse. The scientist's eyes stared blankly skyward.

Zain lowered Jang's eyelids with two fingers and released a weary sigh. "Damn it, Jang…we needed you."

"Stray bullet?" Melyndie asked, moving to kneel beside Zain.

"More likely a heart attack," he replied. "I thought you were helping with the puppies."

Melyndie shook her head, her gaze…and thoughts…on the two dead men next to them. "With their deaths…they take my timeline with them." There was a mixture of sadness and relief in her tone.

Zain reached over, resting his arm around her shoulders. "Your timeline may still be saved."

Melyndie's eyes were wide, haunted by fear. "But what if I don't want it to be? What if I don't want to go back there?"

Zain tightened his hold on her, his voice low but burning with quiet intensity. "Then you stay here. With me. Where you belong. And I'll fight anyone who tries to take you away."

Melyndie's eyes fluttered shut as a trembling sigh escaped her. She leaned deeper into his embrace, pressing her cheek against his chest, uncertainty gnawing at her. They wouldn't know the fate of Dr. Kishida-Guan or her timeline until her set deadline for return. Until that time should would not know real peace.

Finally, they turned away from the stench of death and walked toward David and Amal. The sun sank lower, painting the sky in orange and violet streaks as the four of them moved across the sand—bruised, trembling, yet somehow still standing.

Inside the tent, silence settled around them like a heavy blanket. The puppies collapsed into a panting heap at Melyndie's feet, eyes half-lidded, flanks heaving. Amal lowered herself onto a crate, her shoulders slumping wearily.

Zain scanned the faces of those who'd become his family in battle—dust-smeared, eyes rimmed red, muscles trembling with exhaustion. But behind the weariness, he saw something else flickering there: a glint of defiance, the fragile spark of people who refused to give up.

He drew in a slow breath. "We've won the battle, but the war isn't over…yet. We still need to find a way to stop the rest of the RMPs."

One by one, the others lifted their gazes to him, battered but unbroken, eyes heavy with fatigue yet shining with the stubborn light of those who knew they still had a battle yet to fight.

Outside, the wreckage of the two fallen giants smoldered in the fading light—a promise that humanity could still prevail.

The quartet embarked the next day, heading toward Lieutenant Zhang's former battalion. They needed to let Sergeant Vitelli know about the lieutenant's death, but more importantly, they needed access to an RMP to relay messages to General Takayoshi for aircraft support—and to contact the other battalion commanders. Without an RMP, they'd be stranded on the continent, cut off from any hope of stopping the coming slaughter of every person worldwide.

The sun climbed higher in a bleached sky on the second day as they traced a path westward. Dust spiraled off the wheels of the jeeps like desert ghosts as they barreled along the desolate landscape. The horizon seemed endless, a scorched expanse shimmering under the ruthless sun.

Sweat beaded across Zain's forehead, streaking through the fine film of desert dust clinging to his skin. Every few miles, he checked the rearview mirror for the second jeep trailing behind, a shimmering mirage in the heat radiating off the sand. They drove mostly in silence, exhaustion and worry making idle conversation feel tedious—a shallow diversion against the intrusive thoughts that haunted them. Only the engine's hum and the occasional soft whimper from one of the puppies dreaming in the back seat broke the quiet that dragged on for hours at a time.

Zain, noticing Melyndie's tension, reached over and brushed his fingers against her arm. "We're hours out from Lieutenant Zhang's battalion," he said gently, his voice suddenly loud in the quiet that had settled over them.

Melyndie blinked, startled. She swallowed hard, attempting to moisten vocal cords dry from disuse. Finally, she managed to speak the concern that had her gripping the radio tightly. "It's just...too quiet. Like the whole world's already dead."

Zain had no reply. No comfort to give, so he opted for diversion. He glanced over his shoulder at the sleeping pups, their small sides rising and falling with each breath.

"Those two have been through hell." His smile faded as he stared back at the horizon.

"Tom…he'd probably say they're braver than a lot of humans. And he'd be right," Melyndie murmured.

Zain glanced sideways at Melyndie, a small smile tugging at his mouth. "I don't know. I think the four of us fought valiantly. Don't you?"

Melyndie looked down at her hands resting in her lap, her fingers brushing grit abstractedly from the radio. "Valiant? Or just too stubborn to die?"

Zain let out a short, quiet laugh. "What's the difference?"

Melyndie smiled at him, then fell quiet again, releasing her death grip on the radio. "I miss Tom."

"Me too."

"We could have used him by our side," Melyndie murmured.

"You called Tom 'him'," Zain noted, a smile lighting his face. "I think *he* would have liked that. Especially as, in the end, he was just as human as most." He leaned back in his seat, squinting at the wavering horizon. "But yeah, we could have used him now, since this isn't over yet. Not by a long shot."

Melyndie studied his profile, the set of his jaw against the desert light, grateful that at least Zain was by her side.

Later that day, Zain slowed the jeep and pulled to the roadside under a sliver of shade cast by a crumbling signpost. As the vehicle settled into stillness, dust drifted around the tires in lazy spirals. David's jeep rolled to a halt beside them.

Melyndie shot Zain a questioning look. "Why stop now?"

Zain cracked his neck. "The puppies need a break. And so do we." He gestured to Amal and David. "Stretch your legs. Eat something. Refill your canteens. We've got a way to go yet. Amal, Melyndie is handling the puppies. Could you grab some MREs and water for everyone? Take care of any personal needs as well. We won't be here long. David, let's try to reach the battalion over the radios; give them a heads up that we're headed their way."

"Think we're close enough?" David asked, reaching into the back seat to grab his handheld device.

"We're near the Lieutenant's last reported location," Zain replied. "Between the two of us, we can check the channels quickly. I'll start with channels one to seventy, and you take seventy-one to one-forty. Don't linger too long waiting for a reply. Call out, wait no more than thirty seconds, and move on. We need to get a lock on their position so we know we're still headed in the right direction."

"If we're even within range to contact anyone," David reiterated. Zain chuckled, remembering a conversation with Tom about how pessimistic the major was—and how perfectly he'd summed him up.

"I did mention that, yes, David," Zain retorted, heading back to his jeep and settling into the driver's seat. He quickly cycled through the channels, barely pausing even when Amal brought him an MRE and a bottle of water. He balanced the radio in one hand and ate with the other, his attention locked on the static-laden signals.

After about twenty minutes of zero responses, David called across the gap between the two jeeps, "Got something on one-three-nine. It's faint but definitely human."

At David's words, Amal and Melyndie both froze mid-motion, Amal clutching a half-open MRE pouch, and Melyndie stilling as she reached to adjust the puppies' water dish. Both turned toward the radios, listening intently.

"Copy that," Zain replied, immediately switching over to the indicated channel. "This is Colonel Zain Belhasa calling for Sergeant Vitelli. Please respond."

A long silence followed. Then a voice finally answered:

"This is Sergeant Vitelli. Go ahead, Colonel."

Relief washed over Zain as he exhaled sharply, his chest loosening, and he hastily waved for everyone to reboard the jeeps. Melyndie quickly shooed the puppies into the back seat and climbed aboard, buckling in. Zain hit the accelerator without pausing his communication with the sergeant.

"Sergeant Vitelli, we are en route to your position. Please confirm coordinates."

"Understood, Colonel. Hold one while I get the coordinates."

Zain shot a glance in the rearview mirror to ensure that David and Amal were close behind, then returned his focus to the landscape ahead.

After a stretch of tense silence, the sergeant got back on the line. "Coordinates of our current location: 30°35'N 32°16'E."

"Melyndie, can you plot those coordinates into the onboard mapping system?" Zain asked, then turned his attention back to the radio. "Question, Sergeant. Are your RMPs still moving in alignment with their current mission parameters?"

"Accompanying the battalion, scooping up animals big and small. Creepy, if you ask me."

Zain's face registered immeasurable relief. "Do you have any RMPs in your complement currently not following that mandate?"

"Coordinates entered," Melyndie spoke up.

"No, sir," the sergeant replied simultaneously.

Zain looked at the readout. "Looks as if we'll be at your location inside of an hour, Sergeant."

"Yes, sir! Um, might I ask what this is all about, Colonel?" the sergeant queried.

Zain glanced at Melyndie and then back to the road, weighing how much to disclose. "I think it's best to wait to brief you in person, Sergeant. See you soon."

"Yes, sir!"

Zain looked into the rearview mirror. David acknowledged that he had heard the conversation by raising his radio in a confirming gesture, then casually tossed it onto the back seat. Zain mirrored the gesture, then handed his radio to Melyndie.

As the jeeps sped forward once more, the desert blurred into a wavering tide of heat and dust. Melyndie rested her elbow on the armrest, the rhythmic vibration from the engine offering a small distraction from her thoughts as their small convoy drove onward.

"It's reassuring that the RMPs didn't get orders to trigger the chips," Melyndie commented after a while.

Zain nodded, pondering. "It's possible the signal was disrupted due to the RMPs' sudden destruction, or maybe the order was sent but couldn't be confirmed, so it wasn't carried out. At this point, we're just guessing though. We have to hope that whoever's in charge of the RMPs hasn't realized President Saltzer and Dr. Jang are dead and three units have been destroyed—and doesn't manually activate the others."

"You really think that's possible?" Melyndie asked, her eyes widening with worry.

"I don't know, but I do believe that if the technicians notice the missing units, they'll likely try to reach out to Dr. Jang."

"Oh…" Melyndie whispered, dread curling in her stomach.

"Yeah, and if they can't reach him…or President Saltzer…then they may decide to take matters into their own hands."

"Which is likely why nothing has happened yet in the two days since we destroyed the RMPs," Melyndie murmured thoughtfully. "They likely are still awaiting word…from someone."

"That's why it's crucial for us to reach one of the units immediately and send out a message to the battalion commanders as soon as we get there. We must warn them about the situation and subtly advise them on how to destroy the RMPs before it's too late."

"Unless their RMPs don't have armor-piercing—"

"That won't necessarily be a problem. They just need to get their hands on some armor-piercing rounds—preferably steel-core carbine bullets. The RMPs that killed Tom—and each other—were using those rounds. If soldiers can get the same ammo, they can send the RMPs straight to hell."

The discussion faded, their thoughts turning to what lay ahead.

As the afternoon waned, the endless sands began to give way to an astonishing sight—a vast, dazzling expanse of water with sunlight flashing like diamonds across its surface, stretching seemingly without end.

Melyndie's breath caught in her chest as she leaned forward, eyes wide. Her fingers curled tightly around the edge of her seat, as if she feared the sight might vanish if she blinked. "Oh…oh my God."

The Gulf of Aqaba spread beneath them like liquid sapphire, reflecting streaks of molten orange from the descending sun. Wind rushed in through the open windows, carrying the sharp tang of salt and cool moisture. Waves rippled far below, catching the last light like shards of glass.

Melyndie pressed a hand to the glass. A strange ache swelled in her chest, so intense it felt like it might break her apart. Tears welled in her eyes, spilling silently down her cheeks. "I've never… never seen this much water in my entire life."

Zain blinked at her, stunned, and instinctively eased off the gas, coasting the jeep to a crawl. "Wait—what? You're from centuries in the future. How could you never have—"

Melyndie shook her head, words trembling as she interrupted. "In my world…we only had rationed water. If you didn't have your bucket beneath the spigot at precise times, you went without. Oceans…rivers…these were words I'd never known until I arrived here, and then they were only…words…with little meaning." Her voice broke.

Zain felt his throat tighten. His brain scrambled for words. How could a world like hers even exist? "For the love of all that's holy! That sounds…" he trailed off, unable to express how insane her time seemed.

He reached over and gently wiped away one of her tears. "You know what," he continued, trying to replace her tears with a smile. They'd had too many tears over the last few days. "When all this is over, I'm going to take you to see more bodies of water. And…mountains—"

"A mountain?" Melyndie asked, her tone changing to one of childlike eagerness.

Zain laughed, as he remembered the time she had brought Omar's tablet to him and asked if they could visit one of the mountains shown in its picture gallery. "You bet. More than one of them too."

The puppies barked softly from the back seat, alert to the slowing of the vehicle and the sounds of joy drifting to their ears.

"We're not stopping yet, pups," Zain quipped then gave Melyndie a reassuring smile as the radio crackled, shattering their peaceful moment. He reached over and took the radio from her.

"Zain, I see equipment in the distance. We're nearing the battalion. Want me to radio ahead?"

Melyndie blinked the moisture from her eyes, their moment of tranquility shattered. She gave a final glance out the window at the rapidly receding water and sighed heavily, then turned her attention back to Zain.

"Go ahead, David," Zain replied. "Just let me know if we meet any resistance, not that I'm anticipating any."

A few minutes passed before David's voice crackled through the radio again. "Sergeant Vitelli's given the all-clear. He's driving out to meet us."

"Roger that. GPS has us arriving in eight minutes," Zain replied. A moment later, a thought struck him. He grabbed the radio again, urgency creeping into his voice. "David, pull up beside me."

Zain decelerated until his vehicle halted. David pulled alongside seconds later. The two jeeps idled side by side in a rising wind.

Zain turned sharply to Melyndie. "Take the pups. Ride with David and Amal."

Melyndie's eyes flared. "Zain—"

"Not up for debate," he snapped, his voice carrying an edge that brooked no argument.

Melyndie reluctantly whispered for the pups and crossed to David's jeep.

"Expecting trouble so soon?" David asked.

Zain leaned closer. "I don't know, but I do know that you and Amal are still chipped. So, I need you far enough away that if this goes bad…you're out of range of an RMP. Turn around and head back the way we came. Just stay close enough for radio, so I can signal when it's safe."

"Understood." Without question or hesitation, David obeyed.

Zain locked eyes with Melyndie as David's vehicle roared away. He knew there was no logical reason to send her away—her chip was gone, same as his. But if things went sideways, he'd rather it be him alone in the line of fire.

He offered her a fleeting, determined smile before leaping back into his jeep and finishing the last few miles with no company but his growing trepidation.

He was about to stake his life—and humanity's future—on an RMP that might already have orders to terminate him. Every yard closer set his pulse hammering, knowing he could be one dune away from death.

He spotted Sergeant Vitelli's vehicle cresting a small knoll—and behind it—

An RMP.

Zain's chest seized. His knuckles whitened around the steering wheel. For half a second, he saw Tom's face superimposed over the machine—eyes full of questions, as if still waiting for orders that would never come.

Grief knifed through him, sharp and sudden. He forced a shaky breath, wrestling the surge of emotion back under control. Now wasn't the time for weakness—not with an RMP approaching that might already be set to kill him.

They rolled to a stop, nose to nose.

Zain moved his hand to turn off the ignition, then hesitated. Something was gnawing at his inside, a worry that things wouldn't remain quiet and peaceful. After another second, his eyes pinned to the ignition switch, he pulled his hand away. He closed his eyes to calm his nerves, then opened his jeep door.

"Sergeant Vitelli?" Zain called, stepping smoothly from his vehicle and extending his hand. Vitelli hesitated, eyeing the handshake—a gesture at odds with his instinct to salute. He searched Zain's face, as if seeking approval, then reached out and clasped his hand.

"Colonel. It's good to meet you."

Zain gripped Vitelli's hand, but his attention slipped past the sergeant as the RMP eased out from behind the jeep and approached, its visor pulsing softly with each measured step.

Zain let go of Vitelli's hand, his gaze fixed on the RMP. "Sergeant, I'm going to need the use of your RMP to send some urgent communications."

Vitelli blinked, surprised but attentive. "Of course, Colonel. Just tell me what you need."

"Just permission to address your RMP—and your order for it to acknowledge my authority."

"Absolutely. RMP. Acknowledge authority of Colonel—"

"Wait! Just…'Colonel' is sufficient," Zain interrupted, his heart skipping a beat. If the RMP were to ascertain his full identity before he got those messages sent…he closed his eyes, praying the abrupt interruption hadn't triggered the RMP to scan him for identification. He held his breath and waited.

"Authority acknowledged," the RMP replied after a pause that stretched far too long for Zain's comfort.

Zain took a steadying breath, fighting the tremor in his voice. "Relay message to base command. Brigadier General Takayoshi. Request emergency extraction. More details upon arrival. Confirm when sent."

The RMP's visor pulsed, a cool, synthetic glow. "Communication sent. Awaiting confirmation."

Zain swallowed, the dryness in his throat like sandpaper. "Now relay communication to all battalion commanders to cease operations immediately."

A long, taut silence settled over them. Wind whispered across the dunes. Zain's pulse hammered in his ears. He could feel Vitelli's eyes on him—sharp, curious, listening intently—but the sergeant held his tongue, knowing it wasn't his place to question a colonel's orders.

Finally:

"Communication sent. Awaiting confirmations."

Zain seemed to visibly deflate before the sergeant.

Vitelli stared at him, brow furrowed, then cast a quick look back toward Zain's jeep, as if suddenly remembering his own commanding officer wasn't there.

"What's going on, Colonel Belhasa? Why didn't Lieutenant Zhang accompany you?"

At the mention of his last name, Zain froze, dread scraping down his spine. For an instant, panic flared. What if word of his rebellion had already filtered through to the other RMPs? His muscles tensed, ready to react, but when the robotic unit remained still, he exhaled a shaky breath, relief flooding through him.

He forced his features back into a mask of detachment before facing Vitelli again. "I'm afraid the lieutenant was killed…in action," he replied, his voice a strained attempt at calm while his insides roiled with fury over her murder at the hands of an RMP.

The sergeant's eyes widened, confusion twisting across his face. He struggled to reconcile the idea of someone being "killed in action" with their current mandate: pushing reluctant conscripts into clearing debris. How could such routine "actions" claim the life of a senior officer?

Zain registered the bewilderment on the sergeant's face, but he couldn't risk explaining the true circumstances of the lieutenant's death with the RMP standing close enough to hear every word.

Then, without warning, the RMP cut into their fraught silence, its voice cold and metallic. It abruptly raised its weapon toward Zain and stated, "The lieutenant was terminated due to actions that opposed the mission's directive. Zain Belhasa, you are now under arrest for actions leading to the destruction of three RMP units."

Time seemed to fragment. The barrel gleamed in the sunlight. A low hum vibrated through the metal frame of the RMP.

"Shit!" Zain cursed, his voice a low growl of frustration. The RMP hadn't missed his name; it was likely just running his name through the database. Making that connection between him and Xiu. But with Saltzer and Jang dead, who was giving it the orders to arrest him?

The questions flew through Zain's brain, but he knew the answers didn't matter. His time was up. He only hoped the RMP didn't retract the messages he'd already transmitted; if it did, humanity would be doomed.

Without waiting for the RMP to finish him off, Zain dove into his jeep and slammed his foot on the accelerator, sand exploding behind him in a geyser.

His heart thudded against his chest as he nervously checked the rearview mirror, half-expecting to see the RMP closing in with its robotic efficiency. To his surprise, the machine turned smoothly, beginning its steady march back toward the worksite it had originated from. Suddenly, his senses were shaken by distant but intense screams echoing through the air, sending chills down his spine, and he realized...

The chip protocol had been activated.

Over the coming months, as the RMPs marched relentlessly across the vast expanses of continents, an apocalyptic wave of death followed. Their path was marked with desolation, extinguishing life on an unimaginable scale. Billions of lives—each a unique tapestry of memories and dreams—were snuffed out as easily as candles in the wind.

The world shuddered beneath their advance. Once-thriving cities became silent graveyards, streets littered with bodies that had fallen where they stood. There were no screams left, only the hush of a planet dying.

And still the RMPs pressed on, tireless and precise—until whispers began to spread that they could be stopped, that armor-piercing rounds could bring the machines down.

The march of death continued, but for the first time in two years, hope flickered that the slaughter could yet be stopped.

## *Epilogue*

"In a democracy, the well-being, individuality and happiness of every
citizen is important for the overall prosperity, peace and happiness
of the nation."

— Abdul Kalam

The transport carrier arrived inside five hours. The four
weary combatants—Zain, Melyndie, David, and Amal—traveled
with the two German Shepherd pups, as the massive craft carried
them on the long journey back to Icelandic base command.

A sense of urgency pressed in on them, each hour an agony,
dread stretching taut as they imagined what awaited. They might find
only death when they arrived…or, for David and Amal, meet death
themselves.

As the transport touched down, the grim scene they feared
unfolded. A handful of bodies lay sprawled across the base, twisted
in unnatural positions, their frozen limbs stiff as marble. The rest of
the soldiers had been deployed in the field, spared the slaughter—for
now.

Melyndie's breath caught as her eyes swept over the lifeless
forms. A thin, keening sound escaped her—a fragile, trembling note
caught between sob and gasp. She pressed closer to Zain, as though
trying to hide from a past she'd once only studied in dusty archives,
but was now living through.

The RMPs once stationed there, were gone, leaving behind
an eerie silence that seemed to pulse like a wound in the frozen air.

Zain's mind flickered to the image of those machines—their
visors catching the sun like mirrors, eyes empty of all but lethal

calculation. Relief that David and Amal were safe—for now—warred with the finality of the tragedy, sinking in like a dagger twisting deeper with each breath.

The pilot staggered out, initially unable to grasp Zain's explanation of how the RMPs had triggered the chip in everyone's neck, killing them. The words seemed impossible, unreal. When realization struck, he dropped to his knees, vomiting violently onto the icy ground. The acrid bite of bile hung in the brittle air, causing the others to feel mildly nauseated also. Only they weren't certain it was the smell...or the lingering effects of battle.

Since everyone who knew the location of the laboratory controlling the RMPs was dead, they had no choice but to set out on a path to destroy them—RMP by RMP, bullet by bullet, fighting with whatever weapons they could scavenge. Frantic possibility inched through their despair, igniting them with a dire resolve.

"Don't leave a single tent unchecked," Zain ordered, his voice low but edged like a blade honed on grief. "Even one box of armor-piercing rounds could save thousands of lives. I'm going to the command tent to see if there's a radio I can use to contact the battalion commanders. We've got to get word out on how to take down—"

"Sir! If I may?" the pilot interrupted, stepping forward, jaw tight.

Zain turned to him, scanning his face with mild irritation at the interruption.

"I'm fairly certain the only communication is through handheld radios and the RMPs," the pilot said, eyes glistening with the effort of holding himself steady. "I can take the plane and try to reach as many sites as possible. Only land if I see signs of life. Pass the word to as many people as I can to take cover and look for ammunition."

"You won't make it to many sites before running out of fuel, Major."

"I know," the pilot shot back, a bitter humor flickering in his eyes. "But if I've got some ammo with me when I ditch, I can take out whatever RMPs are in range. And I'll be able to tell the troops how to fight back. Hell of a retirement plan, right?"

"It's risky—"

"Risks are all we have left…and we have to take them. We can't just roll over and die…sir!"

Zain gave a grim nod. "Let's see about finding what we need, Major. Without ammo, your sacrifice would be moot. We'll go over the logistics after we've done a thorough search. You three, with me. Major, I'm assuming you know how to refuel a plane?"

The Major grinned, then turned and bolted for his aircraft.

"I sure as hell hope we find what we're looking for," David murmured, glancing toward the bodies, his voice barely above a whisper. He shifted closer to Amal, his hand brushing her arm as if silently offering strength.

"We'll find it," Zain replied, fierce certainty blazing behind his dark eyes. But as he turned away, a shadow crossed his face—a flash of guilt for the soldiers he'd never command again.

The four scattered, a burst of frantic life in the barren stillness, searching every tent, footlocker, and shadowed corner. The search was relentless, fueled by desperation and the thinnest thread of hope.

More than half an hour passed, hope dwindling, until Zain heard a faint call from across the base. He sprinted toward it, breath hissing in the icy air, and found David, Melyndie, and the major converging on the same point.

"Over here!" Amal called as she waved them closer. "Please tell me I found the right thing?"

David reached her first, instantly flipping open the boxes she'd discovered. His eyes widened, and he let out a breath that quivered between relief and disbelief. "Six boxes of armor-piercing rounds," he whispered, then glanced at Zain. "That might be enough…for at least a fighting chance."

A huge grin split his face as he grabbed a weapon and began loading it. The others joined him, their fingers stiff from cold. Melyndie's eyes glittered with new resolve as she murmured, "For every life we couldn't save."

The moment hung heavy between them—grief, purpose, and fire sharpening into one.

Zain looked at his rag-tag band of fighters for a moment longer, his gaze meeting each in turn. Then he spoke, with a final nod of resolve. "Let's get airborne." Then turned and started walking toward the carrier. "The RMPs will probably make a beeline for the nearest inhabited city—"

"I recommend we fly a slow circular pattern rather than a straight path," the pilot interjected, voice taut with focus. "We'll have a better chance of spotting survivors and RMPs that way… unless you're set on hunting down those specific RMPs from this base, Colonel."

Zain flashed a grim grin. "Collect as many weapons as we can carry. We'll load everything onboard. What we don't use, we'll distribute to survivors. Since Melyndie and I are the only ones unchipped, I recommend David and Amal stay here. Until it's safe to join us in the field. As for you, Major…"

"I know," the pilot said, rolling his eyes with a half-grin. "But since we're not getting far without me, I'll do everything I can to stay alive."

Amal opened her mouth as if to protest, but paused, pressing her lips together. She studied Zain's face, reading the strain etched into every line, then gave a single nod. There would be time for diplomacy later—right now, survival had to come first.

David inhaled shakily and reached out to clasp Zain's hand. "Just…come back. All of you. We've got enough deaths already."

**********

For six grueling months, Zain, Melyndie, and their pilot crisscrossed the globe in a desperate race against time and death. Their efforts often felt inches from futility as each day ticked by— but still, they persevered.

They offloaded weapons to anyone willing to fight, with one critical instruction: surprise was essential. Launch the assault before the RMPs could pause and activate the chip protocol.

Time's cruel march left devastation in its wake. Under relentless assault by the RMPs, countless lives were extinguished as city after city fell. Yet slowly, as word spread, the tide began to turn. The RMPs were destroyed one by one—felled by armor-piercing bullets or goaded into firing on each other, just as Zain's team had done.

When the first RMPs were gunned down, the news blazed a trail of hope, igniting hearts and minds like wildfire. By the time the final RMP fell under a hail of armor-piercing bullets fired by an enraged mob, the devastation was complete. A world that had once teemed with more than eleven billion people now stood decimated, leaving the survivors to grapple with the unimaginable task of disposing with over nine billion bodies.

Little by little, global communications flickered back to life. Restored news networks buzzed with stories of the Earth's rebirth. From the ashes of destruction rose a determination to forge unity and rebuild smarter, stronger societies—though all knew that rebuilding peace would be as fierce a fight as any battle they'd already won.

Zain, Melyndie, Amal, and David became reluctant symbols of the new age. Their faces appeared across the media, icons of resilience and hope.

Zain assumed the role of Commander-in-Chief of a unified global defense force, creating new safeguards to prevent any threat, like Saltzer and Jang's, from ever rising again. His leadership, marked by unprecedented transparency, laid the foundation for a new era of international cooperation. Yet in quiet moments, his eyes would drift away, haunted by the weight of each life lost under his command.

Melyndie worked tirelessly with environmental scientists and ecologists, spearheading efforts to regenerate ecosystems and advance technologies that balanced human progress with the natural world. She also helped establish facilities dedicated to restoring a disease-free animal population. More than once, she found herself standing in silent wonder at green growth pushing through scorched earth, fingers brushing tender shoots as though discovering life for the first time.

David found purpose working with young survivors, building centers for psychological recovery and helping children and adults alike reclaim hope through community. His voice, always gentle, grew into a steady force of comfort. Yet there were nights he sat alone, tracing invisible scars on his forearms, whispering names of the dead like a prayer.

Amal turned her focus to diplomacy, using her new prominence to bridge cultural divides and foster alliances that once seemed impossible in the wake of catastrophe. Her words soothed grief and built paths toward peace. But in quiet moments, she sat with photos of fallen soldiers, murmuring soft apologies for living when so many hadn't.

Through it all, they were haunted by memories of those lost—and by the scale of human suffering they'd witnessed. Yet those same memories fueled their resolve, transforming grief into an unstoppable force for positive change. They traversed continents and navigated the complex landscape of human emotion, confronting despair with unyielding hope.

There was no remedy for the reminder embedded forever beneath many survivors' necks; a silent witness to how close they'd all come to extinction. But with the RMPs gone, many people eventually stopped thinking about the chips at all.

*********

Five years after the battle ended, Zain and Melyndie, along with their German Shepherds, found a solitary place to call home—a spot nestled against the same mountain Omar had once shown her in a picture. The mountain, once only an image, now loomed solid and real— a reminder that what was once lost could still be reclaimed.

Now, Melyndie sat on their porch, sipping coffee as the sunset poured golden light across the yard. Six-year-old Omar and Luna bounded through the grass, barking and wrestling beneath the vast sky.

Zain joined her, settling beside her with his own mug in hand.

"I never thought we'd see days like this," Zain murmured, his gaze lingering on the mountain silhouetted against the horizon.

Melyndie smiled and set her cup down, reaching for his hand. "Neither did I. Sometimes it feels like we're only just stepping out of…"

"…a long dark tunnel," Zain finished, kissing the back of her hand. "Yeah. It's been a journey, hasn't it? From total chaos to…this."

"For me, it's coming full circle. From sterile labs and algorithms, to sunsets, dirt under my nails and…"

Zain chuckled, eyes softening. "…a future with me and our pups."

Melyndie nodded, her eyes shining with a mix of newfound peace and overwhelming joy.

The sun dipped lower, shadows lengthening into a soft blanket of dusk. Crickets began their nightly song, and cool air drifted around them—a gentle reminder of nature's quiet endurance.

The world lay scarred and empty in many places. Yet in this small haven, they'd found something precious—just as every surviving soul had. Humanity bore deep wounds, but this new timeline carried a glimmer of hope, a beacon shining through the darkness.

# AUTHOR BIO

Barbara is the author of 29 books across multiple genres, formerly published under Barbara Woster, B.J. Woster, and B. Woster. An educator with a Masters in Early Childhood Education, she crafts layered, character-driven stories that invite readers deep into their worlds. Barbara shares her life with her two cats, Kookie and Ellie, and treasures the love and support of her four daughters, who remain central to her life and are her inspiration. Her works continue to explore imagination, humanity, and the ties that bind us. Learn more at **BarbaraPelhamAuthor.com**.

*Also from this author:*

Titles, written prior to 2025, as last name 'Woster'

**CRIME THRILLERS (B.J. Woster):**
36 Hours (psychological crime thriller / a Detective Hardwick novel)
Killing Faith (international crime)
Edge of Insanity (paranormal crime)
Seeker of Justice (psychological crime thriller / a Detective Hardwick novel)

**ROMANTIC Thriller/Comedy/Drama (Barbara Woster):**
Desires of a Deceiver
Fate's Intervention
Only One
Whispers of the Heart
Love Through Time
Dreamer of Destiny
Victim of Love

**SCIENCE FICTION (Barbara Pelham):**
*3-book series:*
Melyndie: a75b99r84GE (book one)
Zain: The Before Time (book two)
Melyndie & Zain: Shadows of Dissension (book three)

**EARLY READER/MIDDLE GRADE (B. Woster):**
Ehtaria: a land of their own
I Am Proud of Who I Am: I hope you are too (15-book series)
The Purple Christmas Tree

**NONFICTION (Barbara Woster):**
Parenting in the 21st Century: a horror story

All titles @ BarbaraPelhamAuthor.com